'Packed with explosive twists and impossible to put down'
WOMAN'S OWN

'So clever, so engrossing, a genuine "just one more page" kind of book'
M. W. CRAVEN

'You think you've sussed it, but you're completely
wrong. I REALLY did not see that coming'
Reader Review ★ ★ ★ ★ ★

'Absolutely addictive. An unforgettable and nuanced cast of
characters, a claustrophobic setting, and a suspenseful and chilling
examination of the dark and destructive power of secrets'
GILLY MACMILLAN

'A page-turner with a final revelation that satisfies by
being unguessable but retrospectively inevitable'
MORNING STAR

'What a tangled web! Brilliantly weaved and then carefully unravelled
for the big revelations at the end. A totally gripping read'
SUSAN LEWIS

'Fast-paced and shocking'
WOMAN'S WEEKLY

ROBERT GOLD

TEN SECONDS

...AND
SHE WAS GONE

SPHERE

SPHERE

First published in Great Britain in 2024 by Sphere

3 5 7 9 10 8 6 4 2

A CIP catalogue record for this book
is available from the British Library.

Hardback ISBN 978-1-4087-3057-7
Trade Paperback ISBN 978-1-4087-3058-4

Typeset in Garamond Pro by M Rules
Printed and bound in Great Britain by
Clays Ltd, Elcograf S.p.A.

Papers used by Sphere are from well-managed forests
and other responsible sources.

Sphere
An imprint of
Little, Brown Book Group
Carmelite House
50 Victoria Embankment
London EC4Y 0DZ

An Hachette UK Company
www.hachette.co.uk

www.littlebrown.co.uk

Robert Gold is the *Sunday Times* bestselling author of *Twelve Secrets* and *Eleven Liars*. Originally from Harrogate in North Yorkshire, Robert Gold began his career as an intern at the American broadcaster CNN, based in Washington DC. He returned to Yorkshire to work for the retailer ASDA, becoming the chain's nationwide book buyer. He now works in sales for a UK publishing company. Robert now lives in Putney and his new hometown served as the inspiration for the fictional town of Haddley in his thrillers.

Also by Robert Gold

Twelve Secrets
Eleven Liars

In memory of my mum, Christine

TEN
SECONDS

One

*'With no time to think, all she
could do was fight or die.'*

Lying still on his bed, he felt a drop of rainwater land on his cheek. He turned his head and let the water roll across his face onto his dry lips, before carefully capturing the moisture with his tongue. Above him, torrential rain continued to bounce off the rotting skylight window. Dark clouds rolled across the night sky, and he caught a brief glimpse of the moon. He closed his eyes and imagined himself racing through the stars, before setting foot on the moon's rocky surface.

Through the break in the clouds, the moonlight illuminated his bare room. She'd told him he was lucky to have the big room at the top of the house, especially as he had it all to himself. He didn't feel lucky. Stacked in the corner of the room were three boxes, each one filled with old clothes. The clothes smelled like vinegar. She'd promised him she'd take them to a charity shop when she had time, but she didn't know when that would be. He found it hard to believe the room had ever been a bedroom before. She'd told him he had so much space to play in, he could build himself a den. He couldn't. He had nothing to build a den with. Didn't she understand?

Under his duvet, the skin on his legs itched. He pushed off the cover, feeling its cardboard newness, straight out of the packet. He sat on the side of his bed and scratched his legs, before pulling on his joggers over his pyjama shorts. The wooden floor was hard beneath his feet. She'd told him she'd bought an animal-patterned rug to cover the bare boards – did she think he was five years old, not nearly ten? – but the rug was still to appear. She had given him some old slippers of his dad's to wear until it did arrive, but they were far too big for him. He'd never worn slippers and he would never wear these. And he'd never call the man Dad.

He reached across and picked up his football clock; a present from his grandad as he'd hugged him goodbye. Looking at the clock, he felt tears creep into his eyes. Then, angrily, he threw the clock onto his bed. He didn't want anyone thinking he was a cry-baby. All he'd brought with him was his clock, a carrier bag filled with clothes, his small photograph album and his secret notebook, with his name spelled out in capital letters across the front cover. Hidden under his bed, he'd only take his notebook out when he felt very sad. It was where he wrote about all the places he'd visited with his grandad. He never wanted to forget them.

He stood at the bedroom door and edged it open. From the ground floor, he could hear voices rising through the house. Leaning forward, he could see a light reflecting off the hallway mirror on the floor below. The steps down were steep, and he had to grip the banister to steady himself. When she'd first shown him his room, he'd told her he didn't like stairs. Stairs made him feel dizzy. She had told him he'd soon get used to them and smiled. He'd known her smile wasn't a real one. He never looked at people's smiles, only their eyes. Each time he'd met her, her eyes had never smiled at him.

The door to their bedroom was open. He'd never seen cushions on a bed. Running his fingers over them, he felt their

4

velvet softness. Beneath the window, perched on the corner of a dressing table, was a small silver box; dried flowers pressed inside its glass lid. He opened the box and picked up two gold chains. He wound them slowly around his fingers, letting them fall across the back of his hand. He looked back inside the box and carefully lifted out a gold ring with a green stone. He held it up against his eye, twisting his head until the moonlight, creeping through a chink in the curtains, shone brightly through the stone. When he pressed his eyes closed, he could still see the bright green light swirling around inside his head.

Behind him, in the hallway, he thought he heard a noise. He turned quickly but there was nobody there. Perhaps it was the voices still talking downstairs. He put the ring back inside the box before laying the chains on top, just as he'd found them. He closed the lid, gently resting his fingers on the flowers trapped inside the glass.

Standing on the landing, he waited for his eyes to adjust to the bright light. The small bedroom next to theirs belonged to his brother. The corner of the room was dark, but he could just make out his brother sleeping in his bed, curled up beneath his Spider-Man duvet. The room smelled freshly painted and on the floor was a huge Spider-Man rug. That rug had arrived on time, he thought. It did look quite cool, but only for a little kid. Spread across it was a racing-car track and some toy cars. Stuff for children, he thought. He didn't need toys.

He went back onto the landing and sat down at the top of the stairs. Looking through the banister, he could see the living-room door. It was closed but he could hear them both speaking, as well as two other voices he didn't recognise. Again, *he thought he heard a noise and turned towards the far end of the corridor. That was where their boy slept, but his door remained firmly shut. He leaned forward to try and hear what they were saying downstairs. They were laughing but he didn't know why. He rested his head against the banister and closed his eyes. For a moment, he imagined himself back with his grandad. First, on a windy day, flying his bright red kite, and then eating toast by the fire and watching* Mr Bean *on television. He wondered what his grandad was doing now, but when he felt his tears rising again, he stopped. He listened instead to the voices coming from downstairs, until he heard a rattle on the living-room door.*

When he opened his eyes, hers were staring straight back at him.

THURSDAY

CHAPTER 1

I push a gift-wrapped bottle of Talisker single malt whisky into my backpack, exit the off-licence and step onto St Marnham village high street. Outside, evening shoppers mingle with a steady stream of London commuters wearily heading for home. At the end of the high street is Freda's fish and chip bar, and I manoeuvre past a long queue that snakes away from the shop. Empty chip boxes scatter down a dimly lit side street, which separates the shop from the back entrance to one of St Marnham's many riverside pubs. I catch a glimpse of two men failing to conceal themselves behind an industrial bin. Both probably in their thirties, they're hastily snorting cocaine off an empty fish wrapper. St Marnham and my neighbouring hometown of Haddley are no exception to the drug culture now seemingly a casual part of daily life.

Heading out of the centre of the village, the high street turns onto Terrace Road, which runs adjacent to the River Thames. It begins to spit with rain, and I fasten my jacket before pushing my hands deep inside my pockets. I cross through the congested traffic, dodging a speeding Deliveroo driver, before dropping down onto the river path. Beneath the railway bridge, it is suddenly silent until a train rattles overhead and into St Marnham station. Ahead of me, seeking shelter beneath the Victorian structure, is a homeless man making his cardboard bed for the night. From behind, I hear footsteps approaching, at first walking quickly but then sprinting past me towards the homeless man. The two men from the back of the chip shop shout at the man before grabbing the paper cup he has positioned on the ground in front of him. Robbing him of what little he has, the two men scream with laughter before disappearing into the night. I walk towards the homeless man, but he only shrugs wearily. I feel in my pocket for a ten-pound note and push it into his hand.

Only once the path has followed the bend in the river do I emerge at the far end of the village, where streetlights return. With the rain becoming heavy, I'm delighted to see Mailer's restaurant brightly illuminated before me. Standing on the banks of the river and housed in a converted stone warehouse, Mailer's has become something of a local institution. Owned by East Mailer and his partner Will Andrews, over the last decade the restaurant has garnered outstanding reviews both locally and now nationally. Last Christmas, East published his first cookbook and made his debut appearance on the BBC's *Saturday Kitchen*. His inventive recipes, combined with his maverick character, mean he is slowly moving from local celebrity to national recognition.

I turn up the side of the warehouse and enter the paved

courtyard at the front of the building. Cars enter and exit through a giant stone arch and even on a wet February night, floodlights fill the space with a bright warming light. I shelter briefly beneath a winding, first-floor canopy. Looking at my phone, I see a message from my boss, Madeline Wilson, telling me she is two minutes away. She's one of the highest profile and most influential figures in British media, and I've worked with her for almost ten years. For the first five, I worked as a reporter at the national newspaper where she served as editor; in the five years since, as an investigative reporter at the UK's leading online news site, which she runs. Every day I've worked with her, I've learned something new. She is both creative and inventive, and always brutally honest. While at times this means she runs our news site with what might feel impossibly high expectations, she refuses to ever compromise on the accuracy of what she publishes. Throughout her career she has campaigned for fairness and justice, and she expects the very same from all her team. Truth sits at the heart of every story she tells, a commitment she inherited from her father, Sam.

Sam is an old-school newspaper man, owner and editor of the *Richmond Times*, where, like Madeline, I began my career. He took me under his wing after the death of my mother, now almost eleven years ago. Having had no real relationship with my own dad since I was three years old, Sam has become something of a fatherly figure in my life.

'Ben,' calls Madeline, stepping out of her car. I greet her with a brief hug before immediately her phone starts to ring. She glances at the screen before dismissing the call.

11

'Timewasters,' she says to me, before ducking her head back inside her car to retrieve a large parcel from the rear seat. 'Dennis, I'll message you when I'm ready,' she tells her driver. 'It'll probably be sometime around eleven.' He nods in agreement before Madeline and I walk towards the restaurant's entrance.

'No Sam?' I ask.

'I offered to stop by and pick him up, but he was determined to make his own way here.'

'Still obstinately independent,' I reply, opening the door for Madeline.

'He's coming on the bloody bus. I told him I'd pay for a cab, but, oh no. You know Sam, he always knows best.' I smile and can't help thinking how much of Sam's stubbornness his daughter has inherited. 'Seventy-four,' she continues, 'and he's still editing the paper every single week. I've no idea how he does it or how he makes it pay.' I raise my eyebrows and Madeline keeps talking. 'I offered to arrange for a deputy editor to work with him, paid for out of my own bloody money. Do you know what he said?'

'No?'

'Told me he wasn't a charity case. I never said he was, but I can see it's getting harder and harder for him, and he refuses to slow down. Who's still buying ad space in local newspapers? Any offer of help he rejects out of hand, and not just at the paper. I said I'd arrange a cleaner for him at home, just a couple of mornings a week, but he doesn't want anybody coming into his flat and meddling with his things. One day he really will give himself a heart attack.' Madeline smiles

12

as we both remember her night-time race to the hospital last autumn after her dad suffered a suspected heart attack. Fortunately, Sam's *heart attack* turned out to be nothing worse than too much cheese and far too much vintage port.

Madeline's phone rings again.

'I don't know how people get my bloody number,' she says, again dismissing the call. 'I'll kill Carolyn if she's given it out to some random claiming to have a world exclusive.' Working as Madeline's assistant is a position that requires a large degree of patience. She moves forward and gives her name to the maître d' for our reservation but before he can show us to our table, East Mailer steps out of the open kitchen.

'Madeline!' he calls, approaching with his arms open wide. At six foot seven, his long black hair gripped back in a tight ponytail and held in place by an oversized bright red chef's bandana, he is not a figure easily missed. 'Why didn't you tell me you were in tonight? I would have prepared you something special,' he says, cheerfully reprimanding her, as diners from across the restaurant turn to observe their host.

Madeline greets East with an air kiss before wrapping her arm tightly around his waist. 'Everything's always special here,' she replies, laughing. Madeline and East formed an unbreakable friendship in their final years of school and have remained close ever since. 'We're here to celebrate Sam's birthday, if he ever turns up,' she tells him as he walks us to a table with spectacular river views. 'A low-key celebration this year,' she says, 'but don't forget, Sam doesn't need an excuse to enjoy a second helping of your fish pie.'

13

'Leave it with me,' he replies. He raises his hand towards the barman working in the crowded cocktail bar. 'Champagne on the house. My gift to the birthday boy,' he continues, spotting Sam, who has arrived at the restaurant and is being welcomed by the maître d'. East greets Sam by placing a giant hand on his shoulder, almost tucking him under his arm. 'Mr Hardy, I hear we're celebrating.'

'I'm not here to be made a fuss of,' replies Sam, as he lifts his hands in mock protest.

Our waiter pours three glasses of champagne before stepping away. 'Join us for a glass,' says Madeline to East.

'I wish I could, but I'm running the kitchen tonight.'

Sam's eyes light up and he looks towards East. 'Fish pie?'

'Already on it,' he replies, before squeezing Madeline's hand. 'Can I grab you for five minutes later, if you can slip away?' he says, dropping his voice. 'I could do with a quiet word.'

'Everything okay?' she asks.

'Absolutely. Enjoy your dinner,' he replies, before disappearing back to the kitchen.

'Apologies if I'm late,' says Sam, downing half a glass of champagne before he even sits down. 'Connie popped round for a late lunch and the time got away from us.'

'Don't tell me you've spoilt your appetite?'

Sam shakes his head and smiles. 'Maddy, I'm ravenous. I haven't eaten a thing since breakfast.' He continues drinking his champagne. 'When I say Connie popped round for a late lunch—'

Madeline holds up her hands. 'Dad, we know exactly

what you mean, and we don't need any more details.' She turns to me and shakes her head.

'I thought Mrs Wasnesky was your special friend in your block of flats?' I ask.

Sam grins. 'She is but she's visiting her mother in Poland, back tomorrow night.'

'Her mother?' asks Madeline. 'What age is Mrs Wasnesky?'

'Same age as me, a sprightly seventy-four. Her mother was a hundred and one last week. They make them tough in Warsaw.' He shows us a picture of Mrs Wasnesky's mother celebrating her birthday with a shot of vodka. 'I was invited to join them, but Poland in February is too much even for me.' Sam reaches into the ice bucket and refills his glass.

Madeline smiles before bending down beside her chair. 'Happy birthday, Dad,' she says, passing Sam the parcel she brought from her car.

'What have we here?' he replies, stretching across the table for what looks like a large picture frame. While Sam tears into the expensive wrapping paper, a group of four women sat at the cocktail bar capture my attention. As they rapidly make their way through a stream of gin martinis, I'm sure I hear one of them mention my name. Madeline briefly catches my eye but says nothing.

Sam rips away the last shred of paper and rests the frame on the table in front of him. The frame hides his face from Madeline, but I can see him bring his hand to his cheek.

'It's your very first—' says Madeline.

'I know what it is,' he replies, wiping his eyes. 'My very first page-one story, September the twenty-eighth, 1973. I never thought I'd see it again.' Sam passes me the framed edition of the *Richmond Times* from over fifty years ago, before getting to his feet and hugging his daughter. 'Where on earth did you find it?'

'You might not believe me, but I do have the odd contact,' she says, her arms wrapped around her father.

'I've every edition since October '73 . . . '

'Stored in your bloody garage,' adds Madeline, laughing.

'But I lost this one when I first moved in with your mother. She was always tidying up, throwing important things away.'

'I'm sure she misses you too,' says Madeline, blowing her dad a kiss as he resumes his seat at the table. I've never met Madeline's mother, her parents already being long divorced when I first knew her, but she has hinted that their relationship was a feisty one.

I turn again as from behind me I hear a screech of laughter. This time I'm certain one of the women has called my name.

'Ignore them,' says Madeline, overhearing the same comment. She reaches across the table. 'They're not worth it, Ben.'

CHAPTER 2

Throughout my adult life I've grown accustomed to sideways glances, along with the occasional pointed finger, particularly in and around my hometown of Haddley. Over twenty years ago, the murder of my brother, Nick, when he was only fourteen, became infamous on an international scale. A year later, two girls from their school class were convicted of killing Nick and his best friend, Simon Woakes. At the time of the murder, I was only eight years old and while this year will mark the twenty-third anniversary of Nick's death, the crime still holds a morbid fascination for many. With my recent discovery of the truth behind my brother's killing, social media interest in my family's story has again spiked.

'What are you both looking at?' asks Sam, twisting in his chair.

'Nothing for you to worry about,' replies his daughter.

Sam turns back to our table. 'Are we ordering?' he asks, before I catch the waiter's eye.

'I was sorry to hear about your grandfather,' he says to Madeline, after the safe dispatch of his order of fish pie to the kitchen.

'Pops had a great life. Ninety-six was quite an age.'

'You'll be pleased to know I messaged your mother,' he replies, leaning back in his chair and folding his arms. 'Only a brief message, mind you.'

'She'll have liked that,' says Madeline. 'Her father always meant a lot to her.'

'He was a grumpy old sod, and we all know it. Even your mum would admit that. Only reason he lived so long was to stop anyone else getting their hands on his money.'

Madeline laughs. 'I always found him to be very generous.'

'Please,' says Sam. 'When was the last time he gave you anything?'

'I never needed his money,' replies Madeline, her steely independence never far from the surface.

'Your mum will be a wealthy woman now, assuming it's all gone to her?'

Madeline nods. 'A couple of our *rivals* even ran stories on the passing of Britain's so-called Warren Buffett. I wish that was bloody true, but I do hope Mum enjoys herself, takes the chance to travel the world in style.'

'Sounds like the perfect plan,' replies Sam. 'Keep her as far away from London as possible.'

'You should have stuck with her,' I say to him. 'You'd be a gentleman of leisure now.'

'No amount of money could've persuaded me to stay with Annabel.'

'Or her with you,' adds Madeline. 'You were both far too independent. Compromise is not a word I'd associate with your marriage.'

'Something else we passed on to you.' As Sam raises his glass, we hear another scream from the cocktail bar. I turn to see one of the women fall gracelessly off her stool. Two of her friends clamber down to help, but both are unsteady on their feet. In trying to lift her, one of the women falls backwards, crashing a bar stool onto the floor. Two waiters cross quickly.

'I only want help from Nathan,' cries the woman lying prone, her words slurring as she swats away offers of help. Slowly she sits upright, resting her head against the side of the bar. 'Nathan's strong hands taking hold of me,' she says, giggling to herself.

I glance back towards Madeline, and she shakes her head. Sam remains captivated and reaches for his phone to record the scene.

'Dad!' says Madeline, slapping his hand.

'How quick you forget. In local news, everything's a story.'

'Woman falls off stool?' says Madeline. 'Surely things aren't that bad?'

'Drunken brawl in celebrity chef's flagship restaurant,' replies Sam, smiling at his daughter. 'I could sell that to a couple of the nationals. It's all in the spin.'

Grabbing hold of the edge of the bar, the two women haul themselves to their feet. All four women are laughing hysterically as they reach for their glasses to continue drinking. I watch the barman move towards them but before he can say anything, the woman who originally fell to the floor staggers in our direction.

'You are him, aren't you? You're Ben Harper?' she says to me as she approaches our table. 'I'm so, so sorry about what happened to you and your family. You seem lovely.'

Her friend is now at her side. 'Do you know Nathan?' she asks, sniggering. 'You know he works here? He might be the spawn of a child murderer, but he can come home with me any night of the week. Someone posted a video of him on TikTok, running without a shirt. He's gorgeous.'

The two women laugh again but Madeline's run out of patience. She steps around our table and says, 'We're here for a quiet dinner. I think you've all had quite enough to drink and it's time for you to go home.' She picks up her phone. 'Let me call you a cab.'

'Who are you calling a cab for us? We're just getting the party started.'

'I can assure you, your party is well and truly at an end.'

'You should keep your bloody nose out of it,' replies the first woman, lurching in Madeline's direction. Madeline steps quickly sideways and instead of landing a blow on her, the woman falls flat across our table.

Sam grabs his phone and captures the image of the woman, splayed across the table, her face resting in our bread bowl.

'Happy birthday, Sam,' says Madeline, rolling her eyes and smiling at her father before she pulls an empty chair from a neighbouring table. With the help of our waiter, she raises the woman up before lowering her down onto the seat.

'Let me go,' shouts the woman, twisting and turning in an attempt to wrestle herself free.

Madeline crouches beside her. 'It's time for you to go home,' she says, remaining calm. 'I'm going to pay for your taxi, and when you and your three friends wake up in the morning, hopefully you will feel suitably embarrassed.'

'I want a selfie with Ben,' says the woman, arguing like a child.

Unperturbed, Madeline replies, 'Ben doesn't want a selfie with you.' She takes hold of the woman's arm. 'Let's get you outside. The fresh air will help clear your head.'

'Take your hands off me!' yells the woman, directly into Madeline's face. Madeline jerks her head back and in that split second the woman's friend grabs hold of her arm. My boss shakes herself free, but the first woman is on her feet and stumbling towards me. She throws her arms around my neck to steady herself before shakily holding up her phone in front of our faces. She's unable to open the screen. Hanging on to me, she turns to her two other friends still sat at the bar.

'Natasha, Kyla! Come and take a photo of me with Ben.'

The two women sit frozen at the bar, vacantly staring at the chaos unfolding in front of them.

'Let me help,' says Sam, getting to his feet.

'Sam!' says Madeline.

'Let's give her a photo, make her happy and then get her out of here,' he replies.

'Thanks, old man,' says the woman, a look of triumph crossing her face.

'What's your name?' asks Sam, as the woman passes him her phone.

'Abby,' she replies, her arm tight around my waist.

'Smile, Abby,' he says.

'Hold on!' she replies, laughing at herself as she straightens her black cocktail dress and flicks away a pat of butter stuck to her breast. I can't help smiling at Sam as he clicks the phone and captures the moment.

'Do another couple,' says Abby. 'I wasn't quite ready.'

'Get out of my restaurant!' shouts a voice coming from the kitchen.

Madeline steps around our table, crossing quickly towards East. She puts her hand on his chest. 'Don't cause a scene, it will only make things worse,' she says, quietly.

East shakes his head and pushes past her. I see Madeline briefly close her eyes as his giant frame runs towards the two women. 'Did you hear me?' he yells, loud enough for the whole restaurant to hear. 'I said get out of my fucking restaurant.' He takes hold of Abby's arm and before she's able to respond barrels her towards the exit. Two waiters rush forward and quickly usher the other woman off the premises.

'And you two,' continues East, turning his attention to the two women at the bar. 'Out, now, before I call the police.'

'Boss, they haven't paid,' says the barman.

'I don't give a rat's arse if they've paid or not.'

Dumbfounded at East Mailer expelling them from his restaurant, the two women uneasily climb down off their bar stools. One woman stumbles forward, the heel of her shoe collapsing beneath her. Falling towards East, he catches her in his giant forearms. Fellow diners watch in astonishment as he scoops her up and carries her lengthways out of the restaurant.

Madeline turns to her father, who is capturing the scene on his phone.

'I think this one might even go viral,' he says.

CHAPTER 3

Will Andrews put down the book he'd hoped to finish that evening. He gazed out of the floor-to-ceiling window that looked out on the River Thames. Listening carefully, he could hear snatches of his husband's voice in the furious exchanges taking place in the restaurant below.

'What do you think?' he said to his son, Nathan. 'East clashing with another journalist?'

Lying flat on an oversized sofa in the loft apartment where he'd lived for just the past six weeks, Nathan stopped typing. He put down his phone. 'God knows,' he replied. 'I thought after I gave up my shifts in the restaurant, they'd stop coming in.'

Less than a year before, Nathan Beavin had arrived in the London Borough of Haddley burdened by the new-found knowledge that his birth mother was one of the two schoolgirls convicted of killing Nick Harper. Given up for adoption after his mother's conviction, he'd grown up as part of a small family in the town of Cowbridge, outside Cardiff. At university, while studying for a law degree, he'd successfully had his sealed adoption record opened and soon after, aged only twenty-one, had arrived in Haddley in search of his biological father.

Will had lived those first twenty-one years of his son's life with no knowledge of his existence. A paternity test had ultimately confirmed Nathan was his child, although seeing the two men together would have left few people in any doubt they were father and son.

'East has zero ability, and at times very little inclination, to control his temper,' said Will. 'When he gets like that, he's not a nice person.'

'I wonder if me taking some time away from St Marnham might help calm things down.'

Will shook his head. 'I don't want you to do that,' he replied. 'I want you to think of St Marnham as much as your home as Cowbridge.'

'I already do,' said Nathan, but the hesitation in his voice left Will increasingly worried he was about to lose the son he'd only so recently discovered. Social media had feasted on Nathan's story. He'd never sought any attention, but TikTok detectives knew no boundaries. Still only twenty-two, the product of a notorious child killer and her then fourteen-year-old classmate, Nathan had unwittingly become a figure of morbid fascination. Despite her recent return to custody, theories of Nathan discovering his birth mother's new identity and of them together plotting a vile new crime abounded. Even with zero foundation, the online abuse of Nathan had at times become vitriolic. Will could understand how his son might regret ever seeking to

24

discover the identity of his birth parents, and he worried that if Nathan returned to Wales there was nothing to ever bring him back.

He leaned forward in his chair. 'Things will soon settle down. Promise me you won't ever let East drive you out.'

'I don't want to come between the two of you.'

Will said nothing.

Despite the shock of Nathan arriving in his life only last spring, Will had relished the time he'd spent with his son. Discovering they had so many stupid things in common – a love of Ben & Jerry's Cookie Dough ice-cream, NBA basketball, marathon running (at very different speeds), the music of Paul Weller, the TV series *The West Wing* – had helped them establish an easy relationship. Fatherhood was not something Will had ever imagined, but when it had been thrust upon him, he'd loved every moment. Recognising it was harder for East, he'd gone out of his way to include his husband in their relationship. It was East who'd suggested Nathan work with him at the restaurant and, at first, Will had delighted in the growing bond between the pair. Then, over recent weeks East's attitude had changed. Nathan's notoriety brought unwanted attention to the restaurant but, rather than support him, East had suggested Nathan leave. He also suggested he move out of the art deco home Will and East shared in St Marnham village and into the small loft apartment above the restaurant. Will could feel his husband pushing Nathan out of their lives.

He sat and watched as Nathan typed another message on his phone. 'Are you and Sarah definitely done?'

Nathan turned over his phone. 'However hard I try, I think we are.'

Relentless social media pressure had proved too much for Nathan's nascent relationship with a local Haddley woman to withstand. Will knew his son had returned on multiple occasions to visit Sarah Wright, as well as her six-year-old son, Max, in the two months since he'd moved out of her home on Haddley Common.

'You keep messaging though?'

'I thought I'd see if she was about this weekend.' There was a melancholy in his voice. 'Just to hang out with her and Max.'

'Give it time,' replied Will.

Nathan nodded. 'We're going to stay friends.' Will smiled and his son's face reddened. 'We are,' he protested.

With Sarah being almost ten years older and with a six-year-old son, Will knew the chances of his son's relationship surviving for the long-term, even without all the external pressures, were limited. He simply smiled and agreed.

'I'll still want to be able to call by and see Max,' said Nathan. 'I never imagined being a dad, but I really will miss him.'

'One day you'll make a great dad,' replied Will, 'just not yet. Thirty-seven is far too young for me to think about becoming a grandfather.'

Nathan laughed. 'Don't worry, I'm not planning on my own family any time soon. I think right now that's a bit too much to inflict on any child.'

'Whenever it happens, your child will be part of *your* family, not mine, and most certainly not hers.'

Nathan sat upright and reached for his trainers. As his son pulled on his shoes, Will knew both he and his son were thinking of Josie Fairchild, the woman who killed Nick Harper, and the shadow she still cast over their lives.

'I'm going next door for a beer.'

'Give me five minutes and I'll come with you,' replied Will.

'No, I might wander up into the village, get a bit of air.' He picked up his phone. 'I'll drop you a message if I find a quiet spot.'

Will saw the sadness in his son's eyes. 'All of this will pass.'

'I wish I could believe that was true,' he replied, once again typing into his phone before he headed out of the room.

CHAPTER 4

Detective Constable Dani Cash felt a cold shiver run down her spine. Sitting at her desk at the back of Haddley's deserted CID offices, she pulled her jacket off the back of her chair. After zipping it to the collar, she reached towards the ancient iron radiator behind her desk. It was stone cold. Vigorously, she rubbed her hands up and down her arms; anything to stifle the chill of a late February evening. She decided a hot cup of tea would help.

Wandering into the tiny galley kitchen at the top end of the office, she switched on the kettle before opening a small cupboard above the sink. She stretched for the battered Golden Jubilee tea caddy and dropped a teabag into her blue striped mug. When she picked up the kettle, behind her, the door snapped open. She flinched, spilling boiling water across the narrow kitchen surface.

'I don't bite,' said Chief Inspector Bridget Freeman, the station's commanding officer.

'Good evening, ma'am,' she replied, hurriedly unravelling a roll of kitchen towel.

'I'll have a cup if there's still water in the kettle.' Freeman crossed to the small fridge and pulled out an almost empty carton of milk. 'Builder's tea it is.'

Dani smiled. Looking at Freeman, she could only ever remember seeing her impeccably presented; her jacket buttoned, her epaulettes polished. This evening, however, she was dressed in a Metropolitan Police-branded sweatshirt and tracksuit trousers.

'Twenty minutes in the gym,' said Freeman, 'for all the good it'll do me.'

Dani realised she'd let the surprise show on her face. 'Sugar, ma'am?'

'That I absolutely shouldn't do, but a small one won't hurt.'

'Long day?' asked Dani, stirring her own tea.

'In my job, every day feels like a long day – endless paperwork, urgent communication back to the chief superintendent or yet another set of questions on conviction rates from the bigwigs at Scotland Yard.'

In CI Freeman, Dani saw a senior officer with a vast capacity for work. During her time leading the station, Dani had grown to respect her. She admired her ability to be cognisant of every case, while simultaneously allowing officers the freedom to run their own investigations. But the high regard in which Dani held the station's senior officer made her lingering suspicions about her honesty even more suffocating.

'Life was a lot simpler, and dare I say a lot more enjoyable,' continued the chief inspector, 'when all of my time was focused on solving cases.' Freeman picked up her cup and took a sip. 'What's keeping you here so late, constable?'

'I've come from reinterviewing last weekend's intruder victim.'

'Shannon Lancaster?'

'That's right, ma'am.'

'How's she doing?'

'Putting on a brave face, but I can see she's scared.'

'She woke in the middle of the night with the intruder by her bed?'

Dani nodded. 'Opened her eyes to find him leaning over her.'

'Terrifying,' replied Freeman. 'Send me your notes when you're done. Do you definitely think it's the same man?'

Over the past three years, a series of sporadic break-ins had increasingly spread fear across Haddley. What had started out as seemingly innocuous burglaries had escalated to women waking to find a masked intruder in their bedrooms.

'Everything surrounding last Saturday's break-in suggests it's the same man,' replied Dani. 'He was dressed in the exact same way – ski mask, zipped hoodie, leather gloves – and he found his way to the woman's bedside.'

'Anything yet to link the five victims?'

Dani shook her head. 'The pattern of the attacks has been so unpredictable, but they only happen when the women are alone.'

'He's opportunistic?' said Freeman.

Dani agreed. 'Yes, in Shannon Lancaster's case, her two daughters were away, having a sleepover at their grandmother's.'

'Somehow, he finds out. Keep searching for a link between

the victims. We know his behaviour is escalating and we need a breakthrough.'

'Yes, ma'am. I'm starting to work through social media posts tonight.'

'And Shannon Lancaster? She was simply lucky?' Freeman stood in the kitchen doorway.

Having woken to find the man standing over her bed, with no time to think, Shannon Lancaster had thrown herself, screaming, at the intruder. When she'd plunged her fingers into his balaclava, he had run from the room. As he'd fled through the back door of her home, the intruder had dropped a set of black plastic military-style handcuffs.

'Lucky, only in the sense she was still able to fight back.'

CHAPTER 5

A hush of restaurant chatter returned to Mailer's main dining room. Waiters busied themselves taking orders for the very best seafood in London, while offering complimentary glasses of champagne to soothe any frayed nerves. Sam rapidly helped himself to another glass, before reaching for a second and passing it to Madeline.

'Thanks, Sam,' she said, but she'd already placed her napkin on the table and was getting to her feet.

'Where are you going now?' he asked, his wait for his dinner his overriding concern. 'We'll never get served at this rate.'

'Don't worry, I'm sure your fish pie is on its way.' She moved quickly away from the table, past the cocktail bar and out through the warehouse-style doors, which led on to the restaurant's riverside terrace.

'Bloody hell, that stinks,' she said, stepping outside to where East had lit a highly potent spliff. 'If you're going to smoke all of that, I hope you've already cooked my dinner.'

East stared out at the fast-flowing river. Beneath the

waterproof awning emblazoned with his name, Madeline pulled a wrought-iron chair close to his. She looked at her best friend. When they'd first met in sixth form, nearly a quarter of a century ago, they were two outsiders; maverick characters determined to succeed. In some ways, little had changed. Now, he was a successful chef with a bestselling cookbook that she'd encouraged him to write. And anyone who had ever read the news almost certainly knew the name Madeline Wilson or, if not, had read a story she'd written.

'What's going on?' she asked.

East inhaled deeply on his spliff but still said nothing.

'Something's wrong because you just hauled a woman horizontally out of your restaurant. And it's bloody cold out here but you seem hell-bent on sitting outside and getting stoned. You said you wanted to talk to me?'

He licked his fingers and squeezed the end of his smoke. 'I'm scared.'

'Of losing Will?' she replied, knowing their marriage was going through a rough patch. 'You need to talk to him. And you need to get over the tiny bit of attention that comes with Nathan.'

'You call that escapade in the restaurant a tiny bit of attention?'

'East, you made it a thousand times worse. You made the story about you.'

He turned away from the river. 'You made a promise to me. All I would have to do was one TV appearance and that'd be it. I never signed up for this constant attention. If it wasn't for you, I'd never have done that bloody book.'

'Hang on,' replied Madeline. 'Is this what you wanted to talk about? That book sold a lot of copies and made your restaurant super successful.'

'I told you I couldn't handle being famous.'

'East, darling, you're anything but. You're a B-list celebrity chef with a half-decent restaurant. Nigella you're most definitely not.'

He didn't even smile but simply shook his head. 'You can't tell me that.' He paused. 'You've no idea what it's like; every day a different story, another part of my life rifled through. I can barely sleep.'

She could hear the panic in his voice. 'You need to calm down.'

'What do you think this is for?' he replied, holding up his smoke.

'I'm not sure that will help.'

'I don't need you to tell me what will or won't help.'

'East, you're overreacting, I promise you. That video will be a two-day wonder. After that, everyone moves on to the next story. And the wonderful thing is half the people who see the clip will think you did the right thing, and you know what, you'll probably sell a load more cookbooks.'

'Don't tell me that. I should never have let you persuade me.'

'You're being ridiculous.'

'Am I? The tiniest thing and there it is on Twitter or TikTok. Nothing is private. I feel trapped.'

'If I read everything that was said about me on social media, I'd have jumped off St Marnham bridge years ago.'

East walked across the terrace and stood looking out towards the water.

'I'm sorry, I shouldn't have said that.' Madeline stood beside him, resting her hand on his back. 'The truth is you have to learn to ignore it, and if you can't do that, take yourself off social.'

'It's not social I'm scared of,' replied East, snapping at Madeline, 'it's the crazy people it attracts. My face is everywhere. I'm caught in a never-ending vortex; one that you helped create.'

'That's not fair. I gave you a bit of publicity to help sell your book. I could just have easily helped somebody else.'

'Let's be honest, Madeline, you've built a career by exploiting other people's lives.'

She took a step back, watching her friend relight his spliff. At times he could become incredibly self-centred, and she knew there was very little point in arguing with him when he did. For East, it was a defensive reaction, but that didn't make it any more palatable. 'What you said isn't true but I'm not here to argue with you. I'm here to help.'

East drew heavily on his joint. 'Helping? Is that what you call it? It's a feeding frenzy.'

She turned and began walking back towards the restaurant.

'No, wait. I'm sorry.'

'I don't want to hear any more,' she replied, pulling open the door to the restaurant. 'I'm going to enjoy my dinner before you say something you might really regret.'

CHAPTER 6

Sam lifts his napkin and wipes his mouth.

'Dee-licious,' he says, finishing his second helping of fish pie.

'As it's your birthday, shall we order another bottle?' asks Madeline. 'I think I could do with it.'

'However delightful that would be, I'm going to have to love you and leave you,' he replies, pushing back his chair.

'You're leaving already?'

'Going on,' he replies, laughing.

'Who're you seeing now?'

'A couple of the boys promised to buy me a nightcap at the pub next door.'

'No. No. No,' replies Madeline, firmly. 'I take it these are the same good ol' boys who stayed up with you half the night playing poker and getting you so drunk you thought you were having a heart attack? Absolutely not, Dad. No.'

Sam downs the last of his wine before grinning at Madeline. 'My darling daughter, this has been the most glorious evening. The fish pie was wonderful, the company second to none and,' Sam stands and taps his phone in his jacket pocket, 'the *Richmond Times* is the owner of a video clip going viral as we speak.'

I bite my lip.

'One drink,' says Madeline, pointing her finger at her father, 'and then I want you straight home.'

'Two, but I have sworn off port. And I promise you, I'll be in a cab and heading home before midnight.' Sam squeezes me on the shoulder before reaching down for his birthday gifts. 'I don't suppose,' he says, resting the framed newspaper on the table and looking at his daughter, 'one of your lovely people could drop my wonderful birthday gift home for me?'

'Not a chance in bloody hell,' she replies.

'Can't kill a man for trying.' He blows Madeline a kiss and she does the same before he shuffles off towards the exit, a slight sway in his step as he goes.

'One of a kind,' I say to Madeline, as she carefully watches her father step out of the front of the restaurant.

'He'll never admit it, but he is getting older. I do worry he does too much.'

'He wouldn't be Sam if he didn't.'

Madeline signals to our waiter for one last drink before leaning forward, her elbows on the table. 'Can I ask you a question?' she says. 'Did you feel pressured into recording your podcast?'

'Never,' I reply. At the end of last year, I recorded a podcast telling the true story of my brother's murder and my mum's death a decade later. Much to Madeline's delight, it took our network's true-crime podcast to the top of the

Apple charts. She was, however, nothing but supportive throughout the recording process and it was always my decision to broadcast the story.

'And in writing the original story?'

'If you remember, I wrote the story I wanted to tell, even if it wasn't quite what you wanted at the time.'

'You needed to tell the truth for your mum?'

I nod. 'Why do you ask?'

'No reason. The attention on you tonight set me thinking.'

I can see she's being evasive. 'One of the first things you ever taught me was a good story only ever starts with the truth. In the world of social media that becomes harder, but without it everything we do becomes redundant.'

Madeline sips on a glass of Japanese whisky before passing her credit card to the waiter. 'What time are we seeing the new deputy commissioner in the morning?'

'Ten,' I reply.

I first met Dame Elizabeth Jones when I was working on a story of migrant murders in Dover, and she was chief constable of Kent. Recently moving into her new role at the Metropolitan Police, she began by instigating a review of policing standards. She agreed to meet with Madeline and me after I wrote an article implying corruption in the Haddley Police. While the article did nothing to increase my popularity with the local force, Dame Elizabeth has promised us an honest discussion.

'You still think she's one of the good ones?'

'I trust what she says,' I reply. 'She might not like everything we ask but she'll give us a fair hearing.'

'I'll take that,' Madeline replies. 'How're things progress-ing with Dani?'

I smile. 'She's still married to her police-officer husband, if that's what you mean.'

Dani and I first met during the reinvestigation into my brother's death. Then, more recently, we worked together to help clear her late father's name. Over that time, we've become increasingly close. 'It's a tricky situation right now,' I tell Madeline.

'Another thing I taught you,' she replies, with a glint in her eye, 'is nothing is impossible, especially not when you're in love.'

CHAPTER 7

Madeline stood beneath the overhanging canopy at the front of Mailer's restaurant.

'Meet you on the Embankment at nine forty-five,' she called to Ben, as he stepped down onto the river path to make the short walk back to his home in Haddley. 'And don't be late!' She saw him raise his hand in acknowledgement, but she already knew he'd be there on time. That was something else she'd taught him. She clicked on her phone. Her driver was four minutes late. About to message Dennis and ask him if he'd sloped off for a quick pint, she thought better of it. It was only four minutes.

Crossing the cobbled courtyard, she stopped and turned back to face the striking building. Hundreds of tiny light-bulbs, strung around the outside of the stone warehouse, illuminated the spectacular space. She looked towards the small first-floor apartment where she knew Will's son was living but could see no sign of life. Before leaving the restaurant, she'd peered into the open kitchen, hoping to catch sight of East, but he hadn't returned. She hated when they argued. She hoped he'd simply made his way home to Will. In the past, the pair had seemed so incredibly happy, she'd felt almost jealous. Recognising she'd sacrificed much of her own happiness to her career, she wished East could see what he had was worth fighting for. She sighed and, feeling the late evening chill, wrapped her coat tighter around her and looked back at her phone.

Two further missed calls from the same unknown number. In the morning, she'd ask Carolyn to trace the caller. She slipped her phone back in her pocket and, as she did, she saw her car approaching. On the opposite side of the road, the 419 bus to Richmond pulled up at its stop. She imagined Sam staggering across the road and clambering on board, his birthday present tucked beneath his arm. Perhaps she should have said she'd drop it home for him. She waited at the edge of the pavement as her black S-Class Mercedes slowed on its approach, only to stop ten feet past her. Under her breath she chided Dennis, clicking her tongue. Arriving at her car, she distractedly reached for the embedded door handle, but it failed to extend. She rapped on the window. After a moment, the handle extended. She slipped quickly into the rear seat and closed the door.

'What's going on with you tonight, Dennis?' she asked.

The fist slammed into the bridge of her nose. Blood spurted upwards and her head flew back. Frenzied lights swirled before her eyes. Dazed, she fell forwards, crashing into the video screen on which she watched rolling news whenever she was in the car.

A body scrambled from the front seat. Her head was

41

pushed down into the footwell. Desperately turning on the floor, she reached her hand up towards the door, searching for the handle.

'Go!' screamed a voice. The car accelerated rapidly, locking the car doors as it did. The weight of a man's body held her down but, twisting, she caught a glimpse of him.

A grotesque pig's face stared back at her. Only the unhinged eyes were real.

Her best chance of survival was now. With no time to think, all she could do was fight or die. From the footwell, she launched herself upwards, landing her knee in the man's groin. He squealed in pain. She plunged her fingers into the eyes of the pig's face. The man grabbed hold of her arms, but rolling she again landed her knee. She freed her arms and reached forward for the driver's face.

The car swerved across the road, horns blared, and she braced for a collision. Desperately, she felt for the driver's eyes. Instead, her fingers hit against his glasses and the car swerved back across the road.

Then she felt the impact.

A glass bottle smashed onto the back of her head. For a moment she was weightless, drifting backwards until she crashed onto the rear seat.

As her eyes slowly closed, all she could see was the pig's bloodshot eyes staring down at her.

Two

*'It's impossible for us to know
what he might do next.'*

'Get back to bed, now!' she yelled as soon as she saw him peering through the gaps in the banister.

Running up the stairs, he fell, scraping his knee on the wooden floor. His knee bled but he didn't cry. He licked his hand and, wincing, he tried to rub it clean. Back in his room, he tied a dirty sock around his leg to stop the blood.

He lay in bed, letting his eyes follow the swirling clouds across the dark night sky, until he heard footsteps approaching his room. It was the man. He closed his eyes tightly to make him think he was asleep. The man had no sooner put his head around the door than he heard him turn, pull the door closed and walk back down the creaking stairs.

He waited a minute before he slowly pushed back his duvet, crawled across his bed and edged his bedroom door back open. He'd quickly learned if he left his door slightly open, lay perfectly still in his bed and breathed in and out very slowly, he could hear almost every word they were saying in the room below. He closed his eyes and waited for their voices to float up to him. It was her voice he heard first.

'We need to do it now, not wait.' Her voice was little more than a whisper, but it still carried.

'I don't know if we even can,' was his reply. 'Don't we have to talk to somebody first?'

'They're our boys now. We decide what's best for them and

no child of mine will be called Travis.' It was his brother they were talking about.

'But can we just change his name? What will we say?'

'He's five years old. We'll tell him it's a game. He'll be excited about it. And his brother's too daft to realise.'

He hated it when people called him dim. Or stupid. Or slow. Or daft.

He kept listening.

'We say nothing to the adoption agency. We start using his new name straight away. If anyone ever asks, we say it's a nickname. Once it's stuck, we get it changed officially.'

'If you're sure,' the man replied.

'We're here to give him every opportunity in life. "Travis" is not a good opportunity.' He heard her laugh.

'You're probably right.'

'I promise you, it's for the best. He's a bright boy. We need to set him on the right path.'

'We need to set them both on their way.'

'And we will.'

He didn't believe her. He watched his football clock click over a minute until she spoke again.

'You need to accept what each of them can achieve in life will be very different. That means they will need different things from us. Of course, we'll help him, but Travis can make something of his life. It's down to us to help him become a success. Dopey upstairs will never amount to a hill of beans.'

46

CHAPTER 8

I take the long way home. The air is cool, and the sky is beginning to clear. Streetlights illuminate the shuttered shops through St Marnham, before I follow the winding path around the village pond and out onto the Lower Haddley Road. From there the road snakes through the woods, emerging onto Haddley Common, the only home I've ever known.

St Stephen's sixteenth-century church looms into the dark sky, its bell tower still swathed in scaffolding following a recent fire. Outside the church gates, a giant sign announces that the vicar's fundraising efforts to create a garden of remembrance on disused land by the river have now reached 50 per cent of her target. I briefly met the new vicar last week and she seems both incredibly young and enthusiastic. I make a mental note to donate, otherwise she will be on my doorstep seeking not only a contribution but also attendance.

I walk onto the deserted common and follow the path that runs across the wide-open space. My home sits in the middle of a terraced row, looking out on the grass and the woods beyond. Along the south side of the common stands a series of Victorian villas, each one residing in its own grounds and commanding views down to the river. I flick on my phone and message Dani. I share Sam's video from the restaurant, knowing it will make her laugh, I can't stop myself wishing she'd been able to join us for dinner, but I understand the impossible situation in which she finds herself. Dani admits she married her husband, DS Mat Moore, for no other reason than her own feelings of guilt. Sixteen months ago, a brutal knife attack at which she was present left him facing life-changing injuries. Although their lives are largely separate, she is determined to help him rebuild his. I can only admire her for that. The nights she spends with me feel like moments stolen in time. However much I want us to be together, I know I must be patient and can only hope that one day it might be possible. After a moment I type another message.

Can you get away this weekend?

As I wait to see if Dani replies, a figure, emerging from the narrow footpath that runs across the top of the woods, captures my attention. Only occasionally used by locals as a shortcut to St Marnham station, the path is now rarely taken. Dressed all in black, his collar up and with a baseball cap pulled low to conceal his face, he hurries along the dark lane. Passing in front of the row of Victorian villas, he moves quickly from one house to the next. When he approaches the home of Sarah Wright, a friend and neighbour of mine

48

for the past seven years, he slows. His rapid walk becomes little more than a nervous step before he stops at the end of Sarah's driveway, peering towards the house.

I step off the pathway and walk slowly across the grass. I watch the man take two further steps before he stops again. Positioned on the driveway is a builder's skip, half filled with discarded kitchen units. The man crouches behind the skip before suddenly hurrying towards the house. To keep him in sight, I move rapidly forward and when I reach the edge of the common, I'm running.

In front of me, Sarah's house stands shrouded in darkness. Having recently split from her partner, Nathan, she embarked on a much-delayed renovation project. She's been living only in the upstairs rooms of her home and cooking for herself and her young son, Max, on an electric hotplate, and she told me she is desperate for her builders to finish the job. I stand behind the skip and watch the figure pass the stone steps, which lead up to the home's imposing black front door. The man stops at the bay-fronted sash window, briefly attempting to prise it open with his hands. Immediately my mind jumps to the intruder Dani and I spoke of at the start of the week. I move out of the shadows and am about to call to him when he darts away, disappearing down the side of the house.

I follow him. He scampers past the home's side door before pushing open a gate and scurrying into the back garden. He jumps over the scaffolding erected at the rear of the house and stands in front of the boarded-up patio door. Reaching up, he rips down the timber loosely secured in place.

49

'What do you think you're doing?' I shout.

He turns towards me. The darkness hides his face, but I see him reach down for a short piece of scaffolding. He brandishes the metal bar at me.

I step back onto the lawn and feel for my phone. 'I'm calling the police,' I yell.

He says nothing in reply, but before I can pull my phone from my pocket he charges forward. Raising the metal bar high, he swings towards the side of my head. I duck and jump sideways, landing on the grass. As I fall, he hurls the bar towards me. I'm able to deflect it with my shoulder, but as I scramble to my feet he's already sprinting away towards the back of the garden.

'What the fuck do you want?' I call, racing after him. He's halfway across the back lawn, but I can see I'm catching him. I run harder, and summoning all my schoolboy memories, launch myself forward in a flying rugby tackle. As I fall towards the ground, I grab hold of his ankles but when I try to drag him down, he kicks himself free, knocking me sideways as he does.

I stagger back onto my feet but he's ahead of me now. All I can do is stand and watch as he clambers up into Max's treehouse, before dropping from the platform and over the rear garden fence. He lands on the gravel path that runs behind the garden, and in the still night air I hear the crunch of his footsteps slowly fade into the distance.

CHAPTER 9

Sarah Wright puts her finger to her lips. We're standing silently in the bedroom doorway of her six-year-old son. Curled in his bed, a soft, stripy bumblebee sitting sharp-eyed at his head, Max sleeps on, blissfully unaware of the intruder in his garden. Standing on the table beside his bed, illuminated by the light from the landing, is a picture of Max in a football shirt with arms wrapped around his father. Sarah sees me glancing towards it.

'James took him to his first Brentford match,' she whispers. 'Max is their new number-one fan.'

'I'm their number-one fan,' I reply. 'Max can be their number-two fan.'

Sarah smiles and looks across at the selfie taken at the side of the pitch. 'I have to admit James is a far more attentive father now Nathan is no longer around.'

'I can understand how it might be easier for him.'

'Of course, the fact that his student girlfriend dumped him may also have freed up some of his weekend time. Perhaps his midlife crisis is coming to an end. I should be grateful.'

I follow Sarah down the hallway and into a spare bedroom temporarily converted into a living space. She switches on the room lights. 'Ben,' she says, wincing, 'let me get you something for your face.'

'Honestly, I'm fine,' I reply, gently touching the corner of my mouth where the intruder's boot caught me a glancing blow. My fingers come away etched with blood. 'I should probably wash my face.'

'Use that bathroom,' she says, pointing to the ensuite. I hear her flick the switch on a kettle she has set up in the corner of the room. 'Tea?' she asks.

'Thanks,' I call, standing in front of the bathroom mirror. I run the hot water tap, wipe my swollen face, and rub a towel across my hair. After the man escaped along the pathway, I walked back towards Sarah's kitchen where a minute later she appeared. She called the police, only for the operator to tell her that as the intruder was no longer on the premises it could be up to an hour before officers were able to attend.

'I think that might be a little sore in the morning,' she says when I walk back into the bedroom. 'Please let me get you some cream.'

'Really, don't worry, I'll find something when I get home,' I reply, taking a mug of tea from her and sitting on one of the two small sofas. When I lean back, something sharp digs into my lower back, and I pull a Lego speedboat from behind the cushion.

'Max has been looking all over for that,' she says, laughing. 'He built it himself, with only a little help from Nathan.'

'Max must miss him?' I say. I lost count of the number of

times I saw them playing football on the common; just the two of them for hours on end.

'Nathan was brilliant with him, but it's good for Max to be closer to his father now.'

'And you?'

'I divorced a husband who was ten years older than me and then I jumped into a relationship with a man almost ten years younger. Nathan and I have known each other for less than a year.' Sarah reaches for her mug. 'He was fun to be with but he's not much more than a kid, and now he's landed with a shitload of stuff to deal with, none of it of his making. Our lives are in very different places. Max is my number-one priority.'

I tell Sarah what happened at the restaurant and her eyes drift towards the speedboat. 'Nathan's a gentle and caring soul who never signed up for any of this. He struggles with all the attention on social media. I've told him he should get away from London.'

We finish our drinks before heading back downstairs to wait for the police. The back of the kitchen is still open to the garden.

'I can nail that back up if you like.'

'I've messaged James. He said he'd come over.'

'It'll take me two minutes.'

'Are you sure?' she replies. 'Let me run upstairs and close Max's bedroom door.'

I search through the builder's tools, left scattered across the kitchen, but before I've found what I need there's a knock at the front door.

'I'll get it,' I call, quietly.

I move Max's green Frog bike to one side and open the door.

'Ben,' says the officer standing on the doorstep.

'Dani,' I reply. 'I wasn't expecting you.'

CHAPTER 10

I take a step back, and Dani enters the dimly lit hallway.

'Ben,' she says, quietly, her hand reaching up to my cheek, 'look at your face. What happened?' Her soft fingers move across my mouth, and I gently kiss them.

'It's nothing,' I reply. 'I promise, I'm fine.' I pause and take hold of her hand. 'I'm glad you're here.'

Dani edges away from me. 'Karen, PC Cooke, is accompanying me. She's checking down the side of the house.'

'When can I see you?'

'Ben, not now. Karen will be here any second.'

A moment later, PC Cooke pushes open the front door and when Sarah appears down the stairs, the police officers introduce themselves to her. Together, we walk through to the kitchen, and I share my limited description of the man.

'You're certain it was his intention to enter the property?' asks PC Cooke.

'One hundred per cent,' I reply. 'He tried the front window and then, if I hadn't stopped him, would've entered through the kitchen.'

'We do advise caution, rather than heroics, in such situations,' adds Dani, and I smile. She turns to Sarah. 'Mrs Wright, it's not impossible this could have been nothing more than an opportunistic burglar. Building works often signal easy access to a property. He sees a skip in the driveway, the house in darkness, and he thinks he'll chance his arm.'

'The speed he moved down the lane, ignoring all the other properties, it was this house he was targeting.' Dani stares at me and I realise I'm probably not helping.

'It's perfectly possible he scouted properties during the day,' she replies, her eyes focused firmly on me. I say nothing further, and Dani turns back to Sarah. 'However, it's equally possible this wasn't a burglary.'

'You're talking about the intruder?' interrupts Sarah. There's a sudden tension in her voice. 'The one who breaks into women's bedrooms?'

Dani holds up her hands. 'That's not what I'm saying.'

'But he did break into another woman's home last weekend?'

'At this stage, it's impossible for us to say. I am aware of the speculation about last weekend, but we are yet to confirm if that was the same man as in previous attacks.'

Across Haddley, social media is alive with rumours surrounding a new intruder attack. Like me, I'm sure Sarah has read the running commentary on our neighbourhood app. It's over four months since the intruder's last confirmed break-in, but fear still permeates the town that his attacks will escalate. Residents are openly questioning the efforts of the Haddley Police to apprehend the perpetrator. Dani, and all her colleagues, are under enormous pressure.

'Do you think it might've been him?' asks Sarah. 'Up until now, all of the women were alone when he broke in?'

'That's true, but if it was him, he may not have been aware of your son's presence in the house.' Dani stops as, down the hall, the front door of Sarah's home is suddenly thrown open.

CHAPTER 11

'James!' exclaims Sarah, at the sight of her former husband entering the kitchen.

'Sorry. I still have my old key. I'm Max's father,' he explains to Dani and PC Cooke.

'You were just passing?' asks the uniformed officer.

'Sarah messaged and asked me to come over. Of course, I came as quickly as I could.'

'Thank you,' says Sarah, briefly putting her arm around his waist.

'Is Max okay?'

'Sleeping soundly.'

'If I could continue,' says Dani, 'right now we're asking local residents to be extra vigilant, until the intruder is apprehended.'

'I read on Twitter,' James says, 'because he was forced to flee earlier in the week, you think he's likely to attack again.'

'That's pure speculation. As I said, we're yet to confirm anything about last Saturday's break-in,' replies Dani, calmly. 'Social media can be a blessing and a curse. It's impossible for us to know what he might do next. We are simply urging caution.'

James looks at his ex-wife. 'Have you told them about the other stuff?'

Sarah shakes her head. 'I'm sure that was nothing.'

'I wouldn't call a fire nothing.'

'Mrs Wright?' Dani's tone is more urgent now.

Sarah presses her fingers into the back of her neck. 'Last week, some kids started a fire in the skip out front. One of the builders was still here and he put it out in thirty seconds. All very uneventful.'

'You saw the children start the fire?'

'No, but I'm sure that's all it was.'

'And the rest,' says James.

'There is nothing else,' replies Sarah, turning sharply to her former husband.

'Dog shit through the letterbox?' he says.

Sarah sighs. 'Three nights ago. Hardly the world's greatest crime. It was even wrapped in newspaper,' she says, trying to laugh it off.

'But not very pleasant all the same,' replies Dani. 'Mrs Wright, can I ask if Nathan Beavin still resides here?' Dani was one of two officers to first interview Nathan after he revealed the identity of his birth mother.

'No,' replies Sarah.

'That boy attracts all kinds of crazy people. Any one of them might have done this,' says James. 'If you ask me, you're better off without him.'

'Mr Beavin does capture of huge amount of attention

online. As his now ex-partner, there appears to be little logic for indiscriminate attacks upon you. However, strange as it may seem, it can take the TikTok world a little time to catch up with real life. It's not impossible people believe you're still together.'

'Who cares if we are?'

'Some very odd sorts,' replies James. He turns to Dani. 'I take it you'll be stationing an officer here tonight.'

'Resources are limited, I'm afraid, Mr Wright. The most important thing is to secure the rear of the property, and we can send somebody out to help with that.'

'If that's the best you can offer, Ben and I can board up the kitchen.'

'If you're sure.' Dani turns away. 'Mr Harper, if you could show me where the intruder exited the garden, I'd be most grateful.'

As Dani and I step through the patio doors, I hear Sarah agreeing to James's suggestion he stay at the house tonight. Walking across the garden, I whisper to Dani, 'Let's go away this weekend.'

'I'd prefer it if you didn't contradict me when I'm speaking to a crime victim,' she replies.

'That's a bit harsh,' I say. 'I just told you what I saw.'

'I'm too tired to argue.'

'I didn't know we were arguing. How about we go down to Devon? You love the coast.'

'I'm not like you, Ben, I can't just drop everything.'

'Are you working?'

'Hopefully not.'

'Then let me arrange it.'

'I've got responsibilities.'

'You mean Mat?'

'Yes, I mean my husband,' replies Dani. 'And I'm exhausted. I've been on lates for a week and I've another week to go. I need some down time.'

'I want to be with you, Dani. Come back to mine now,' I whisper.

'I'm still on shift.'

'When do you finish?'

She doesn't reply and, in silence, we walk towards the bottom of the garden. Dani lights her torch as we stand beneath Max's treehouse.

'Are you still seeing Dame Elizabeth Jones tomorrow?'

'Is that what this is about?'

'Are you?'

'I've told you, it's my job.'

'And this is my career. What I told you was nothing more than a throwaway comment.'

'A throwaway comment by the most senior police officer in Haddley,' I reply, snapping at Dani and letting my frustration show. 'One which left you anxious, and both of us fearing Freeman could be complicit with the Baxter family.'

Dani briefly closes her eyes and exhales. 'Please can we not do this now?' she asks. 'Whatever I might've said about Chief Inspector Freeman and the Baxter family, it was between you and me. Any decision to share it any further is mine, and mine alone.'

A local crime family, the Baxters, monopolise the supply

of illegal drugs across our borough. Dani's father, DCI Jack Cash, spent his life pursuing them. In posthumously clearing his name, Dani and I discovered a local church minister, the Reverend Adrian Withers, had been complicit in their crimes. Withers ended up dead, but hidden in the vicar's ancient filing cabinet was a stash of illegal drugs. A comment from Freeman told Dani she too was aware of the hiding place. More concerning was the hiding of the knife used to stab Mat in the same filing cabinet, and its disappearance following the vicar's death.

'I get what you're saying, Dani, but your concerns are genuine.'

She moves to stand by the fence at the back of the garden and lowers her voice. 'I can prove nothing. Freeman is a decorated officer and highly respected by everyone at the station.'

I know how much Dani is torn. Her overwhelming urge is for Haddley Police to succeed. While I may be ready to believe corruption exists within the force, for her it is far harder to accept. Haddley Police has been a rare constant throughout her life. In her heart, she doesn't want to believe criminality exists within her team, but I worry she is too quick in her desire to look the other way.

'Somebody took the knife, Dani. You know that as well as I do.'

'This isn't about the knife, Ben. This is about trust. I confided in you and now I'm asking you to leave it. This is about you and me.'

'But what if you're right?'

'I know you'll do anything for a story—'

'Only if it's the truth—'

'You're not listening to me. This is about us. If you so much as hint to Elizabeth Jones about Freeman, I will never forgive you.'

I reach for Dani's hand. 'I won't,' I say, 'I promise.'

She pulls her hand away. 'If you betray me, Ben, that's the end.'

CHAPTER 12

Will Andrews sat on the edge of his bed and looked at his phone. It was 1 a.m. He typed another message to his husband. This was the third message he'd sent since closing the restaurant. All were without reply. From the upstairs flat, after seeing East sitting alone on the terrace, smoking, he'd watched him drift down onto the river path and disappear into the darkness. He still had no idea where he'd gone.

He reached for a sweater from the chair beside his bed and stepped out onto the vast landing of his St Marnham home. He walked downstairs, the cold of the marble steps rising into his feet. Passing the ornate glass front door, he glanced up at the giant Hockney print, which hung at the back of the hall. In the kitchen, he reached for a French crystal glass, filled it from the chilled water tap and sat drinking at the bespoke quartz island. Everything in his home was either chosen or designed by East. Yes, they had bought it all together but, looking around, every bit of it was in East's extravagant taste. Will knew he was lucky to have an art deco home overlooking the village pond, but he'd been equally happy in the two-bedroom flat in Haddley where he'd lived when he first worked in the City. He didn't need all the trappings his wealth brought them. Perhaps East did.

His phone buzzed. His stomach tensed as he quickly opened the screen, only to see it was a message from Nathan.

You awake? asked his son.

Yes, he replied. Where are you?

Just in.

Where've you been?

I've been messaging my mum.

Will could see Nathan was still typing, so he waited.

She suggested I go back to Cowbridge.

Will stared at his phone.

A visit might be nice, he replied after a pause.

She wasn't meaning a visit.

What was she meaning?

I need some time away from St Marnham.

Can we talk it through tomorrow?

I've booked a train for Saturday.

He hated to admit it, but Will realised Cowbridge was Nathan's real home. And the Beavins his real family.

Let me drive you.

Are you sure?

Of course, I'd love to meet your family, was all he could type in reply.

Finding Nathan, however painful it had first been, had brought new and unexpected joy to his life. He'd started to think of his own life and wealth differently, realising he could give his son new opportunities. His only regret was they hadn't found each other sooner.

He heard the front door open, before East let it slam closed behind him. When his husband walked down the hallway towards the kitchen, Will raised his eyes but said nothing.

'Don't look at me like that,' said East, collapsing into a corner armchair. 'I thought you'd be asleep by now.'

'I still have a vague interest in where you might be.' His husband looked exhausted. 'Was it another journalist?' he

66

asked, referring to the disruption he'd heard in the restaurant earlier in the evening.

'Worse. Drunk women googling pictures of him online. It'll be all over social by now.'

'By him, I assume you mean Nathan?'

East dropped his head back. 'I feel as if I'm trapped inside a giant goldfish bowl.'

'How do you think Nathan feels?'

East replied as if he hadn't heard Will. 'Except it isn't a goldfish bowl, it's a murky cesspit of online poison.' He began to pace the kitchen. 'Every inch of our lives trawled through, speculated upon. *How far does the fruit fall from the tree? Is he in touch with his mother?* And in every single post there I am, TV chef East Mailer. I've been on one bloody Saturday-morning show and suddenly it's as if I'm the criminal.'

'You have to learn to ignore it.'

'Really? Do you think it's that easy? You should read what they say about you.' Will said nothing, but with anger quickly burning across his face, East continued. '*Did he rape her?* That's what they're asking. When you were fourteen years old, did you rape the child killer?'

'They can say what they like about me, I don't care. My only interest is in Nathan. And, for the record, no I didn't. I might regret everything that happened, but I'll never regret Nathan.'

'Every fragment of our lives scrutinised. Pictures snatched from the restaurant. And it's getting worse by the day.'

'He's my son.'

'You've only known him ten months! Before that you didn't even know of his existence. How can he mean anything to you?'

Will bit back. 'He's kind, thoughtful, generous. All the things you used to be.' Over the last few weeks his marriage to East had become increasingly strained. He didn't know what East wanted any more or even if he wanted to stay married. 'Whatever happened to the funny, inventive man I fell in love with? When did you become so angry at the world? Nathan's my son and I love him. Have you ever stopped for a single second to consider what his life has become? He never asked for any of this.'

'And neither have I. I can't control who his parents are.'

'What the hell is that supposed to mean?'

'I might feel sorry for him, but not enough for him to fuck up my life. That's why I think he's better off out of my restaurant and out of our lives.'

'I'm going to bed,' replied Will, before stopping at the foot of the stairs. 'You'd do well to remember, without my money there would be no restaurant.'

'My name is what makes that restaurant.'

'What? Because of your two-bit TV appearance?'

East poked his fingers into Will's chest. 'I won't let your son destroy everything I've built.'

Will looked at his husband. 'You signed up for life with me, the good times and the bad. Unless you're telling me you're done?'

CHAPTER 13

Dani Cash stepped off the night bus at the top of Haddley Hill. Most days she walked the twenty minutes from the police station to her home, but tonight she was simply too exhausted. A packed bus had left her with no choice but to stand throughout the journey, and as she watched the bus pull away, she stretched her back and inhaled the cool night air.

As she walked onto the modern estate that housed her two-bedroom terrace, she paused by the multi-coloured bottle bank and assorted recycling bins. Painted signs invited local residents to deposit their waste and make the planet a greener place. Attempting to hide between a giant blue bin, overflowing with crushed cardboard boxes, and a bright red container for plastic bottles, was a group of teenagers. Even before she saw them, she'd already smelled the skunk. The stench left her feeling nauseous and she crossed to the opposite side of the road.

'That stuff will fuck with your brains,' she shouted. One of the older boys yelled something offensive back. 'I'm sure you've got school in the morning,' she replied. 'Shouldn't you be safely tucked up in bed?' The teenagers laughed, and feeling as tired as she did, she simply walked on towards her home.

Whatever they were smoking, there was bound to be a way of tracing it back to the Baxter family. A member of the same family was suspected of Mat's stabbing. Could her station commander really have collaborated with the local crime family to seize the knife used in the attack? Freeman's unguarded comment had made clear to her she knew of the drugs hidden in the ancient filing cabinet, but did that mean she also knew of the knife? Perhaps Dani had made too much of a leap, but the comment still unsettled her. She felt uneasy with herself in doubting her commanding officer, one who led the station with such authority. But, more than three months after the incident, she still found her suspicions impossible to shake.

She'd made the decision to confide in Ben, but now she feared that the desire to uncover a shocking story would prove too irresistible for him. Nobody wanted to root out police corruption more than her, but from her father's experience she'd learned that had to be a waiting game. Ben's never-ending desire to uncover the truth was at times all-consuming and his approach often rash. With her marriage all but over, she hoped her future would be with Ben. But could she trust him?

Outside her home, she stopped and searched in the bottom of her bag for her door key. The living-room light was on, which meant Mat must still be awake. Slipping the key in the lock, she thought of the separate lives she and Mat still somehow shared – him living downstairs, her living upstairs. At least they'd now found a way to be civil with each other. Immediately after the attack, she had married him simply due to feelings of guilt. She still wanted him to be happy, but hoped they both now recognised their marriage had no future.

'Hi,' she called, bringing as much positivity to her voice as she could muster. She put her head around the living-room door.

'Late finish?' asked Mat.

'Another potential intruder break-in. This time on Haddley Common.' Dani relayed the evening's events to her husband.

'Do you think it's him?'

'Shannon Lancaster, I'm certain. He's opportunistic. Saturday night, she was home alone; somehow, he knew. He made it into her bedroom, but for the first time, he'd planned to attack.'

'The handcuffs?'

Dani nodded. 'If she hadn't fought back, I hate to think what we might be investigating now.'

'Brave woman.'

'Incredibly.'

'And tonight?'

'Maybe,' she replied, picking up her husband's jeans from where he'd left them on the floor and folding them over the back of his wheelchair. 'Description fits. Victim has recently split from her partner and, other than her young son, she was alone.'

'Will he go again?' asked Mat.

'We know he wants to escalate, but who the fuck knows what he'll do next.'

'It's the control he wants? The power of watching the women sleep, letting them wake to find him standing beside their beds?'

Dani agreed. 'Until now, everything's been in the threat of what he might do. From here, it only gets worse.' She bent down and kissed Mat on the forehead. 'I'm exhausted so I'm off to bed. I'm on lates again tomorrow but I might see you at the station after lunch.' She stopped at the living-room door. 'Oh, and I think I'll probably have to work this weekend.'

'Don't you ever stop?'

'With you moving on, we'll be a body down.' At the end of the following week, Mat was leaving CID and transferring into the Met's Directorate of Professional Standards. It was no longer sustainable for him to continue working in Haddley's small CID unit, but the DPS, investigating his fellow officers, would have been Mat's very last choice. She couldn't help but wonder how much pressure senior officers had applied before he'd agreed to take the role.

'As long as you're able to get a little bit of time for yourself,' he replied.

Dani felt her face flush.

Mat reached for the light switch at the side of his bed. 'Please don't humiliate me,' he said, before covering the room in darkness.

CHAPTER 14

The jolting of the car brought Madeline back to conscious-ness. She could feel the rough terrain beneath the tyres and realised they were now driving off road. Where were they?

The car jumped again, and she gasped for breath as her head cracked against the broken glass splintered across the seat. Reaching for the back of her head, she felt blood seeping through her tangled hair. She opened her eyes and could see there were no longer any streetlights. Wherever they were, the light of the moon brought the only brightness.

Slowly lifting her head, she saw Pig Face leaning for-ward between the two front seats. With his hand resting on the driver's shoulder, she could see his arms thick and muscled; his back broad and square. What chance did she have? Fleetingly, she smelled the lemon scent Dennis used to polish the woodwork. *Dennis!* Where was he? He'd realise she was gone. He'd send for help. But what if they had hurt him?

'Where's Dennis?' she yelled suddenly, somehow forcing herself upright.

'Shut up,' shouted the driver, 'or you'll go the same way.'

Instantly, she thought of Dennis's kindly manner, never failing to keep an eye out for her. 'Tell me what you want,' she said. The two men ignored her. 'Tell me what you want,' she repeated. 'I can get you money. Let me out here and I can get you a lot of money, tonight.'

'It's over there, on the right,' said the driver to Pig Face.

'I said I can get you money,' she cried.

'And I said shut the fuck up.'

'Do you know who I am?' she said, hearing the panic in her own voice.

The men ignored her. 'Here's the key,' said the driver, reaching his hand back towards Pig Face.

Pig Face took the key and slipped it into his jacket pocket. She seized her moment. Scrambling forward, she dived past him, launching herself head first into the front passenger seat. From behind, Pig Face lunged at her waist, but she was already past him. She kicked her legs backwards against his chest and propelled herself towards the door. The driver snatched at her arm, but she twisted away and clawed at the handle.

The cold air hit her face. She threw herself out of the open door, only to feel, from behind, a giant hand grab hold of her hair and haul her back inside. With the door open, the car spun to the side, its tyres sliding to a stop in the wet mud. The hand dragged her back through the gap in the two front seats. The pain was overwhelming as Pig Face pulled her by her hair. She screamed as he slammed her onto the back seat, his right hand locked around her throat. Held down, suddenly she couldn't breathe. Her eyes closed. He was going to kill her now.

He flipped her over, forcing her face down into the soft leather. His knee on her back, his weight crushed against her spine. He grabbed her hands and held them together.

And then she heard the duct tape ripped from the roll.

Pig Face wound the tape endlessly around her hands, binding them together behind her back. He flipped her over again and slapped more tape across her mouth. He pulled again at the roll. Frantically, she started shaking her head, pushing herself backwards in the seat. He grabbed hold of her hair and knelt on her chest. All she could do was lie still as he bound the tape across her eyes.

Trapped in the darkness, Madeline tried to control her breathing. She thought of her father, everything she'd shared with him, how much she loved him. Even as a child, he was the one she'd run to, the one who would save her. But not this time.

Lying on the back seat, her senses stifled, she heard one of the car's rear doors open. More of the cold night air flooded into the confined space. Pig Face lifted himself up and she heard him climb outside. The driver's door opened, and he followed. The pair moved further away and spoke in whispers.

Could this be her last chance? She edged forward. By resting her head against the front seat, she found her bearings. For a second, she waited. Were they even looking in her direction? She moved again, cautiously, towards the open car door.

The two men spoke in the distance. Could they still see her? Rolling out of the side of the car, she fell onto the cold, wet grass. With her hands taped, all she could do was crawl to the back of the car. From there, she snaked beneath the boot, her legs pushing her forward. When she reached the far side, she leaned against the closed rear door, trying to catch her breath. Then she forced herself upright and started to run.

Run. Run. Run for your life, she told herself.

She kept blindly running, through the wet grass, until her ears rang with the most terrifying sound. The two men howling with laughter, screaming in delight, as she made her desperate charge for freedom.

A blow landed on her kidneys; another across her back. All she could do was gasp for air. When he yanked her hair, inwardly she screamed. He dragged her backwards, her scampering crab like behind him, across the open field. He slammed her against the side of a van. She heard a key turn and the squeak of an opening door. Pulling her forward, he lifted her up and tossed her onto the floor of a transit van. Then, he followed her in.

She scrambled backwards across the cold, metal floor and pressed herself into the far corner of the load space. She heard the man crawl towards her, and she held her body rigid. Together in the confined space, the man crouched close enough for her to feel his rapid breath on her neck. She lifted her head to his. Whatever he was going to do, she would make him look at her face. She drew back her shoulders and even with her eyes hidden, she stared defiantly at her captor.

In silence, Madeline waited for what felt like an eternity but was in reality no more than a few seconds. Was he looking at her? The inside of the van must be pitch black. Did he have a light on his phone? Was he holding it up to her face, her body?

She felt a touch on her cheek: rubber against her skin. It was Pig Face. Even now, alone in the darkness, with her eyes obscured, he still wore his vile mask. He rubbed his face against hers, one animal pushing against another. She swallowed hard but kept her head held high.

Without warning, he grabbed her legs and dragged her forward. The sound of the duct tape rapidly unwinding echoed inside the van. First her feet, then her thighs, tightly bound together. She'd learned in the field that running was pointless; now it was impossible. Pig Face jumped out, slamming the door closed behind him.

Seconds later, the engine fired, and the van pulled slowly forward. Bound and gagged, nothing more than an animal loaded for slaughter, she bounced from side to side, her shoulder crashing against the floor. The van slid across the wet grass before rolling onto a firmer gravel path. When it climbed a sharp bank, she began to slide backwards towards the rear doors. Beneath her she heard the wheels spin, slipping on the loose gravel. The driver pumped the accelerator, revving the engine hard. He crunched the gears, and from behind the wooden partition she heard him cry out. She prayed for the van to stall, for it to fail to mount the sharp bank, but when he slammed the accelerator again, the van jumped forward. As it lurched over the top of the rise, she bounced into the air; a sharp pain shot through her spine when she crashed down onto her back.

The terrain flattened, and she began to imagine them travelling along Haddley's river road. Feeling with her arms, she wedged herself between the side wheel and the back of the driver's cabin. Her legs ached, but at least she was able to stop each turn in the road throwing her across the van's empty load space.

Slowing, she assumed at traffic lights, she suddenly found herself kicking at the side of the van, thumping with her knee. The van's acceleration was fast and she realised they must have heard her. She began to kick at the wooden partition. Over and over, she knocked and banged. She didn't know what she was hoping for, but she did know she would fight until her last breath left her body.

The driver slammed on the brakes. Hurled forward, inside she smiled. She was annoying them. Then, she heard the passenger door thrown open and she froze.

'I'll deal with the car,' said a voice, now standing outside the van. It was the driver of the car. She realised Pig Face must be driving the van. 'I've changed your licence plates and spray-painted the sides. You're on your own now,' he said to Pig Face.

And so, she realised, was she.

Three

'It was her relentless pursuit of the killer that led to a conviction.'

Inside his room, the only sound he could hear was of his own slow breath, but from the floor below the sounds they made still drifted upwards. He knew what they were doing. The noise the man made he'd heard a hundred times before; so many men doing the same thing to his own mum.

He'd hated it when the men came into their flat. The flat only had one bedroom. He'd had to sit in the kitchen rocking Travis in his pushchair, waiting until the men left. One of the men had made him stand in the doorway and watch. He'd felt like grabbing a knife from the drawer and stabbing it into the man's hairy back. Instead, he'd stood frozen in the doorway until he felt the warmth run down his legs, soaking his pyjamas. His grandad had bought him those pyjamas. They'd had footballs dotted across the top.

Before Travis, when it had been just him and his mum, he'd been happy. And so had she. They'd play together and he'd soon learned how to make her laugh. Seeing her laugh had made him feel special. He'd wanted to make her laugh all the time. When Travis arrived, she'd stopped smiling. He'd tried everything he'd done before to make her smile, but nothing seemed to work. His songs, his dances, even him pressing his face against the window and squidging his nose only seemed to make her more sad. His fifth birthday came soon after Travis was born. His mum was so tired she'd forgotten. He still made a birthday wish but it never came true.

81

With more and more men visiting their flat, he'd had to learn how to take care of Travis. Making up powdered milk was easy, but once Travis drank real milk, it seemed they ran out almost every day. On the ground floor of the block of flats where they lived was a mini-market. He dreaded walking down the five flights of stairs, but each day he went as quickly as he could, buying whatever his mum could afford. Every time he visited the shop, Mr Puri, the owner, would tell him he'd grow giant muscles carrying the two big bottles back up the five flights. Mr Puri always laughed when he said this. He'd never felt like laughing.

Travis always drank every last drop of his milk. Afterwards, he knew to pick him up to do a burp and sometimes a massive fart, which always made him laugh. Once Travis was asleep, he'd sit at the kitchen table and watch the small TV set that sat on top of the microwave. One hot night, all he had for Travis was half a bottle of milk. He'd pushed him around the kitchen, hoping he'd fall asleep, but he'd kept crying. A man had shouted from the bedroom telling him to 'shut that fucking baby up'. He'd tried turning off the lights to see if that would make Travis go to sleep. It hadn't and pushing him around in the dark had felt stupid. He'd looked at the clock on the microwave and seen it was eleven. That was when Mr Puri closed his shop. Quickly, he'd put on his glasses, grabbed some money out of the jar hidden at the back of the kitchen cupboard and run out through the living room. Another man was sitting on the sofa, and he wondered if he was there to watch.

When he'd arrived at Mr Puri's shop, he found the door

82

locked. He could see Mr Puri inside, still standing behind his counter, so he'd knocked loudly.

'Two big bottles to grow your giant muscles?' said Mr Puri, opening the door. 'Come in and help yourself.'

'I'd thought we were closed for the night?' Mr Puri's wife appeared in the doorway at the back of the shop.

'Just helping out a friend in need,' Mr Puri replied, winking at him.

Reaching for the milk, he'd heard Mrs Puri tut. 'Simple boy,' she'd said. 'All his mother's fault. From what Sita told me, she took drugs while she was pregnant. I'd be amazed if the other boy doesn't turn out the same way.'

Mr Puri turned away from his wife and collected the few coins he'd pushed onto the counter. 'Big strong muscles,' he'd said, laughing, before opening the door.

He'd run back upstairs and poured more milk into Travis's bottle. As Travis fell asleep on his knee, he'd decided he didn't care what people said about his mum. He loved her just the same.

FRIDAY

CHAPTER 15

Detective Sergeant Lesley Barnsdale opened her eyes and stared up at the thin crack running across the length of the white-painted ceiling. With neatly painted lines perfectly connecting the bright ceiling to light grey walls, otherwise the room was immaculate. She lifted her head off the deep pillow and imagined the clothes hanging orderly behind the mirrored wardrobe door. Tracing her fingers across the soft cotton duvet, she suddenly remembered her body lying naked beneath. When she heard water running in the neighbouring bathroom, she pulled the cover tightly around her.

Last night, a few of her colleagues at Haddley Police had suggested a drink after work. That was something she always did her very best to avoid, but somehow, they'd learned it was her fortieth birthday this coming weekend. It'd been impossible to escape. At the Green Man pub at the top of Haddley Hill, she'd deliberately followed her one gin and tonic with a dandelion cordial. After that, she'd made her excuses, only for a small group of officers to join her on the walk back towards Haddley Bridge. Outside the Watchman bar, which looked over the River Thames, the three officers had insisted on one more birthday drink. Ushering her inside, they'd ordered her something called a Pornstar Martini and followed that with a Drunken Bee, in which she felt certain she could taste both tequila and whisky. By the time she'd got up to use the bathroom later in the evening, she could barely feel her legs. Returning to their table, she discovered two men had joined them.

Seated next to her was Phil Doorley, a successful local businessman and co-owner of PDQ Deliveries. She'd met him twice before. Once following a break-in at the PDQ warehouse and a second time when he'd dropped packages at her home on the north side of Haddley Bridge. Sipping on a third cocktail, she'd laughed at his tales of making deliveries only to find homeowners in compromising situations, and listened attentively as he'd explained how difficult it was to find reliable drivers. When he'd suggested they pop to the Italian next door for a pizza, her first instinct had been to make her excuses and hurry home. But, when he'd laced his fingers with hers, she'd surprised even herself when she'd told him how much she enjoyed a pepperoni.

With a glass of white wine, they'd shared a garlic bread before slicing up two pizzas and eating with their fingers. Over coffee she'd enjoyed hearing about Phil's former life as a school geography teacher before, more than a decade earlier, he'd thrown everything up in the air to set up his own business. Two years later, a friend from school, Dominic Taylor, had invested as his partner. When Phil had told her he hadn't regretted it for a single second, he'd smiled so genuinely that Lesley found herself a little envious of his carefree spirit.

Outside the restaurant, he'd walked with her to Haddley Bridge and, standing beneath the Victorian streetlamps, he'd moved to kiss her. Instinctively, she'd turned her face away and he'd stepped back.

'Sorry,' he'd said, 'I thought ...'

'No, don't apologise,' she'd replied, reddening, and fixing her eyes on a brightly illuminated party boat as it passed beneath the bridge. She'd watched the boat cruise down the river and thought of her own birthday plans for Sunday – a phone call from her mum in Durham, perhaps a walk across Wimbledon Common, followed by a roast chicken dinner from M&S. Slowly, she'd turned back to Phil and gently touched his face, before closing her eyes and kissing him.

Now the bathroom door opened, jolting her out of her thoughts, and Phil stuck his head around the door. His highlighted blond hair was soaking wet, and he pushed it back off his sun-blushed face. 'Water's hot if you want to jump in.'

CHAPTER 16

'Mr Doorley,' said Lesley, a towel wrapped loosely around her, 'please explain to me how you became a schoolteacher, and responsible for the moral wellbeing of the teenagers of Haddley?'

Lying naked beside her, Phil laughed. 'I'm not sure I was necessarily the ideal guardian of the school's moral code, but I gave it my best shot. I'd grown up in Haddley and I think I convinced myself I wanted to give something back.'

'You only ever taught here in Haddley?' she asked, turning onto her side, her head resting on her hand.

'I did a year in Huddersfield as a newly qualified teacher. After that I couldn't wait to get back to Haddley.'

'And why geography?'

'It was the only thing I was any good at. Probably explains why I set up a delivery company,' he said, smiling. 'I actually taught geography and sports, but when you sign up for that nobody tells you about refereeing reserve-team matches on freezing-cold Saturday mornings in mid-January.'

'And Mrs Doorley?'

'I can tell you're a police officer.'

Lesley smiled. 'You mentioned her last night.'

'What did I say?'

'Best month of your life was when you set up your business and left your wife.'

'Slightly harsh of me,' he replied. 'I did three, maybe four years at Haddley Grammar, but I'd be lying if I said I ever really enjoyed it. I went into teaching for the wrong reasons. I was only there because I didn't know what else to do. Jane was passionate about education, still is. We started at Haddley Grammar at the same time; met at a new joiners' drinks. We married the following summer. Two years later, we both knew it was a mistake. That was fourteen years ago.'

'No kids?'

Phil shook his head.

Lesley ran her fingers through her dark hair. 'And you've never married again?'

'Never!' replied Phil, rolling on top of her and unravelling her towel.

She reached across and looked at the time on her phone. 'I'm already an hour late for work,' she said, but when she felt Phil's touch, she didn't care.

The smell of fresh coffee drifted upstairs as Lesley tied back her hair. When she walked into Phil's sparkling modern kitchen he handed her a cappuccino, and she kissed him again.

'Your home is spotless,' she said, leaning against a bright white countertop.

'Only me to mess it up.'

'I wish you'd come and clean mine.'

'I can't take all of the credit,' he replied. 'I've a lady comes in twice a week for a couple of hours. I can give you her number if you like.'

'A DS's salary won't pay for a cleaner. My guess is the delivery business is slightly more lucrative,' she said, and looking at Phil's home she felt certain it was.

'Maybe a little. We did well during the pandemic, but it's tougher now. I preferred it when Covid trapped everyone at home with nothing to do but shop online,' he replied.

'It made my life a little easier as well,' she replied, smiling. 'I still see your vans out and about most days.'

'We're surviving. Finding drivers is by far my biggest headache. I'll be out working delivery shifts this weekend.'

'Really?'

'I enjoy it, reminds me of when I started out. The more you put in, the more you get out. Hard work always pays off in the end.'

Thinking of her own job, she wasn't convinced he was right. She decided not to argue and stepped into the hallway in search of her jacket.

'If you're looking for your coat, I hung it on the rack under the stairs.'

Pulling her jacket off the peg, she smiled as she remembered abandoning it on the floor last night.

'I can drop you at the station,' he called, 'if that's where you're heading?'

'Might be a good idea if I show my face.'

'Give me two minutes.' He ran through to the living room, where he'd kicked off his Timberlands the previous evening.

'I don't fucking believe it!'

'What is it?' called Lesley, hovering in the hallway.

'Some bastard's stolen my van.'

CHAPTER 17

The sun reflects off Big Ben's striking new clock face as I walk along the Victoria Embankment towards Scotland Yard. Madeline and I are due to see Dame Elizabeth Jones, the new deputy commissioner, at ten o'clock this morning. Delays outside Waterloo station mean I'm already late for our arranged meeting time, and I hurry towards the Metropolitan Police's imposing riverside offices.

Waiting beneath Scotland Yard's famous rotating sign, I watch two heavily armed officers talk casually, while two further officers stand sentry beside the fortified vehicle gates. To my surprise, there's no sign of Madeline. I flick on my phone, expecting to see a rushed message of explanation, but there's nothing. Instead, I message my boss, asking if she's close by, but receive no response. I glance through the news headlines on my phone. Our site is leading on the latest government resignation, but I click through to the piece I wrote on Haddley Police at the beginning of the year.

An implication of police corruption runs through my article. While not naming the Baxter family, I tell the story of a drugs ring operating out of Haddley for more than twenty years – and the persistent failure of the local police to dismantle it. Such longevity only occurs with an under-pinning of police patronage. When I drafted the article, I had no idea of Dani's own fear of criminality reaching the highest levels of our local force. Her concerns surrounding the honesty of Chief Inspector Bridget Freeman have only heightened my resolve to uncover the truth. This is why the new deputy commissioner has agreed to talk to us.

I click out of our site and back into my messages. Madeline is yet to read the last note I sent her, but I type her another quick line all the same. I flick through my contacts, searching for her driver, Dennis, and drop him a short message asking him how far away they are. Behind me, Big Ben sounds ten. I check my phone again, but with no response from either Madeline or Dennis, I walk slowly up the front steps and make my way inside. I pass through airport-style security before giving my name, and explaining I have an appoint-ment with Deputy Commissioner Jones. I'm soon escorted to a break-out zone on the third floor. Moments later, the deputy commissioner greets me with a welcoming hand-shake, and we sit together on a bright red high-backed sofa.

'This is all very modern,' I say. 'A little different to the mice running around your old office in Dover.'

She smiles. 'Where you had to keep your foot on the door when you were peeing. Even the loos here are Met Police branded.'

'Madeline was desperately keen to meet with you,' I say, 'but she's been unavoidably detained.'

'I read we've lost another government minister this morning. I'm only glad it isn't the home secretary. I couldn't face breaking in another one, not so soon after the last. I'm sure Madeline is very busy snouting around Westminster. We'll bump into each other sometime soon.'

The conversation turns to the case of Dani's father, DCI Jack Cash. I share my belief that his unrelenting pursuit of the Baxter family resulted in his premature departure from Haddley Police.

'Jack retired after forty years of exemplary service. That was his decision and his alone,' she says, unwilling to engage any further, 'but I do hear good things about his daughter. I'm yet to meet her myself but I understand you've worked with her a couple of times now?'

I nod and, suddenly proud, reply, 'I think she has the makings of a truly excellent officer.'

'You know I've no issue with us working with the press when appropriate, as long as no lines are crossed. I did read your account of your own mother's death. I should compliment you on your excellent police work. I think we might even find a spot for you here, particularly as you already seem so adept at impersonating a police officer?'

I feel my face flush. 'Only in certain circumstances,' I reply.

'But be careful,' she continues, gently raising a finger. 'Not all of my colleagues are as forgiving as me.' Dame Elizabeth's assistant brings us both a steaming cup of coffee. Our conversation moves to the male-dominated culture of the Met Police and the outdated attitudes Dame Elizabeth is determined to stamp out.

'I've made it clear I'm going to make changes, but I thought you were reaching a bit in your recent article,' she says.

'How so?' I reply.

'Your implication around the Baxters and Haddley Police is clear.'

'All I'm saying is, as a family, the Baxters have survived an awful lot over a very long period of time.' I pause before adding, 'If only we had the knife used to attack DS Mat Moore.'

She puts up a hand to stop me. 'Ben, you can ask me as many questions as you like, but don't provide your own answers. Haddley has one of our highest rates of conviction across the whole city. CI Bridget Freeman is one of my best-performing officers and she leads an exemplary team.'

I drink my coffee. I'm desperate to challenge her opinion of Freeman but then I think of my promise to Dani and the future I want us to share. 'I'm sure she's a very effective officer,' is all I say. After a moment, I move on to my next question. 'Do you believe there are officers in your force dealing drugs?'

She raises an eyebrow. 'You're probably going to tell me you have a list of ten officers from southwest London alone.' I shake my head before she continues. 'It's possible, and equally likely there are still examples of theft or fraud, but we are doing everything we can to drive it out of the force. If any officer has concerns, they should feel comfortable in stepping forward. My door is open. I'm here to ensure honesty enhances careers, rather than inhibits them.'

I tell her I recognise the vast majority of officers are doing a tough job in difficult circumstances.

'And they do it every single day.'

When our conversation ends, I thank her for her time and promise to speak with her again before publishing any future articles. She walks me to the lifts, but as we shake hands to say goodbye, she steps in beside me.

'I should show you out of the building.'

'I'm sure I can find my own way,' I reply, but Dame Elizabeth hits the button.

'Thanks for your time,' I say, as we step out into the ground-floor lobby.

'Let me walk you outside.'

'There's really no need,' I say, turning towards the giant floor-to-ceiling glass windows and looking out at the endless traffic on the Embankment.

'No, Ben, I insist.' Dame Elizabeth holds my eye and I hear a firmness in her tone I know not to oppose. I say nothing further. Together we exit through the security gates and move away from the building. Dame Elizabeth walks briskly beside me until we are some distance from Scotland Yard. I realise she wants a conversation away from the building.

'I'm genuinely sorry Madeline couldn't join us this morning, but I would like you to convey my very best wishes to her.' She stops and faces me. 'I've long followed her work. Like you, Ben, while she can be a thorn, she has championed some excellent causes during her career. I remember one in particular.' Dame Elizabeth's sharp eyes lock onto mine. 'The Aaron Welsby murder case. It was her relentless pursuit of the killer that led to a conviction. She took us to task, but as a result some of us within the Metropolitan Police respected her all the more. We needed to change.' I nod again, aware of the controversial case that helped establish Madeline's uncompromising reputation, but unsure of why the deputy commissioner is raising it now.

Dame Elizabeth holds my arm. 'Due to the diminished responsibility nature of his conviction, information is severely restricted.' Elizabeth Jones is breaking police protocol. 'However, my belief is Madeline needs to be aware on a personal level. Two weeks ago, Billy Monroe was released from prison.'

CHAPTER 18

I walk into the neighbouring Whitehall Gardens where I spot an empty park bench. I reach for my phone, type the words *Billy Monroe murder case* and click search. Instantly, a tabloid newspaper headline from thirteen years ago screams out at me.

KILLER ROAMS FREE

This newspaper accuses Billy Monroe of killing Aaron Welsby.

If Monroe wants to deny the allegation, let him sue us. And if not, on this the first anniversary of Aaron's murder, we call upon the Metropolitan Police to arrest Monroe NOW!

Beneath a blurry image of a man labouring on building-site scaffolding, the full story is written by the newspaper's then deputy editor, Madeline Wilson.

Twelve months ago, on a late November evening, Aaron Welsby walked across the Thames footbridge from St Marnham to Baron's Field.

Following the steps down on the north side of the river, he was oblivious to Billy Monroe's murderous intention.

Concealing himself in a stone alcove halfway down the steps, Monroe, 24, was waiting to launch his deadly attack. Appearing from the shadowy recess, he shouted Aaron's name and ran quickly towards him.

Three times he plunged the eight-inch blade into Aaron's body.

Heroically, Aaron, 27, fought back.

Using all his energy, he pushed Monroe backwards down the stairs. With blood pouring through his clothes, Aaron desperately made his way back up the steps and onto the deserted bridge. But severely wounded, his pace was slow.

A genuine coward, Monroe returned and pounced on the injured man. Dragging Aaron off the graffiti-covered walkway, he forced him over the barricade.

Aaron plunged to his death, falling from St Marnham Bridge and into the River Thames.

Hours later, Aaron's lifeless body washed up on the shore.

In the following twelve months, the Metropolitan Police have stumbled through their investigation.

Despite mounting evidence, the force has done little more than dismiss the case as a 'gay hook-up gone wrong'. They have failed Aaron and failed the community with their inability to make a conviction – or even bring charges.

Now is the time to give Aaron the justice he deserves.

Thirteen years ago, the front-page story made Madeline internationally famous. At the time, even in my last year of sixth form, I was aware of the controversy the headline created. Through her newspaper, Madeline relentlessly championed the case of Aaron Welsby, demanding justice for the innocent man stabbed to death on St Marnham Bridge. Madeline argued institutionalised homophobia ingrained within the Metropolitan Police had prevented a comprehensive investigation. In the weeks that followed her first headline, Madeline published countless articles hounding the Met. She accused the police of a dereliction of duty in failing to investigate Billy Monroe as a potential suspect.

I've never known what made Madeline so certain of Monroe's guilt, but the man she drove the Metropolitan Police to convict is now free.

CHAPTER 19

Lesley Barnsdale stepped out of the front door and, together with Phil Doorley, walked down the path at the front of his house. They waited at the roadside until a metallic blue BMW raced up the road, coming to a quick stop directly in front of them.

Phil opened the rear passenger-side door. 'Go ahead and slide in,' he said, before introducing his business partner, Dominic Taylor. As Lesley buckled herself in, Phil climbed in after her. 'Thanks for swinging by,' he said. 'Dom likes to think of himself as the "D" in PDQ Deliveries, but I'm not sure I ever agreed to that.'

'I feel more like your bloody chauffeur this morning.' Dom laughed. 'Nice to meet you,' he said to Lesley.

'Lesley's with the Haddley Police,' said Phil.

'Lucky you were close at hand,' replied Dom, catching his partner's eye.

'You'll need to file a stolen vehicle report,' she said, turning to Phil. 'I can send someone up to the warehouse if you like. It shouldn't take long.'

'Thanks.'

'Was it parked out front?' asked Dom, as they pulled out onto the Lower Haddley Road.

Phil leaned forward, resting on the front passenger seat. 'On the strip of land, down by the side of my house. Same place I always leave it. I must admit when we got in last night it wasn't on my mind to check. And I was in the warehouse all day yesterday, so it could have gone any time in the last twenty-four hours.'

'They're scum,' replied Dom. 'And the police will do eff-all. Always too busy ticketing delivery men on yellow lines.' He stopped himself. 'Oops,' he said, looking at Lesley. 'But I'm sure you know what I mean.'

She smiled. 'Do your vans have GPS tracking?'

'Only on the newer vehicles,' replied Phil. 'Mine was the oldest of the lot. I only use it for knocking about.'

'Make the report and at least you'll be able to put in an insurance claim. Probably the best you can hope for.' She touched Dom on the shoulder. 'Don't you dare quote me on that.'

The car slowed when it approached the traffic lights by Haddley Bridge, but as they changed to green, Dom raced through, turning sharply up the high street. Her stomach tensing, Lesley smoothed the imaginary creases in her black pencil skirt. Suddenly she was in a situation in which she so rarely found herself. Work dominated her life, with her only escape a monthly train trip to Durham to visit her mother. Now, she was desperate to ask Phil when she might see him again, but didn't want to appear too eager, especially not in front of Dom. They were fast approaching the front of the police station.

'If you take the next left, you can drop me in the car park at the back of the building. Wouldn't want you to get done for stopping on the double yellows out front.'

As the car turned off the high street, Lesley squeezed Phil's hand. He leaned across and kissed her on the cheek. She felt his breath in her ear, and he whispered, 'See you again tonight?'

When she stepped out of Dom's BMW, her fellow officers would have barely recognised DS Lesley Barnsdale as a bright smile lit up her face.

CHAPTER 20

I throw my jacket onto the beaten-up old sofa that fills the back corner of my kitchen. Switching on my coffee machine, I grab some milk from the fridge and, with a double shot, brew myself an extra-strong cup of coffee. I reach for my phone and dial Madeline's number. Again, it goes straight to her voicemail and, while I kick off my shoes, I hear her telling me to leave only a brief message. Madeline hates timewasters. I scroll through my contacts and call Min, who works alongside me at our twenty-four-hour news site. Her answer is instant.

'Hey,' she says. 'Where are you? I'd thought you and the boss would have come into the office after meeting the new Deputy Dog.'

'She's not with you?'

'Who?'

'Madeline. She never showed for the interview.'

'I haven't seen her this morning, but hang on,' replies Min. I can hear her getting to her feet and imagine her looking across our vast open-plan office towards Madeline's

goldfish-bowl corner room. 'She's not in her office,' continues Min, coming back on the line. 'Nobody here's seen her.'

'Odd,' I say.

'A tough lesson for you, Ben, but one we all learn at some
point,' she replies, her tone mocking me. 'Even though you
are her favourite, if she sniffs out a better story, she'll drop
you in a second.'

'You're probably right.' I pause before continuing. 'Can I
ask you a favour?'

'Nothing's ever stopped you before.'

'Can you pull me anything you can find on the Aaron
Welsby murder case?'

'Madeline's finest hour?'

'Certainly her most controversial.'

'What's your angle?'

'Just something Dame Elizabeth mentioned. I'm sure it's
nothing, but whatever you can find would be great.'

'Leave it with me.'

'Will you message me if Madeline shows up?' I ask.

'Trust me,' says Min, hearing the unease in my voice.
'Another story came along, followed by a hugely expensive
Friday lunch for which somebody else will be paying. Have
you called her?'

'Called, messaged, but nothing.'

'And Dennis?'

'The same.'

'That's not like him, but I can guarantee you she'll be
tracking down a story she doesn't want anyone – not even
you – to get a sniff of.'

CHAPTER 21

Dani Cash turned onto the lane at the top of Haddley Common and came to a halt outside Sarah Wright's driveway. Standing at the front of the house were Mrs Wright and her former partner, Nathan Beavin. The two were engaged in conversation, and Beavin had his hand on Sarah's shoulder. Neither noticed her until she was already walking up the driveway but, as she approached, Beavin dropped his arm to his side. He took two steps back.

'You've got to do what you think's right,' she heard him say to Sarah. 'Why don't you just go ahead and give Max a farewell hug from me?' He moved away and walked directly past Dani. Hanging his head, he was barely able to lift his eyes to hers. She watched Beavin follow the narrow lane away from the house towards Haddley Woods, and when he'd disappeared out of sight, she approached Sarah.

'Have you found him?' Sarah asked, immediately.

Dani shook her head. 'Sorry, no, nothing yet. I was passing and thought I'd check-in. Were you able to get some sleep?'

Sarah shrugged. 'Max was awake before six. For once it

was nice to be able to send him down the corridor to find his father. In fact, James is still here now.'

'Oh, I see. I'm guessing he and Mr Beavin don't really hit it off?'

'Nathan called by to tell me he was returning home to Wales tomorrow. He asked to see Max but, if I'm honest with you, I couldn't face it. Max would get upset and Nathan only brings out the worst in James.'

'Mr Beavin is leaving Haddley?'

'Probably for the best. He needs some time with his family and friends; people who know him as Nathan, not as fodder for social media. I hope he gets the support he needs. He's still young and he's had to deal with a lot.'

'You and he are definitely over?'

'We both said we'd stay friends and I think we meant it. Nathan is a genuinely sweet guy.'

Dani thought of her own break-up. Although she and Mat would remain colleagues in the Met Police, she'd be surprised if they were ever friends. 'I did want to ask you one question about last night.'

'Go ahead.'

'What time did you turn your lights out?'

'These days, I can barely keep my eyes open past ten.'

'So, the house would have been in darkness for around an hour when you heard Ben?'

'That was close to eleven-thirty, so probably a little more.'

'Thanks,' replied Dani. 'You have my number. Anything at all, please call me.'

CHAPTER 22

I hear a tap on my front door. I toss my phone down onto the sofa, run across the kitchen and, in my socks, slide down my tiled hall. I open my front door and step outside to greet Dani. She looks exhausted.

'You came,' I say excitedly as I take hold of her hand.

'I don't have long. I'm back on shift in an hour.'

When a delivery van stops at the front of my house, I let go of her hand and run quickly down to the roadside.

'Short of drivers?' I say to Dominic Taylor from PDQ Deliveries, who passes me an Amazon parcel.

'Phil and I are on shift all weekend. Give me a shout if you know anyone who wants a job!'

I run back up to my house, where Dani stands in the doorway. 'Get inside, or your feet will freeze,' she replies.

She leans against the hall radiator, and I kiss her. 'I've missed you,' I say, quietly.

A soft smile lights her bright blue eyes. 'I might have missed you too. A little bit.'

'Only a little bit?'

'Don't push your luck. I'm still annoyed about last night.'

'Sorry,' I say.

'Me too. I guess I was a bit shirty. I'm exhausted with all these lates. How was the deputy commissioner?'

'Are you just here to check up on me?' I snatch another kiss before sliding back down the hall and into the kitchen.

'Ben!' calls Dani.

'Don't worry,' I say, when she walks into the room, slipping off her jacket. 'I was on my best behaviour. Scout's honour.'

'Were you ever a scout?'

'Never,' I reply.

'This is all a big joke to you, isn't it?'

'No, of course not,' I say, offering her a coffee.

'I'm fine, thanks,' she replies, before reaching for a glass and running the cold water tap.

'Something to eat?'

'I'm good with this,' she says, and drops onto the sofa. 'Tell me what you said.'

'I avoided what you told me about Freeman, I promise.'

'Thank you.'

I sit beside her. 'You do know I'd never betray your trust?'

'I know,' she replies, a little too quickly. 'Did she have anything of interest to say?'

'Only what you'd expect. She did ask about you. I told her you have the making of a first-class police officer.'

Dani laughs. 'Thanks for the endorsement.'

'She also told me Bridget Freeman was one of her *best-performing officers* across the whole of the city.'

'Haddley tops the league in conviction rates.'

'Except when it comes to the Baxter family.'

Dani sips on her water. 'When I look at Freeman, all I see is an exceptional officer leading a very strong team.'

'That's pretty much what she said,' I reply. 'And I'm not saying that isn't true, but somebody took that knife out of the filing cabinet.'

'Even if there is a grain of truth about her and the Baxters, she has influence way beyond anything I can ever hope for.'

I lean forward. 'But Dani—'

She shakes her head. 'No, don't even say it. She made a throwaway comment into which I could easily have read too much. I will make my own judgement over a period of time. I'm sorry.'

'Will you tell Mat?'

'Never,' she replies, sharply. 'And if you ever see him, you must promise me you never will. He'd never let it go. It would destroy him.'

'He doesn't deserve to know your suspicions?'

'That's all they are. You have to promise me.'

'I promise.' I reassure Dani and change the subject. 'When I left Scotland Yard, an odd thing happened.' I tell her of my conversation with the deputy commissioner outside the famous building.

'Was she asking for Madeline to run a story?'

'Possibly, but somehow it felt more than that.'

'If your site ran a story, it would give Dame Elizabeth a chance to say how much the Met has changed and is still changing.'

'True.'

Dani pulls off her boots, curls her legs onto the sofa and yawns.

'Long shift last night?' I ask.

'Bloody endless. I'm making zero progress with the intruder.'

'The man I saw last night, the way he entered her driveway, I'm certain Sarah's was the only house he was interested in.'

'You think she was the target?'

I nod.

'But she wasn't alone in the house,' says Dani. 'Up until now, he's always been so careful. Even the women who had partners, or kids, he targeted them when completely alone. He takes his time and needs to be certain he won't be disturbed.'

'Sarah and Nathan broke up recently. Perhaps he picked that up somewhere and didn't realise Sarah had a child.'

'Possibly,' replies Dani. 'I've had a look on social this morning and there's a huge amount of comments on both Nathan and Sarah.'

'I'm guessing not all of them very pleasant?'

Dani shakes her head. 'Turns out living with the son of a child murderer doesn't make you the most popular person, and bizarrely makes others jealous.'

'And the other five women. Anything to link them?'

'Not yet. People share so much of their lives online, and you never know who's reading it.' Dani reaches for her glass. She drinks again from her water, before resting her head back on a cushion and closing her eyes. 'I need to spend more time searching through their posts.'

'Do you think he'll try again?'

'If it was him last night, he's been thwarted twice in a week. He won't like that.'

'Are you worried?'

'He's escalating,' she replies. 'We haven't shared it publicly, but when he fled from Shannon Lancaster's last weekend, he dropped a set of military-style handcuffs.'

'Fuck, he planned to assault her,' I say, under my breath. 'You need to find him.'

Dani lifts her head and opens her eyes. 'I know.'

Resting her feet across my legs, she drops her head back down. 'I wish I could stay like this for ever,' she says. I hear her breathing slow and think she's falling asleep, but then she continues. 'I told Mat I had to work tomorrow night.'

'And you might not have to?'

'I'm allowed a few hours off once in a while.'

'We can go away for the night.'

'If you like, but let's not travel too far. I'd rather be spending the time with you. Somewhere just outside London?'

'A nice spa?'

'I'd kill for a back massage.'

'Let me see what I can do.' I lean across the sofa and push the curls off her face. 'I love you,' I whisper. She touches my face but says nothing. 'This is the point where you're meant to say I love you, too.'

Dani's face is pale. I worry she looks worn out. Before I can kiss her again, she abruptly sits up. 'I think I need some air.'

CHAPTER 23

'I'm fine, honestly,' says Dani, holding a mug of sweet tea and standing at my open kitchen door.

'At least have something to eat before you go.'

She shakes her head. 'One too many long shifts, that's all. What I need is an early night.'

'Stay here and call in sick.'

She shakes her head. 'We can't all tell our boss we're researching a new article and working from home.'

'As if I would!'

'And anyway, I said I'd see Mat at the station.' I turn away. Dani comes and stands beside me, resting her hand on my back. 'There's no point in us pretending he doesn't exist. I should be able to get away by mid-morning tomorrow. Meet you here?'

We agree to meet for a late breakfast. I walk Dani to her car, parked on the lane at the top of the common. When she climbs in, she turns and smiles. Watching her drive away, I realise I love her in a way I've never loved anyone before in my life, and it terrifies me. Throughout my life, the people

115

I've loved have been stolen away from me. I've been scared to ever love anyone else again, but with Dani it's impossible not to.

When her car turns into the traffic on the Lower Haddley Road, I step back inside. I slump down onto my kitchen sofa and feel for my phone, which has fallen between two cushions. I flick on the screen and see I have four missed calls. Each one of them is from Madeline's father, Sam. I click on WhatsApp and see Sam has sent me ten messages.

Where are you?

I've left you a telephone message

I've left you another telephone message

I need to speak to you

Don't you answer your phone?

I realise I had my phone on silent.

I've called you again

Can you see this message?

It's Sam

I need to speak to you

About Madeline

I call Sam's number, but it goes straight to voicemail, so I leave a message telling him I'm heading straight over to his flat. I grab my jacket and search briefly for my car keys before finding them hidden behind a loaf of days-old bread. I arrive at Sam's apartment block, having tried and failed to get through to him twice on the drive over, and park my car in front of garage number 3, a space I know he rents from Mrs Wasnesky to house his fifty-year archive of the *Richmond Times*. I hurry to the rear door of the flats, arriving just as Connie Shields, Sam's close acquaintance, is leaving. Greeting me with a bright smile, the grey-haired septuagenarian always has a twinkle in her eye. I can see why Sam enjoys lunch with her each week.

'Ben, are you here to see Sam?' she asks, holding the door open.

'I'd said I'd pop by,' I reply, wanting to avoid a long conversation.

'He does so enjoy seeing you, although of course he'd never admit that to you,' she says, touching my arm as I pass.

I smile and head quickly inside. Exiting the lift, I follow the corridor to Sam's top-floor apartment and rap on his door. He opens it instantly.

'What's going on?' I say, stepping inside. 'I've called you back three times and you don't pick up.'

'You left me a message saying you were coming over.'

'And?'

'So, I knew we'd speak when you got here,' he replies. 'And if you must know, the first time you called me I was in the loo. That's a more frequent occurrence for gents of my age, as one day you'll probably find out.'

I push my hand through my hair. 'What's going on, Sam?'

He passes me his phone and suddenly I see his hand is shaking.

'Read the last two messages.'

'What's your code?'

'What code?'

'To open your phone.'

'Oh,' says Sam. 'One, two, three, four.'

'That's not secure,' I reply, quickly typing in the number.

'It's easy to remember though.'

'And around four million people in the UK have that same code.'

'Because it's easy to remember. I use the same number at the bank.'

I widen my eyes at Sam but say nothing more. I click on his messages and scroll to the top two, both of which have come from an anonymous number. Reading the first message aloud, I feel my pulse start to race.

We have your daughter. Call the police and
she's dead.

'I didn't think it was real,' says Sam, his voice cracking. 'Madeline gets all kind of crazy threats. The things people say about her on the internet, you wouldn't believe. She's always said if I ever received anything to call her straight away. That's what I did, but she didn't answer.' He stops and looks directly at me. 'Then I got the second message.'

I click on Sam's phone and open a brutal image of Madeline. Her face beaten black, her mouth covered in blood and her eyes despairing.

It's time to settle the score.

'Ben, crazy people can do all kinds of things with photos these days. It might not be real,' says Sam, shaking his head, trying to hide the fear in his voice.

Instantly, I'm terrified what this might mean. I think of my meeting with the deputy commissioner. Madeline would never simply skip such a high-profile interview. And then I think of Dame Elizabeth's warning.

I want to reassure Sam, but I can't. 'I think this is real.'

He holds my eye. 'Then we have to find her.'

Four

'What if this time I can't rescue her?'

The cold rain felt like ice. He pulled the fur-trimmed hood of his parka over his head. She'd never wanted him to have the coat – he'd heard her say it made him look like a drug dealer – but the man had bought it for him anyway. When he'd unwrapped it, he'd rushed across the room and hugged him. Putting on the coat, he'd felt her eyes on him, but he still wore it every day, even in the summer. Some of the older kids laughed at him, but he didn't care.

Standing at the school gates, he watched his teacher, Mr Holroyd, leaving through the side door. He didn't want Mr Holroyd to speak to him, so he crouched down behind some nearby bushes. He saw Mr Holroyd exit through the front gates and climb into a little red car. His teacher sat beside a woman with long, blonde hair. He watched him kiss the woman on the lips before the car raced away. He'd liked Mr Holroyd until the last parents' evening. She'd come home furious and said he wasn't trying, that Mr Holroyd said he was failing in both maths and English. All he knew was he was doing his best.

Every Wednesday, he had to wait forty minutes after school finished for Travis to have one of his extra lessons. Travis was having lessons in both maths and English. He'd heard her say she wouldn't let him go the same way.

Suddenly, there was a hand on his shoulder. 'Why are you

123

hiding?' Two girls from his class were standing beside the bushes. 'You were hiding from Mr Holroyd.'

'No, I wasn't,' he replied. He felt his face flush bright red.

'Yes, you were,' one of the girls replied, laughing loudly. 'You're scared of him because you're his most stupid pupil.'

'No, I'm not,' he yelled, stumbling forward out of the bushes. The two girls screamed and began to run. 'I'm not scared of him,' he shouted, chasing after them. Running in front of the school, he soon began to lose his breath. Knowing he couldn't keep up, he slowed to a walk.

'Come on, fatty,' called the girls, who'd stopped a short distance ahead of him. Taunting him, they cried, 'You'll never catch us.' They turned, running again, but as they did one of the girls stumbled over her drawstring gym bag. She caught her foot in the cord and fell to the floor. In a second, he was on her. He grabbed her bag, swinging it above her head. Cowering on the floor, she had nowhere to go; she was no longer laughing. Faster and faster, he swung the bag, closer and closer to her face. When she held up her hands, he saw the fear in her eyes. And her fear made him feel powerful.

He slowed the bag, letting it fall to his side. He placed the bag on the ground beside her, turned and walked back to the school in search of his brother.

CHAPTER 24

A leather-topped reporter's desk, rescued from the *Richmond Times* two decades ago, fills much of the space in Sam's spare bedroom. I stand behind him as he logs on to his computer. We both need to read the information Min has found, so we wait for the screen to come to life.

'Sam,' I say, resting my hand on his shoulder, 'I think we should call the police.'

'The message said no police,' he replies, staring at a square monitor that already feels a relic from another lifetime. 'Absolutely not.'

'Madeline's a high-profile figure. It's not impossible this could be an elaborate hoax.'

'If it's a hoax, where is she?' He turns in his chair. 'You've seen the picture, Ben. She's in trouble.'

I can't keep the vile image from my mind – Madeline's face black with bruises, her mouth covered in blood. 'But even so,' I say, 'the police have specially trained officers to handle a situation like this.'

'When did you become such a fan of the boys and girls in

blue? I said no police.' His eyes have the same steely flash of determination I see in Madeline when she's intent on being first to a story.

'How about I call Dani?' I ask.

He shakes his head and faces his screen.

'You're thinking of Alaka,' I say. Alaka Jha was a reporter who worked for Sam thirty years ago. 'Hers was a very different situation.'

'The police became involved, and she ended up dead. I won't make the same mistake with Madeline.'

I pull a chair from the corner of the room and sit beside Sam. 'I know you're scared. So am I.' Sam stares at the hourglass timer slowly rotating in the middle of his prehistoric screen. 'We need to do what's right for Madeline.'

I have no choice but to tell Sam of Billy Monroe's release.

'Then he's our man!' he replies, a sudden hope in his voice.

'We shouldn't jump to conclusions.'

Sam ignores me. 'If we already know who we're after, that's half the battle.'

'If it is Monroe,' I insist, 'finding him is a hell of a lot bigger challenge.' I think of all the opportunities given to me by Madeline. I would do anything to save her, but if I am to help Sam, I must believe we are her best chance of freedom. 'We need to understand more about who we're dealing with,' I say.

'Billy Monroe? Madeline got him convicted. Right from the very start she was certain he was guilty.'

'I reread her most famous article this morning,' I say. 'She didn't hold back.'

'It was her bravery that forced the Met to act.'

'Publishing a piece like that, accusing Monroe of murder, she must have been certain? With no charges pending, she opened the paper up to a huge libel claim.'

'Can't libel the truth.' Still now, I can hear the pride in Sam's voice. 'She pushed and pushed, running a story every couple of weeks, and in the end a guilty man ended up inside.'

'She hounded the police?'

'Pretty much.'

'What was it that made her so certain?'

'You know Maddy better than anyone – always the best sources, and then she discovered the CCTV that ultimately led to his arrest.'

When Sam is finally able to open his emails, I point to a message I've forwarded from Min. Sam clicks on the link to an article published by Madeline the day after Billy Monroe's conviction, twelve years ago.

GUILTY – AT LAST!

Our campaign leads to the conviction of Billy Monroe for the killing of Aaron Welsby.

An Old Bailey jury yesterday found Billy Monroe guilty of the killing of Aaron Welsby.

The jury took less than two hours to convict Monroe of voluntary manslaughter with diminished responsibility.

The prosecution of Monroe only occurred after

this newspaper produced evidence previously dismissed by the Metropolitan Police.

We found the CCTV evidence proving Monroe's presence in St Marnham on the night of Aaron's killing.

Only then did the police pursue Monroe, finally uncovering the DNA evidence that led to his conviction.

'Click on the next link,' I say.

Sam opens the newspaper's editorial page, also published the day after Monroe's conviction. Madeline wrote:

The killing of Aaron Welsby was a hate crime.

Billy Monroe lay in wait for a single man crossing towards the picturesque Baron's Field pasture on the banks of the River Thames. At the time, Baron's Field was a known meeting place for gay men.

When Monroe saw Aaron approaching, he charged at him with only one thought – to kill him.

Almost two years later, justice is now done.

While Monroe might suffer from some minor mental incapacities, he knew enough to lie in wait for his victim. His actions on that night were premeditated and planned.

Monroe will now spend many years in prison. Sentencing will take place in four weeks' time.

This newspaper calls on Judge Malcolm Charles

to deliver Billy Monroe the maximum sentence of twenty-four years.

'That sentence didn't happen?'

'The judge was a stickler, gave him a decent term, something close to twenty years, but these days we seem to let murderers out with a pat on the back after not much more than a couple of years served.' Sam turns and looks up at me. 'Sorry,' he says, remembering my brother's killers served only a decade, 'but you know what I mean.'

I read aloud the final two lines of Madeline's editorial.

Justice is served. Now let it be lasting.

In Aaron Welsby's memory, it's time to settle the score.

CHAPTER 25

Sam reaches across his desk and grabs his phone. He points at the same words in the kidnapper's message.

It's time to settle the score.

I stare at the message. Taken directly from Madeline's own words, the threat can only come from Billy Monroe.

'For Monroe, this is all about revenge,' says Sam.

'Why a manslaughter conviction, not murder?' I ask, knowing a murder conviction would have kept Monroe imprisoned for many more years than the twelve he served.

'He was charged with murder,' replies Sam, 'but his defence argued he suffered with significant *developmental issues* from birth. If you ask me, he was a bit slow, nothing worse than that. He certainly wasn't crazy. His mother took drugs when she was pregnant. In court, the defence played out the whole sob story.'

'Did she stand by him, his mother?'

'She was long since dead. His grandfather stuck by him, though, sat through every day of the trial.'

Sam clicks on the last of the links sent through by Min. It shows a series of photographs published by Madeline's newspaper the day after the trial's conclusion. I lean on the back of Sam's chair as he scrolls through pages of pictures, many of Billy Monroe with his dark eyes staring straight at the camera.

'There!' I say, spotting an image of an older man, his collar upturned, walking away from the Old Bailey. 'See if you can zoom in any closer.'

Sam looks at me and raises his eyebrows. I take hold of his mouse, double-click, and zoom in on the image. Beneath the picture is the caption, 'Monroe's grandfather, Tosh Monroe, 63, hurriedly leaving the court after yesterday's verdict. He refused to make any comment.'

'If he's Billy's only family,' I say, 'that's where we need to start.'

CHAPTER 26

'Thanks, Min,' I say, clicking off my phone and opening my car door. 'Tosh Monroe lives just outside Nottingham, in a place called West Bridgford,' I tell Sam, as we pull out of his driveway and into the London traffic.

'How did you find out so quickly?'

'Don't ask,' I reply, smiling. 'Let's just say we have very good contacts.'

'Not in the police?' says Sam.

'No, don't worry. And I didn't tell Min why I was asking.' I glance towards Sam. 'You're sure we're doing the right thing?'

'One hundred per cent. We let him set the rules. It's the only way we can be certain of getting Maddy home safely. I couldn't live with myself if something happened to her.' Sam looks to me. 'Nearly every Friday, she buys me lunch at the Cricketers. When the weather's nice, we sit outside, looking over Richmond Green. It's a million miles away from the pressure-cooker life she leads the other six and a half days a week. She thinks she's checking up on me. She's

132

never clocked it, but, in reality, I'm the one checking up on her.' Listening to Sam, I realise how protective he remains of Madeline, surely as much as he was on the day she was born. Looking at me, he reads my thoughts. 'She'll always be my little girl, Ben.'

As we join the M1, my satnav tells us, in the late afternoon traffic, we're still more than two hours' drive from West Bridgford. Sam reaches for the controls beneath his seat and eases back his chair.

'Make yourself comfy,' I say.

'I am,' he replies, before twisting to reach into the back seat.

'What are you after?'

'My phone,' he replies. 'I put it in my jacket pocket.' He grabs his coat and starts feeling in each of the pockets. 'Shit,' he says. 'I'm sure I brought it with me. What if he sends another message? We'll have to go back.'

I look quickly over my shoulder and see Sam's phone. 'It's on the back seat.'

'Thank God for that.' He unbuckles his seatbelt and twists backwards, almost knocking the gearstick.

'Do you need it now?' I say, as the seatbelt warning begins to sound. 'Why don't I stop at the next services?'

Sam ignores me. 'I can't reach the fucking thing.'

'Just leave it,'

'No,' he replies, snapping at me. 'What if he messages again?'

I move into the inside lane. Sam is slowly sinking between the seats, and when I look at him, I have to bite my lip to stop myself from laughing.

133

'You're going to have to stop on the hard shoulder,' he says.

'There isn't a hard shoulder.'

'How do you mean, isn't?'

'It's a smart motorway.'

'What the hell's that?' he shouts, stuck on his side.

'Two minutes and we can stop,' I say.

The car park at the motorway services is busy, but I find a space opposite a Starbucks coffee shop. I unbuckle my belt before helping Sam ease himself back into his seat. I reach into the rear and pass him his phone. He is silent, holding his phone in his hands as if he were praying.

'Sam?' I say, gently.

'Who am I fooling?' he asks, and there's a tremor in his voice. 'I'm seventy-four years old and can't even reach my bloody phone.' He sniffs, rubbing his hand across his reddening nose. 'As a child, Maddy never spent a night away from home, not until she was thirteen. There was a school trip to France, one of those outdoor, adventure holidays. Her mother and I both told her she'd hate it, but even then Maddy knew best. I'm sure there was a boy involved somewhere along the way. First day in France and the whole class have to learn to roll in a canoe. She hates it. I drove twelve hours to bring her home.'

Listening to Sam, I realise he has memories of Madeline I can barely imagine. When I hear the love in his voice, all I can do is nod.

'I was there for her, Ben. Every single time.' Sam turns to me, and there are tears in his eyes now. 'What if this time I can't rescue her?'

CHAPTER 27

Dani Cash pulled into an empty space in the car park at the back of Haddley police station and checked her reflection in the rear-view mirror. She puffed out her cheeks and ran her fingers across the dark circles beneath her eyes. The clock on the dashboard told her she still had another four hours on shift. Taking a deep breath, she scrunched her hair, grabbed her bag, and reached for the car door. A tap on the passenger-side window caught her attention. She climbed out of the car and walked around to speak to her husband.

'Just checking your make-up?' he said as she leaned against the car.

'Very funny,' she replied. 'I do look shocking though.'

'You're probably being a little harsh on yourself,' he replied, reaching up to touch her arm.

'Thanks,' she said.

'Where've you been?' he asked.

'Barnsdale sent me up to the PDQ warehouse to make a stolen vehicle report. A complete waste of my time. Uniform could have dealt with it in ten minutes.'

'You know my views on Barnsdale.'

Dani didn't have the energy to argue. Mat believed Barnsdale only ever did anything by the book. Dani felt more generous towards her superior's abilities, and often wondered if it was that very approach which made Barnsdale a successful officer.

Edging back his wheelchair, Mat smiled. 'A little bird tells me Barnsdale has a new special friend who works at PDQ. My guess is she wanted to impress him by sending a detective.'

'I'm Barnsdale's date bait?' replied Dani, laughing with her husband.

'One of the owners,' said Mat. 'Hooked up with him after her birthday drinks. CCTV images of her cracking on with him in the middle of Haddley Bridge.'

'Is nothing private in this place?' said Dani. 'Who showed you?'

'I can't reveal my sources, but I have it on very good authority he dropped her at the station this morning.'

Dani felt certain it would be PC Karen Cooke gossiping about the detective sergeant. Cooke had an encyclopaedic knowledge of the private life of every officer across the station. She wondered how long it would be until Cooke was spreading gossip on her and Ben.

'I'm pleased for Barnsdale,' said Dani, turning away and walking towards the station entrance, 'and it's nobody's business but her own.' Most inside the station thought Barnsdale uptight. She certainly kept to herself, but Dani enjoyed working with her. She felt she could trust her supervising officer. 'Are you coming or going?' she asked her husband.

He held up a small shopping bag from the local supermarket at the back of the station. 'Thought I'd have a change from Deliveroo and cook myself a pizza.'

'Opening a box and putting a pizza in the oven does not count as cooking.'

'It's a step forward.' Laughing, Mat wheeled himself up the ramp towards the rear door. Dani reached across with her access card to open the automatic doors. 'Thanks,' he said, moving ahead.

Three months ago, Mat would have vented in rage at his wife for even opening the door for him. His pride, combined with his unwillingness to accept the reality of his situation, had left him frustrated and angry. She was relieved to see him moving on with his life. While the job he was starting next week would never be his first choice, it would give him his own investigations and with that, hopefully, a renewed purpose. He rolled through the second set of doors leading directly into the CID offices, and stopped beside Dani's desk. 'You going to be late again tonight?' he asked, as she hung her jacket on the back of her chair.

'Hopefully not as late as last night, but it'll be after ten, probably later.'

'I'll leave you a light on.'

She smiled. 'You don't have to wait up.'

'Nothing else to do.'

Dani turned away and logged on to her screen. She hated

the thought of Mat holding on to the hope their marriage might have a future. 'I should get on,' she said. 'I need to log this stolen vehicle and then keep ploughing through the social media of the intruder victims.'

'Any progress?' said Mat, remaining beside her desk.

'Nothing yet.'

Dani looked up to see Chief Inspector Bridget Freeman enter the room. Mat turned and followed his wife's gaze. The station's commanding officer spoke briefly with DS Barnsdale before walking towards them.

'Your final week next week, DS Moore?' she said to Mat as she approached.

'Don't worry, chief, I'm not slacking off.'

'Never entered my mind that you would,' she replied. 'DC Cash, I read your report on last night's break-in on Haddley Common.'

'Sarah Wright, ma'am.'

'Yes,' replied Freeman. 'If we take Shannon Lancaster as a definite, all our intruder break-ins occurred between two and four in the morning. Mrs Wright's was some time before midnight.'

'Yes, ma'am. I confirmed the timings with Mrs Wright earlier today.'

'Might be nothing, but worth noting. I must dash. I've a dinner with the chief superintendent. Have a good evening, both.'

Dani watched Freeman hit the security button to open the rear doors. She couldn't help but admire the confidence and authority with which she led the station. Somehow, she constantly managed to keep herself fully acquainted with every element of the unit's operation.

Any officer would tell you how she remained fair, balanced and on top of every detail. She never seemed to make mistakes. But it was that very ability to be across every detail of each investigation that left Dani with the unsettling thought she couldn't shake.

CHAPTER 28

Approaching seven o'clock, evening traffic heading into Nottingham is heavy. We crawl past the university, where students crowd around a bus stop ready to embark on a Friday night out. We follow the road along the River Trent, then away from the city and into the suburb of West Bridgford. With the lights of the football ground shining in the distance, I turn down the tree-lined Musters Road and stop outside a local sandwich shop, Mrs Bunns Cob Emporium. Sam looks again at his phone. It's six hours since the last message from Billy Monroe.

'Anything?' I ask.

He shakes his head. I feel uneasy. What does Billy Monroe want? With no financial demand, I can't stop myself worrying he might have a very different motive.

'Let's find Tosh's flat,' I say, dismissing my thoughts.

Sam points at a road in front of us, leading off to the right. 'Is that the one?'

I nod. 'Millicent Road.' We step out of the car and walk down the neatly kept street.

'Pleasant neighbourhood,' says Sam, as we pass a small church where a single light shines through the evening mist. Sam zips up his jacket and rubs his hands together. We cross a side road before stopping to stand in front of a carefully maintained Georgian house, now divided into four flats. At the side of the building is an old-fashioned metal fire escape, more at home on a Brooklyn brownstone than in a Nottingham suburb.

'Is this the place?' asks Sam.

'Flat four,' I reply.

'What do we do now?'

'Exactly what we always do in our jobs – knock on the door.'

Sam follows me up the narrow driveway. We squeeze between a blue Honda, displaying a disabled badge in the front window, and a small city van with an advert for a local carpet-fitting company plastered across its side. I press the buzzer for number four. Resting beside the front door is a black grocer's bike, with a vintage wicker basket fastened to the front. The sound of Sam repeatedly ringing the bicycle's bell fills the night air.

'Is that in case Tosh Monroe didn't hear the buzzer?'

Sam smiles. 'I thought maybe Mrs Bunns was out delivering.'

I'm about to press the door buzzer for a second time when a heavily accented voice greets us over the intercom.

'Is that Mr Monroe?' I say.

'Who's asking?'

'My name's Ben Harper,' I reply, 'I was wondering if it might be possible to ask you a couple of questions about your grandson.'

141

'You a journalist?'

'I am, but I'm here with my colleague . . . ' I look at Sam and he raises his eyebrows, ' . . . and we were hoping we might have just five minutes of your time.'

'I don't talk to journalists.'

'I appreciate that, Mr Monroe and we're not here looking for a story, we simply want to speak to you about your grandson.' Tosh Monroe is silent, but I can hear his breath through the speaker. 'Mr Monroe, we know Billy's been released and we only want to help him.' I wait a moment before continuing. 'Either we come up to your flat for a conversation or we wait here until you come out, but one way or another we are going to talk to you.'

After a brief pause, we hear his sharp response. 'Five minutes, no more.'

The lock buzzes and Sam quickly pushes open the door. We stand in a small entrance hall, where a red floral carpet follows the stairs up to the top floor.

'No lift?' says Sam. Slowly, we begin to make our way up. 'Living here would bloody kill me,' he continues, his breath becoming shorter as we climb the stairs.

We stop halfway. 'When we meet him,' I say, establishing our story, 'we're journalists researching an article on the impact of crime on the relatives of offenders.'

'Who works for who?'

'What?' I reply.

'Do you work for me, or do I work for you?'

'We're partners.' I start walking up the next flight of stairs, and look back over my shoulder towards Sam.

'I'm not sure partners ever works,' he says. 'Somebody needs to be in charge.'

'Shut up.'

The stairs steepen and turn again. Tosh Monroe's flat is housed in the eaves of the building and reaching his door I have to bow my head. The door is ajar. I look back at Sam and he whispers, 'Go slowly.'

I push open the door. With four more steps to climb, there is little light in front of me. I call ahead. 'Mr Monroe, it's Ben Harper.' I follow the stairs up and stand in a dimly lit living room. The room is uncluttered with just one small wicker sofa and a large-screen TV. I step forward, Sam at my side, and we both turn quickly when a door behind us is opened.

'Mr Monroe?' I say with a start.

'Thought we might need another seat,' he replies, walking past us with a fold-up kitchen chair. He seats himself in front of the television, leaving us with the sofa.

'I'm Sam Hardy,' says Sam, walking across to Monroe and offering his hand. 'And this is Ben Harper.' He explains the article we are supposedly working on.

'Sit down,' says Monroe.

We do as instructed; Sam and I finding ourselves nestled closely together.

'It can't have been an easy time for you,' I begin, 'with your grandson's release?'

'Haven't seen him.'

'He hasn't been in touch?' asks Sam.

'No.'

'Does that surprise you?'

Tosh shrugs.

'You stood by him though,' I say, 'throughout his trial. You attended every day. Did you ever believe he was guilty?'

'Not for me to judge.' Sam and I remain silent, waiting to see if Monroe will say anything more. After a moment, he does. 'I was the only family he had left, so it felt right that I should support him. Whatever he might have done.'

'Do you think he understood what he did?' asks Sam.

Monroe laughs. 'Aye, he understood. Whatever people said, he wasn't so stupid.'

'Can I ask what happened to his mother?'

'Mairi wasn't a bad lass, got in with the wrong crowd.' He sniffs. 'She never wanted to hurt Billy. She took some stuff when she didn't know what she was doing. Billy was left to live with the consequences.'

'Did you keep in touch, while he was inside?'

'I did my best. They kept him in a place outside Birmingham, not much more than an hour from here.'

'You still felt a family loyalty?' says Sam.

'He took his punishment.'

'How did he cope?'

'I guess like most of them, over time, he found a way.'

'How often would you see him?'

'Every two or three months.'

'So, you knew he was due for release?' Tosh Monroe is telling us very little, but Sam keeps pushing. 'And even though you'd stayed close, you didn't offer him a place to stay until he was back on his feet.'

Tosh stands and folds his chair. 'I've to get to the station to catch my train to work.'

'Night shift?' asks Sam.

'If you must know, yes. Twenty years ago, I ran a warehouse. Now, I schlep around all night chucking crap into a trolley just to pay my rent.'

Sam nods. 'Can I use your bathroom?' Tosh stares at him but, getting to his feet, Sam continues. 'At our age you have to take every opportunity you can.'

Tosh laughs. 'Try walking around a warehouse all night with your balls freezing off. Through the kitchen and on the left.'

Sam hurries out of the room, and I go to stand next to Monroe. 'You're sure you've no idea where Billy might have gone?'

'None,' he replies, edging towards the kitchen door.

'We need to talk to Billy,' I say, taking hold of his arm.

'I can't help you.' His voice is unwavering, but almost too much. 'I'll leave you to find your own way down,' he continues, when Sam returns through the kitchen.

'If you do hear from Billy, here's my number,' I say, scribbling it down on the back of an old petrol receipt.

'I won't,' he replies, crumpling the paper into his pocket.

We step out of Tosh Monroe's flat and immediately he closes the door behind us.

In silence, Sam and I make our way down the stairs. We step outside and, standing at the front of the house, I ring the bell on the old grocer's bike. 'What do we do now?' I say.

Sam smiles. 'We wait.'

CHAPTER 29

Lesley Barnsdale waved to the desk sergeant as she walked quickly through the front exit of Haddley police station. It was twenty minutes until the end of her shift, and for the first time in her eighteen-year career she was leaving early. It was also the first time she had ever waved to the desk sergeant.

In the fading February daylight, she hurried down the high street, crossed onto Haddley Bridge and, fighting the wind that was becoming increasingly blustery, made her way towards the gleaming glass tower block, which stood imposingly on the north side of the river. At the foot of the tower was the gourmet supermarket she'd heard her colleagues discuss many times. She was yet to venture inside as a customer, but she followed the steps down into the riverside courtyard and walked briskly into the store.

She'd always imagined the place as one frequented by City bankers and wealthy London solicitors, returning to their homes around Haddley Common. Looking at her fellow clientele, she realised she wasn't wrong. Tonight, she didn't care. Braised beef-shin rigatoni, crumbled feta cheese, garlic focaccia and a bottle of Pinot Noir. Or would he prefer beer? She realised she had no idea. She looked at her shopping basket. Ten pounds for garlic bread. Thirty pounds for a bottle of wine. Who was she fooling? Last night on Haddley Bridge, when Phil had moved to kiss her, she'd suddenly found herself confronted by the reality of her own life. After college, she'd joined the police force and worked diligently throughout her career. A promotion to inspector was promised within the next twelve months, and she knew that would make her mum proud. Along the way, she'd dated a couple of fellow officers, but had never been in love. And had never been loved. She'd made her career her focus, until for a split second on Haddley Bridge, faced with her upcoming fortieth birthday, she thought *what the hell*. She looked again at her shopping basket and for a moment she considered putting everything back. But then she took a deep breath and instead reached for a second bottle of wine.

Hurrying through the Victorian side streets and back to her one-bedroom flat above Puddle-Ducks nursery, she felt her phone buzz. She looked at the screen and saw it was her mother calling. About to answer, she stopped. For once, her mother could wait.

After almost running up the stairs into her flat, she began hastily to tidy her home. Phil's house had wowed her, and while she couldn't hope to make the same impression on him, she wanted him to feel comfortable. In truth, this was little more than the place she slept between shifts, but she was determined to make the effort. She hurried into the bedroom, shook the duvet and plumped up the pillows. Closing the curtains, she lit just one lamp and squirted a spray of the perfume her mother had bought her for Christmas. In the living room, she tidied the cushions, making space for two on her small IKEA sofa. She lit two candles on the gas hob and carried them through to the bathroom. Carefully she stood them at the end of the bath before searching for the scented bubbles, another gift from her mum. In the kitchen, she opened the wine and began to prepare dinner. Should they eat at her small kitchen table or together on the sofa? She ate most of her meals in front of the television so, for this occasion, she decided on the kitchen. She set the table with two wine glasses and lit another candle.

When the doorbell buzzed her heart jumped, but later, curled together on the sofa, sipping from her glass of red wine, she couldn't believe she'd worried. Phil was exactly as he'd been the night before – funny, caring, and she already adored every moment she spent with him. He took hold of her hand and slowly led her through to the bedroom.

Then her phone rang. He tried to stop her reaching for it, but she knew she must.

'PC Cooke?' she said, answering the call.

'Sorry to disturb you, ma'am, but an unidentified male body has been recovered in the car park at the back of St Marnham boathouse.'

CHAPTER 30

'Egg mayonnaise or roast beef salad?' I say to Sam as I climb back into the car.

'I'll play safe and stick with the egg mayo.' I pass Sam a packet of Co-op sandwiches. 'No crisps?' he asks.

'Afraid not. I'm following Madeline's instructions to get you on a healthier diet.'

He smiles. 'Which coffee is mine?'

'Take your pick,' I reply. 'Both fresh from a vending machine. Did I miss anything here?'

After leaving Tosh's flat, I pulled the car around the corner. We're now parked in a side road directly opposite his home.

'Nothing,' replies Sam. 'He's still upstairs.'

'So much for being in a hurry to catch his train.'

Sam turns to me. 'Perhaps he needs to check the loft before he leaves.'

When Sam visited Tosh's bathroom, walking through the kitchen he spotted a loft hatch up into the roof. Propped behind the washing machine was a hook-ended pole to open

149

the hatch. Fresh scratches on the paintwork suggested the recent opening of the door.

'Do you think Madeline could be up there?' asks Sam.

'Let's not get ahead of ourselves,' I reply. 'Tosh certainly knows more than he's letting on. I'd bet you good money he's seen Billy since his release, but that doesn't mean he's here now. Or Madeline.' I bite into my sandwich.

'How is it?'

'Chewy,' I reply, my mouth still half full. I drink from my coffee before picking up my phone. I begin to reread Madeline's articles describing the night of Aaron Welsby's murder. The stone stairs leading up from the footbridge, the graffiti-covered walls, the dark alcove where Billy Monroe concealed himself. The killing took place only a couple of hundred yards from St Marnham's Victorian high street, the shops already illuminated by Christmas lights.

I read again the campaigning article Madeline wrote on the anniversary of Aaron's death. Her challenge to Billy Monroe to sue her newspaper, the knife repeatedly plunged into Aaron's stomach, his desperate fight for life as he staggers back up onto the bridge, his final fall into the depths of the River Thames. I scroll back up the page and begin to read the article for a third time.

'Something isn't right,' I say to Sam. 'Listen to this. *Appearing from the shadowy recess, he shouted Aaron's name and ran quickly towards him.*'

'What?' he replies, absent-mindedly pulling the crust off his sandwich.

'*He shouted Aaron's name,*' I repeat. I hurriedly search

150

through the other articles Madeline wrote in the months following. 'Only in that very first article does she use that phrase.'

'And?'

'How did she know? How did Madeline know Monroe shouted Aaron's name? One of the reasons the police investigation stalled was because there were no witnesses. They couldn't place Billy at the scene.'

'We all use a little dramatic licence at times in our reporting. You know that.'

'Not Madeline,' I reply. 'And not on a detail as important as that. She never embellishes, never fabricates. I've seen her tear a strip off reporters for even the tiniest exaggeration.' I twist in my seat. 'Explain to me what happened after the publishing of the first article. How did Madeline get the police to bring the case to trial?'

'She discovered the CCTV of Monroe in St Marnham.'

'That was evidence she found, not the police?'

'Yes,' replies Sam, drinking his coffee. 'In defence of the Met, it was almost impossible to find. After killing Welsby, Monroe lowered himself down from the footbridge and onto the railway line below. The route was difficult to imagine, until you saw the size of Billy Monroe. He followed the railway track through the village, jumped into Bryan Brook, swam half a mile, before finally scrambling out of the water outside St Marnham Primary School.'

'He was captured on the school CCTV?'

Sam nods. 'The school was close to two miles away from the bridge. The police had reviewed all of the CCTV within a mile radius – on the station platform, in the village, pubs, shops – and drawn a blank. Lazily, they assumed the killer left through Baron's Field, which had no cameras.'

'Billy was only ever caught on the school cameras?'

'Yes. Like I said, his escape route was almost inconceivable, but Madeline pieced it together. The footage from the school led to the police questioning Monroe. Not long after, they found a pair of his trainers specked with Aaron's blood.'

I look at Sam. 'How did Madeline learn so much? She built the case for the police and led them to the evidence.'

Sam stares at me, realisation dawning in his eyes. 'It's almost as if somebody was feeding her the information, like she had her own witness.'

I nod. 'Somebody else was there.'

CHAPTER 31

'There was a witness?' asks Sam. 'But why would they share information with Maddy and not the police?'

'Who knows? Perhaps for some reason they didn't trust the police.'

'They were involved?'

I shrug. 'Right now, it's impossible for us to know. We need to understand more about Aaron.' I quickly type a message to Min. I need to know if Aaron has any surviving relatives. The more I can learn about him, and the night of his murder, the more hope there is of tracking down Billy Monroe and of finding Madeline alive.

Sam nudges my arm. 'Tosh's lights are out.'

Seconds later, the front door of his home opens, and he climbs into the blue Honda parked in the driveway. The headlights on the car burn brightly through the mist and we watch Monroe pull away. I open my car door and pour the remains of my coffee into the gutter. Sam does the same, and together we cross the road towards the house.

'I can do this on my own,' I say to Sam, as we stand at the bottom of the metal fire escape.

'No, we're finding her together.'

Knowing it's pointless arguing with him, I jump up and pull down the ladder. 'Be careful on these first few steps,' I say. 'Once we're on the main escape, it'll get easier.'

Sam climbs the ladder far quicker than he did the stairs up to Tosh's flat. Together we make our way up the escape until we reach the very top and stand outside a large sash window.

'It leads straight into the bathroom,' says Sam.

I lift the window and it slides easily open.

'I'm getting good at this,' he says, smiling, as we step through the window. Sam reaches for the cord on the bath-room light, but I grab his arm.

'Let's not announce our arrival,' I say.

We move into the kitchen. Sam passes me the pole to unlock the latch for the loft hatch. I switch on my phone light and Sam does the same with his.

'When I open the hatch, point your light up into the loft.'

'What if Billy's in there?' whispers Sam.

'Only one way to find out.' I lock the pole into place. I look at Sam, holding his breath. He nods and I turn the lock. The door drops down and a short ladder unfolds in front of us.

'Billy?' I call, looking up into the dark space. 'Are you up there? If you are you need to come down.'

'With your hands up,' adds Sam. I turn and stare at him. 'Why not?' he mouths.

'Billy?' I say again, but there's still no reply. Holding my phone in front of me, I begin to climb the ladder. 'Smells damp,' I call to Sam, when I'm halfway up. My head passes the entrance, and I can see inside the loft.

'Ben,' says Sam, in a forced whisper.

'Hang on,' I reply. 'He's not here but somebody's been up here pretty recently.' I climb further up the ladder.

'Ben, wait,' says Sam, his voice louder.

'I'm going in,' I call in reply. 'There's a mattress, a sleeping bag, food wrappers, two half-drunk mugs of coffee. Someone's been living here, and my money is on Billy.'

'Ben, you need to come back down.'

'No, we've definitely got something.'

'You need to come back down now,' shouts Sam.

'Shh! Why?' I call from inside the loft.

'Because I don't want Mr Monroe to pull the trigger on the shotgun he's pressing into my back.'

Five

'Somebody hit him on the back of the head pretty hard. In what circumstance, I'll leave that up to you.'

He carefully closed his book on the planets before placing it down at the side of his bed and lying back on his pillow. Through his open blind he stared up at the bright night sky. He imagined himself hurtling through the stars, escaping in the fastest ever spaceship, until he reached the moon. Always the same dream.

This was the fourth birthday he'd spent in the house and in the loft room. To him, the room felt cold and damp, but she simply repeated he was lucky to have so much space. If he was cold, he could have an extra blanket at night. She'd promised him a heater but, like the rug for the floor, it had never arrived. For his birthday she'd bought him new school trousers. She'd told him it was what he needed, and money didn't grow on trees. The man had given him the book on the planets. He couldn't read all the words but it was packed full of colour pictures, and he loved it.

Three weeks earlier, she told him that if he did better at school, he could take four friends to the bowling alley. He wasn't sure who to invite but had settled on Ethan, who was his only real friend, plus Dylan and Samuel. They were brothers and lived three doors down and, when it wasn't raining, would play football in the street with him. The day before his birthday, he failed his maths test. He'd done better than he ever had before, but that wasn't good enough. She'd told him there would be no bowling alley and it was his responsibility to tell his friends.

He'd screamed at her, yelling over and over how much he hated her. As he'd screamed, he'd started to cry. She'd stared at him, not moving. He'd run out of the kitchen, pushing her out of the way as he did.

As soon as he'd left the room, he'd known it was a mistake. He'd kept running up the stairs to his room, but behind him he could hear her groaning. He'd told himself he didn't care but sitting on the edge of his bed his stomach had felt strange.

Standing outside his room, at the top of the stairs, he'd listened again. She was silent. He'd hoped she was okay. Then she'd groaned again. He'd thought he should check on her, but then he heard her son walk down the stairs and into the kitchen. Thirty minutes later he'd heard an ambulance arrive.

She was back home now. He could hear her downstairs. She was still crying.

Then he heard her shout, 'I want him gone.'

CHAPTER 32

'What are you looking at?' asked Phil as they waited for the traffic lights to change on Haddley Bridge.

'I haven't seen you in glasses before,' Lesley replied.

'Do you like them?' he asked, turning to face her.

Wearing glasses made him look older, she thought. The frames were too dark and heavy. 'Most distinguished,' she replied. She wasn't quite sure what that meant, but it felt both a positive and non-committal thing to say.

'You prefer me without?'

'No, not at all,' she replied. 'It's just they make you look different.'

A hand slammed on the bonnet of the van.

'Sorry, mate,' shouted a drunken voice from the road, before a group of twenty-somethings stumbled towards the river path. It was after nine on a Friday night and Haddley's bars were heaving.

Phil pulled slowly forward, turning onto the Lower Haddley Road. 'I only wear them occasionally,' he said, picking up their previous conversation. She realised she'd made him feel self-conscious. He kept talking. 'And when I do wear them, it's only really for driving; if I've already removed my contact lenses.'

'I like them,' she replied, laughing.

'But you wouldn't have chosen them?'

'Let's say I might have imagined you with a different look. Next time you need a new pair, I could come with you?' Immediately, she regretted saying the words. Phil was sure to see her as too pushy.

'Always good to have a female perspective,' he replied, smiling, and Lesley couldn't stop herself imagining the two of them shopping together. Even so, she doubted it would ever happen. After she'd received the call from PC Cooke, Phil had pulled her slowly towards the bedroom. When they reached the doorway, he'd kissed her, and she'd longed for him to take her into the room. But she'd known she had to leave, and she'd forced herself to step away. He'd followed her into the bathroom, sitting on the edge of the bath, watching her undress and change into her work clothes. Their conversation had been casual – he was interested in her investigation, what might happen next – but those few minutes felt like the most intimate they'd shared together.

'I prefer your hair down,' he'd said, as she'd pulled her hair tightly back and gripped it into place.

'I need it to be practical,' she'd replied. Even though she wasn't in uniform, this was the first time he'd seen her dressed as a detective.

Standing beside her at the bathroom mirror, he'd kissed her on the cheek. 'You should try it sometime.'

She knew that was the moment Phil had realised he was sleeping with a police officer, and, since then, she'd been riddled with doubt.

The van passed through Haddley Woods and on into St Marnham. 'Any idea what time you'll be finished?' he asked as they drove down the deserted village high street.

'Never can say with these things,' she replied, shaking her head.

'I could wait up for you?'

She sucked in her cheeks, knowing it would be longer than that. 'I could be a few hours,' she said. 'It'll be tomorrow morning by the time I get home.' As they turned along the river, she stared at the road ahead. Suddenly it would be obvious to Phil her work had to come first. She didn't want to see his reaction. She'd already told herself what it would be.

'Let's do something tomorrow then,' he replied. 'You must be allowed a few hours off at some point?'

She heard her own nervous laugh, and realised it was in relief as much as anything. 'Perhaps we could get lunch?'

'I've got to take this van back but the PDQ warehouse canteen does a cracking steak and ale pie on a Saturday lunchtime.'

'You know how to treat a girl.'

'Be nice to show you where I work.'

'It's a date,' she replied.

A black cab exited the courtyard at the front of Mailer's fish restaurant and Phil slowed to let the driver enter the traffic. Ahead of them, Lesley could see the blue flashing lights.

'You can drop me here, if you like,' she said when they were still a couple of hundred metres away.

'You don't want your colleagues to see you climbing out of my van?' he replied, before pulling up at the edge of the curb.

'Nothing of the sort,' she said, her tone a defensive one. 'Well, maybe not just yet.' He smiled and leaned over to kiss her. His hand was on her leg. 'I have to go,' she whispered, opening her door.

'I'll see you tomorrow,' he replied, leaning back in his seat. 'Drop me a message when you're on your way up.'

She stepped out into the traffic and hurried across the road. As she approached the boathouse car park, she glanced back over her shoulder, but Phil had already disappeared, back towards Haddley.

CHAPTER 33

A uniformed officer raised the police tape and DS Barnsdale ducked beneath it. Rain began to fall as she crossed the unlit car park at the side of St Marnham boathouse. Fastening her jacket, she made her way towards the river.

'This way, ma'am,' said PC Karen Cooke, greeting her at the top of a shallow bank. 'It's a bit boggy down here, I'm afraid.'

Barnsdale could already feel the damp seeping inside her shoes and wished she'd dug out her boots before leaving home.

'Bit of a trek,' continued Cooke, looking back over her shoulder as she led Barnsdale down a small flight of brick steps before joining a narrow concrete trench. The trench was an inch deep in floodwater.

'Who on earth found a body down here?' called Barnsdale.

'Anonymous tip,' replied the officer. 'Local dealers often use the abandoned boat shed at the back of the car park. My guess is one of them called it in.'

'How public spirited. Make sure somebody goes through the shed, just in case.'

Beneath overhanging trees, one weak spotlight barely illuminated the trench. Crouched over the body was a forensic pathologist.

'Hi,' he said glancing up and smiling. 'DS Barnsdale, isn't it?'

She nodded. She'd met him before but couldn't remember his name. He looked so young. 'George Lennon,' he said, pulling off his blue gloves and offering her his hand. *Of course, the guy with the Beatles fanatics for parents*, she thought.

'What can you tell me?' she asked.

'Sixty to seventy years of age. Initial examination suggests two or three heavy blows to the back of his head.'

'One of those killed him?'

'Tough to say right now. Might well have done, but if not, cardiac arrest immediately following or simply exposure after lying here unconscious for the past twenty-four hours.'

'But somebody killed him?'

'Somebody hit him on the back of the head pretty hard. In what circumstance, I'll leave that up to you.'

She grimaced. 'Any other signs of assault.'

'Nothing I can see right now. I'll take a closer look when we get him on the table.'

'Killed here or dumped afterwards?'

'He's lying in an inch of water. I can't say definitively but my guess is he hasn't travelled far.'

Barnsdale sighed. 'Any identification?'

'If you want to feel in his pockets, be my guest.'

Cooke lifted her light in the direction of the victim's body and looked doubtfully towards her commanding officer.

'Go ahead, constable,' said Barnsdale. Cooke trudged through the water, pulling on a pair of latex gloves before reaching the body.

'Easier if you remove the trousers,' said Lennon.

Cooke swallowed hard before doing as advised. She found nothing.

'Why would he be here?' said Barnsdale, thinking aloud.

'Your guess is as good as mine,' replied Lennon. 'He seems a bit old for the usual boathouse hook-up crowd.' She waited for him to say more but instead he indicated to his colleagues that the body was ready for bagging and removal. 'Good luck,' he said, briskly, before making his way up the steps.

'Let's get a search going of the local area and see if we can find any other way of identifying him,' she said to her junior officer.

'We can run a missing persons check for the past twenty-four hours.'

Barnsdale nodded before making her way back up into the boathouse's gravel car park, Cooke following behind her. As the constable bent to remove her plastic shoe coverings, a woman raised the police tape at the roadside above her six-foot frame and walked towards her.

'PC Cooke?' said the woman, in a soft Australian accent. 'I'm Kate Hoy, the boathouse manager.'

'Thanks for coming so quickly,' replied Cooke. 'This is Detective Sergeant Barnsdale. She's leading the investigation.'

The three women walked across the car park until they

reached the padlocked iron gates at the far end of the property. Barnsdale rattled the gates. 'These are always kept locked?'

'Don't think I've ever seen them open; wouldn't even know if there's a key.'

The gates led directly into the courtyard at the front of Mailer's restaurant. 'So, the only way in and out is through the front gates?'

Hoy nodded. 'Unless you scrambled up the riverbank, but that wouldn't be easy.'

Feeling the cold water in her shoes, Barnsdale agreed. 'Certainly not if you're dragging a six-foot body.' She explained to Hoy the discovery of a male body, most likely in his sixties, by the banks of the river. 'Grey hair, moustache. Could that be anybody linked to the boathouse?'

'Poor bloke. We've a few older rowers, mostly guys who've rowed their whole lives, but I'm afraid he doesn't ring a bell. My dad, back home in Sydney, has a grey moustache, so I'd definitely remember him.'

Barnsdale nodded. 'Any CCTV?'

Hoy shook her head. 'We've cameras in front of the main boathouse, but not for the car park or the old boat shed.'

'I understand that shed is now used for other business?'

Hoy rolled her eyes. 'Hey, I've called that into your lot three times in the last month. There's only so much I can do.'

'We'll still need access to the shed.'

'Be my guest.'

The women walked back to the front of the main building. Cooke's phone buzzed and she stepped away.

Barnsdale remembered the comment made by George Lennon. 'Is the car park ever used for hook-ups?'

Hoy laughed. 'Doesn't everyone meet online these days, sergeant? You might get lucky after a race meet but that's about it.'

'And in the last twenty-four hours, anything unusual?'

'I'm in and out the whole time, but I've not seen anything.'

'Thank you,' said Barnsdale. 'If we need you again, we'll be in touch.'

'Ma'am!'

Barnsdale turned, surprised at the urgency in Cooke's tone. The junior officer was hurrying towards her, pushing her phone back into her pocket.

'Report of a suspected intruder at a house on Haddley Common,' said Cooke, breathlessly. 'A woman has locked herself in her bathroom with her young child but fears the man may still be inside her home.'

'Go!' yelled Barnsdale.

CHAPTER 34

I step backwards down the loft ladder.

'Slowly,' says Tosh Monroe.

I look briefly over my shoulder. Monroe is pointing his shotgun directly at me.

'We're not here to hurt anyone,' I say, stepping off the bottom rung of the ladder, my back to Monroe. I turn slowly with my hands raised to my shoulders. He is holding the gun inches away from me. 'Mr Monroe, please put the gun down and we can explain. All we want to do is speak to Billy.' My eyes dart towards Sam. He is standing at the side of the kitchen; his eyes wide, his hands pressed firmly against the wall. I turn back to Monroe, fixing my eyes on his. 'Please lower the gun and let me explain.' I start to drop my hands, wanting him to do the same.

'The last time I looked, breaking and entering was still a crime,' says Monroe. 'Perhaps I should call the police.' His voice is strong, but I can see a shake in his hand.

'I don't think any of us want the police involved,' says Sam.

'Please put the gun down,' I repeat. 'We need to find Billy, urgently.'

'We want to help him,' adds Sam.

Monroe slowly lowers his weapon and disengages the barrel. Sam rubs his hands across his face and lets out an audible sigh.

'I wouldn't have killed *you*,' says Monroe.

'Good to know that now,' replies Sam. 'I need a drink before I piss myself.'

'Since you're here, how about a whisky?' asks Monroe.

'That would be nice,' replies Sam, with an anxious laugh.

'Twelve-year-old Glenfiddich?'

'Is there any other?'

I glare at Sam, but he raises his palms and shrugs. Monroe carefully places his shotgun on top of the washing machine, and we follow him through to the living room.

'Billy was here,' he says, bending to open a small cupboard before pouring three generous shots.

'Why was he sleeping in the loft?' asks Sam.

'It's a decent space. I use it as a spare room. For Billy, after twelve years in a prison cell, it felt like luxury. And he loved the skylight.'

'How long did he stay?'

'I told him he could stay as long as he liked, get himself sorted, but he was gone within a few days.'

'Why didn't you tell us?' asks Sam, downing his drink.

'Two nosey journalists from London – do you think I'm stupid or something?'

Sam smiles and Monroe tops up his glass. He offers the bottle to me before saying, 'You've barely touched yours.'

'Driving,' I reply.

Monroe turns back to Sam. 'Billy's been through enough. He deserves his chance now.'

'He did kill a man,' replies Sam.

'Aye, and he's done his time.'

I briefly catch Sam's eye. We both know we need Tosh Monroe onside. 'You're right, he's done his time,' says Sam, 'and I know the last thing you'd want to see is him going back inside.'

Monroe slumps in his chair and sips on his drink. 'What makes you say that?'

'It might not be Billy's fault, but we think he's in danger of getting mixed up with some pretty unpleasant folk; people we were already looking at.' Sam pauses. We both know telling Monroe the truth will only set him against us. 'Our story isn't about Billy,' he continues, 'but his name has come up, among a list of names you wouldn't want him connected with.'

I nod at Sam, and he throws me a quick smile.

'He's good-hearted beneath it all, despite what's he's done. But bloody gullible,' says Monroe, with a bitter laugh. 'He's too easily led astray, always has been. Throughout his life, people have used him; his mother probably being the first.'

'All we want to do is talk to him,' says Sam.

Monroe looks at him and then at me. 'Why would you want to help him?'

'We're following a story, that's all,' I reply. 'If we happen to help Billy along the way ...'

Monroe drinks again from his glass. 'He was here for

a week, just over. Came straight here after his release. I gave him some money, bought him some clothes and a cheap phone.'

'Have you got his number?' asks Sam.

'I've been calling him for the last four days, left him umpteen messages, but nothing.'

'It would still be good if we could have the number,' says Sam, trying to disguise his eagerness, 'just so we can try calling as well.'

Monroe disappears into the kitchen, reappearing seconds later with a scrap of paper that he hands to Sam.

'Thank you,' says Sam, folding the paper and slipping it into his jacket pocket.

'I've written my number beneath it. If you find him, give me a shout.'

I nod. 'Do you have any idea where he is right now?'

Monroe traces his fingers across the liver spots on the back of his hands. 'Billy never had many friends but there was a lad he met at school, Ethan Harris. They kept in touch off and on, and then the first two years Billy was inside Harris was already there.' I raise my eyebrows. 'He hadn't killed anybody,' continues Monroe, 'but he drove a getaway from a petrol-station raid. Once he'd done his stretch, I think he did go back and visit Billy a handful of times.'

'And you think Billy might be with him now?' asks Sam.

Monroe shrugs. 'Like I said, Billy doesn't have many friends. I heard him talking on the phone when he was here. I hoped Harris might be a good influence. He's got a decent job; works nights as a forklift-truck driver at a warehouse in

Wolverhampton. Best Billy ever achieved was working as a builder's labourer on a daily rate.'

'Is that what he was doing in Haddley, before Welsby's death?' I ask.

'There was always a lot of building going on in the town. Billy said staying by the river reminded him of home.' Tosh downs his shot. 'Stupid, I know, but I hoped Harris might now help him find something more permanent.'

'Have you got an address for Harris?' asks Sam.

Monroe reaches into his back pocket and pulls out another scrap of paper. About to pass it to Sam, he hesitates.

'If we can get to Billy first,' says Sam, 'and set him straight, he'll be far better off than getting involved with the police again.'

Monroe looks at Sam and slowly nods, before handing him the address.

CHAPTER 35

'Sarah, are you still with me?' said Dani. She slammed her hand against the button at the rear of the CID office and ran out into the car park.

'I think I can hear him coming up the stairs,' replied Sarah Wright, who'd called the detective's number directly.

'Stay where you are,' replied Dani, aware Sarah had locked herself in the bathroom. 'Uniform are on their way.' She jumped into a patrol car and, under lights, raced her way towards the high street. 'I'm three minutes away,' she said. 'How's Max doing?'

Sarah had hurriedly carried her six-year-old son from his bed, after hearing breaking glass in her living room.

'You're doing okay, aren't you, Max?' Sarah said to her son.

'I wish Nathan was here,' Dani heard him reply to his mum. 'He would come and rescue us. He's Super Nathan.' Dani couldn't stop herself smiling as she passed through a red light at the bottom of the high street before turning along the river road.

'Mummy,' said Max. 'Nathan would grab hold of the bad

man and punch him in the face. Will Nathan come and visit us soon?'

There was silence on the end of the phone.

'Nathan sounds very brave,' said Dani, wanting to keep the conversation alive.

'He is very brave,' said Sarah to her son. 'I'm sure he'll come and visit soon.'

'He should come now!' shouted Max.

'Shh,' said Sarah, 'we must be quiet. But, yes, it would be nice if he did.'

'Phone him then,' said Max to his mum. 'Or if not, call Daddy. He'll come and rescue us.'

'The police are on their way,' replied Sarah to her son.

Dani accelerated along the Lower Haddley Road and, as she approached Haddley Common, she saw blue lights arriving in the opposite direction.

'One minute away,' said Dani. 'Tell Max he's being incredibly brave.'

'He is,' replied Sarah, before whispering to Dani, 'braver than me.'

'I'm almost with you. Can you hear the intruder?'

'No, nothing. I'm scared, Dani.'

'Hold on.'

'Oh my God,' said Sarah, suddenly.

'What is it?' asked Dani, as she raced up the side of Haddley Common.

'The bedroom light's gone out. He must be in the next room.'

'Stay where you are. Don't open the door.'

The sound of a hand slamming against the bathroom door echoed through the car, causing Dani to jerk her head back.

She heard Max scream.

And then the line went dead.

CHAPTER 36

'How far to Wolverhampton?' asks Sam, as I click open the car doors.

'Not far, sixty miles.'

'Let's go,' he replies, before reaching for his phone and dialling the number Monroe gave him.

'What are you going to say if he answers?'

Sam looks at me and lowers his phone. 'I don't know. What do you think?'

'We're pretty certain he's got Madeline,' I say, and Sam nods. 'Therefore, chances of him answering the phone are fairly slim, but if he does answer, the danger is all we do is spook him. And we still won't know where they are.'

'I think we should call all the same. If he answers, we tell him we've spoken to his grandfather and we're on to him. We tell him to give himself up before it's too late and then we head straight to Wolverhampton.'

'Okay, if that's what you want.'

Sam dials the number again before hastily passing the phone to me. 'You speak,' he says.

I listen to the tone, but it simply rings out. 'Nothing,' I say. 'He's probably ditched the phone already.' I can see the disappointment in Sam's face. He sniffs and then inhales deeply.

'Let's get going,' he says, nudging my arm before buckling his seatbelt. 'We can be there in an hour.'

My phone buzzes. 'One second,' I say, reaching for my jacket. There's a message from Min. 'Aaron Welsby's parents are still alive,' I read aloud. 'Since their son's death, Barbara and Patrick Welsby have lived in the small Cotswold town of Winchcombe, not far from Cheltenham.' As I glance at the dashboard clock, the time ticks past 10 p.m. 'If we leave now, we can be there before midnight.'

'What about Wolverhampton?'

'Ethan Harris works nights.'

'Thank God one of us was paying attention,' replies Sam.

I start the engine. 'We can see the Welsbys and still be outside Harris's home in Wolverhampton before he comes off shift.' Sam nods his agreement and I copy the address Min has sent me into Apple Maps.

Late-night motorway traffic is light, and soon we are racing around Birmingham. Sam drops his head back onto his headrest. 'Twenty-four hours ago,' he says, his eyes resting closed, 'we were all celebrating my birthday in East's restaurant. Madeline offered me a ride home, but I just wanted to go on drinking with my buddies. I should have been with her.'

'You can't blame yourself.'

'But, if I'd been with her, I could have done something.'

179

'If Madeline couldn't—' I stop myself as I realise I'm probably not helping.

'I know you think she and I bicker, because we do. We argue and wind each other up but only because we love each other.' Sam pauses. 'When she was a kid, she wanted to be a photographer. We both encouraged her. She took some great pictures. Her mother wanted her to go into fashion, but I always knew. Whenever I took her to the newspaper office, she'd always have an idea for a story. Before she was ten, she knew how to set the front page.'

'It was in her blood,' I reply, half smiling as I look over at Sam. Under the bright motorway lights, for the first time ever, I see an old man sitting next to me.

'What if we can't find her, Ben?'

'We will,' I reply, still trying to inject confidence into my tone. 'We're making progress but, Sam, if we don't find her in the next twenty-four hours, we go to the police.' Sam says nothing. I'm desperate to find Madeline but know the longer we go the harder it will become. 'Agreed?'

'Agreed,' replies Sam, his voice faint.

We leave the motorway and begin to follow a dark road into the Cotswold countryside.

'Do remember Aaron's parents from the trial?' I ask.

'They sat through every minute,' replies Sam. 'I'm not sure that's something I could've done. The prosecution presented some horrendous details. Once the trial was over, they never said a word.'

'No victim statement?'

'Nothing, not even from their solicitor outside court.'

I find it strange the Welsbys decided to stay silent, and that the couple chose to offer nothing in tribute to their son.

'They'd probably had enough of the press by then,' continues Sam, reading my thoughts.

'Or they didn't want to be put in the spotlight.'

'What are you hoping they might tell us?'

'Either at the trial or before, they must have met Madeline,' I reply. 'Maybe they can shed some light on who was feeding her so much information.'

CHAPTER 37

Dani Cash couldn't stop herself smiling as Sarah Wright's young son told her how he'd scared away the intruder from their home.

'Super Max shouted at him, and he ran away,' said Max, animatedly, as he pulled his superhero pose.

'You were so very brave,' replied Dani, taking the seat opposite Max and his mother in the temporarily converted bedroom. She looked at Sarah and asked her to recount the break-in to her home.

'I was watching TV in here, just on my iPad, when I heard a rattle on the window downstairs, followed by the sound of breaking glass.' Yawning, Max curled into his mother's side, and she wrapped her arms around him.

Dani briefly turned towards PC Karen Cooke, who was standing behind the sofa, waiting for the kettle to boil. From what Sarah had just said, it was obvious the intruder was becoming increasingly brazen.

'I've been meaning to have the lock fixed on that window,

but I always assumed nobody would dare break in at the front of the house. It's in clear sight of the road.'

'You'd be surprised,' replied Dani.

Karen walked from the back of the room with a mug of tea. 'Here you go,' she said to Sarah, before perching on the corner of the sofa. 'I've had a quick look at the window. Looks like he levered it up, probably with not much more than a screwdriver.'

'Stupid of me,' replied Sarah, stroking her son's hair as he drifted back to sleep.

'Not your fault,' said Dani, 'but probably worth getting all the locks checked.'

Sarah recounted carrying Max from his bed before bolting themselves in the bathroom and calling Dani. 'When he slammed his hand on the door, I think both Max and I screamed, and I dropped my phone. Max yelled at him to go away, and then, incredibly, he did. I could hear your police sirens coming up the common, so I guess he heard the same.'

Dani nodded. She'd been first on the scene with Cooke arriving just a couple of minutes later. They'd entered the house through the living-room window. Moving through to the kitchen, they'd found the temporary boarding removed and the room open to the garden.

'It appears he left the same way as last night, out through the back and over the fence. We've officers searching the area now, but I'm afraid he's probably long gone.'

Sarah looked down at her son, now sleeping beside her. 'Why is he targeting us?'

'It's impossible for us to know what his motivations

are. With him being scared off yesterday, and knowing the way out through the garden, he might simply have chanced his arm.'

'I was frightened, Dani,' said Sarah. 'It felt like he was coming for us, coming for me.'

'We will leave an officer outside but is there anyone who might spend the night here tonight?'

'I'll call my ex-husband,' replied Sarah.

'You might even want to consider moving out for a couple of days, just until we get hold of this guy.'

Dani walked downstairs and into Sarah Wright's living room. A cool breeze blew through the room, causing the dust sheets that covered most of the furniture to billow eerily. She stood beside the forensic technician who was working on the window.

'Pretty easy,' said the man, pointing to the single lock on the sash window. 'One good shove and he was in.'

'We'll get it boarded over properly once you're done,' replied Dani, turning to see Cooke standing in the doorway.

'He's definitely getting bolder,' said the uniformed officer.

'That's my worry,' replied Dani, before looking back at the window. 'Why break the glass when the lock was so weak?' she asked.

'Levering up the window and slipped?'

'Possibly,' said Dani, as she ran her hand thoughtfully across the back of a covered sofa, 'or perhaps his aim was to strike a maximum level of fear?'

CHAPTER 38

Approaching midnight, we drive down a deserted Winchcombe High Street. We pass an antique shop, a fine-art studio, a florist and, next door, a traditional hardware store. Winchcombe is an old-fashioned English town, idyllic and peaceful. I can understand why the Welsby's chose to escape here after the trauma of their son's murder.

I nudge Sam, who is sleeping beside me.

'Are we there?' he asks, stretching his arms.

'Couple of minutes away from the house.'

He rubs his eyes and looks out of the window. 'I can't imagine anything ever happens here,' he says.

I smile, and as the street narrows further, we pass a long row of Cotswold stone cottages. The impressive St Peter's Church, its striking tower reminding me of the one neighbouring my home in Haddley, follows at the end of the high street. We drive a short way out of the town centre until the Corner Cupboard pub comes into view.

'They're still open,' says Sam, suddenly alert when he sees a man staggering down the pub's front steps.

'One of the upsides of country life,' I reply.

'Perhaps I should reconsider my views.'

We pass the pub but almost immediately I pull up onto the pavement on the opposite side of the road. With few streetlights, I have to peer out of the window until I spot a small terrace cottage with a bay-fronted window. The number 78 is fixed at the top of the home's neatly presented narrow green door.

'This the place?' asks Sam, looking up at the cottage. 'No lights on.'

'Probably asleep by now. I think they're both in their eighties.'

Sam stands beside me before reaching for the cast-iron door knocker. 'I'll just knock quietly,' he says.

'Why?

'So as not to startle them.'

'Whatever you think's best,' I reply.

He gently taps the door.

'If they are asleep, that will never wake them.'

He knocks again, this time with slightly more gusto. 'Let's give them a minute,' he says. 'I know it can take me a minute or two to get my bearings, and I'm still a vibrant septuagenarian.'

I step back into the road and look up at the front bedroom window, but it remains in darkness. 'Knock again,' I say.

Sam taps the door with even greater timidity than his first knock.

'For Christ's sake, Sam,' I say, before rattling the knocker.

'That will wake the dead,' he says, 'or, if not, kill them.'

A light goes on upstairs. A moment later I see a figure crack the curtains. I call up to the window. 'Mr Welsby? I'm sorry about the hour . . . '

He pulls the curtain sharply closed.

Sam looks at me and raises his eyebrows, but as he does his phone buzzes. He scrambles for it in his pocket and, huddled together on the narrow street, we stare at the screen.

Midnight tomorrow. St Marnham Bridge.

'Twenty-four hours from now,' I say to Sam, just as a second message appears.

Two million in cash.

CHAPTER 39

'What now?' asks Sam, with a look of despair.

'We're not done yet,' I reply. We hear bolts on the inside of the door sliding open. When the door opens narrowly, a metal chain holds it in place. Sam steps forward and peers through the gap.

'Mr Welsby, my name is Sam Hardy. You don't know me, but I desperately need your help. My daughter's life is in danger.' Sam speaks with a renewed urgency. Welsby tries to push the door closed, but Sam is quick to keep it open with a wedged foot. 'Mr Welsby, please. I think you may know my daughter. Her name is Madeline Wilson.'

Sam waits before removing his foot from the door. The door closes gently before we hear the chain sliding off.

'You'd better come in,' says Patrick Welsby, opening the door fully.

I lower my head and follow Mr Welsby and Sam down a narrow hallway and into a small living room. Wooden beams line an uneven ceiling. Welsby, dressed in pyjamas and a dark red dressing gown, invites us to sit beside a wood-burning stove. Although extinguished, its embers still bring some warmth to the stone-walled room.

'Patrick, what's going on?' calls a voice from upstairs.

'We're in the living room, dear,' he replies, and moments later an older woman appears, her long, grey hair pulled loosely back behind her head.

'Barbara, this is Sam Hardy. He's Madeline Wilson's father.' I see an immediate flicker of recognition from Mrs Welsby at the mention of Madeline's name. Both of the Welsbys are aware of who she is, but I'm still unsure how well they know her personally.

'And this is Ben Harper,' says Sam, introducing me as he stands to greet Barbara Welsby. 'He works with Madeline at her news site. We wouldn't have disturbed you at this late hour if it wasn't urgent.'

'Please, sit,' says Mrs Welsby, and waits for us to do so before taking a seat next to Sam on the sofa.

'We believe Madeline's life may be in danger,' I say, leaning forward from the opposite armchair.

She holds my eye. 'This has something to do with Billy Monroe?'

Mrs Welsby glances at her husband, and I turn in his direction. With only one small light illuminating the room, darkness shadows his face, but when I look closely at him, I realise now how frail he is. I can see his eyes have become glazed, the emotion of his son's death still raw. I turn back to his wife.

'Are you aware of Monroe's release?' I ask.

'Twice we spoke against his parole,' she tells us, 'but this third time we were unsuccessful. The authorities informed us two weeks ago.' She looks towards her husband, but his eyes drop to the floor, and she continues. 'We both felt Madeline should be made aware. We tried calling her on numerous occasions but to no avail. Perhaps we should have left a message. I'm sure she's a very busy woman.'

'Thank you for trying,' says Sam.

'Your daughter is a very special woman. Her campaigning for Aaron helped win him the justice he deserved.'

'Can I ask,' I say, quietly, 'if you knew Madeline before the trial?'

Mrs Welsby shakes her head. 'We met her briefly at the Old Bailey, but only once. We thanked her for all she'd done to bring attention to Aaron's murder.'

'It was only a short conversation,' adds Mr Welsby, sitting in a high-backed armchair, tucked in the corner of the room, 'but we wanted to express our appreciation.'

'That was the only time we met her. She gave us her phone number and said to call if we ever needed her help.'

I've no reason to doubt what the Welsbys are telling us, but I still can't fully fathom the conviction with which Madeline championed Aaron's case, nor the risks she took.

'Sam's daughter is in genuine danger. To help us, we need to understand as much as we can about Aaron's death.' Mrs Welsby's lifts her eyes to mine and I continue softly. 'The night of Aaron's murder. We've reread Madeline's articles, and when describing that night, she offers details that seem impossible for her to have known. It's almost as if she was there.' Mrs Welsby sways gently in her seat but says nothing. 'But, of course, Madeline wasn't there.'

Barbara Welsby's breathing is laboured, her hand held against her chest. 'Madeline's in real danger?' she says, quietly.

'She might die.'

'We want to help, both of us do, but there are certain confidences we've sworn never to betray.'

'Please.' Sam's voice is little more than a whisper. 'We're running out of time.'

CHAPTER 40

'We were both over forty when Aaron was born. We knew then he'd be our only child,' Barbara Welsby tells us, her hands now resting in her lap. 'Still now, I would do anything to protect him.'

'I can understand that,' replies Sam. 'Madeline is my only child.'

'Mrs Welsby,' I say, quietly, as she gently touches Sam's hand, 'perhaps you could tell us a little bit about Aaron's life? He didn't grow up here in Winchcombe?'

'No, no. He was born in Hampton, in west London, a stone's throw from the palace. He attended the local Catholic primary school, and then went to Hampton School. Patrick had an accountancy firm in the town. Hampton was very much our home, but after Aaron's death we needed to get away from the whole area.'

'Was Aaron still living in Hampton when he was killed?'

'No, he had his own home by then. For as long as I can remember, all he'd ever wanted to be was an architect. After university he worked for a firm in Richmond, before setting up his own practice along with two other colleagues. They worked together for a couple of years before Aaron's murder.'

'The firm continues now, very successfully,' says Mr Welsby, adding his voice to the conversation. 'We still hear from the two remaining partners.'

'Just occasionally,' adds Mrs Welsby.

'It was Aaron's idea to set the firm up. He brought in their first major client.' I can hear the pride in Mr Welsby's voice.

'Those early years are so important for a business. I'm sure Aaron was integral to their future success,' I reply. 'Can I ask who that client was?'

'Haddley Grammar School,' replies Mr Welsby. 'A major building project.'

'Really?' I say. 'That's where I went to school.'

'Aaron designed the sports pavilion.'

'The one with the glass roof? I'd moved to the sixth-form college by the time it opened, but I remember it being built.'

A brief smile lights Mr Welsby's face. 'Yes, I believe it's still standing.'

'It is indeed,' I reply.

'We never doubted he'd go on and achieve great things.' Mr Welsby's voice cracks. 'Excuse me,' he says, pushing himself to his feet and hurrying from the room.

Sam and I both shift uncomfortably in our seats.

'He still finds it very difficult to talk about Aaron,' says Mrs Welsby.

'We understand that,' replies Sam. 'I can't begin to imagine the pain, but that's why I'm so desperate for anything you can tell us.'

'We knew Aaron was homosexual – gay,' she tells Sam, as if still familiarising herself with the language. 'I met one or two of the men he knew.' Her voice is quiet. 'I don't know how serious they were. One of them was a sports journalist, travelled the world covering all the big sporting events. I liked him. It was difficult for Patrick, but he never loved Aaron any less. He couldn't have been prouder of everything he achieved.' She pauses and I can see her thinking of her son's death. 'Aaron was a good person. He wasn't the kind of man to go and have sex with a stranger in a park by a river. Not that they're bad men, it just wouldn't be Aaron. Everyone assumed that's why he was walking across the footbridge to Baron's Field, but it wasn't.'

'Why was he on the bridge?' asks Sam.

'I don't know,' replies Mrs Welsby. 'I honestly don't.'

'Please tell us what you do know,' says Sam.

'While he was working on the school pavilion, Aaron began work on a second major project,' comes a voice from the doorway. Mr Welsby has returned, seemingly composed again. He crosses to his chair, and I try to catch a glimpse of his expression before his face is lost in shadow once more.

From the corner of my eye, I can see Mrs Welsby cover her mouth with her hand.

'On the banks of the Thames, in St Marnham, there was a stone-built warehouse, left derelict for five, maybe ten years. New owners purchased it with a plan to fully refurbish. Aaron was delighted to win the job, both as architect and project manager. He was on site almost every other day for over six months. He became close to the man who owned the building.' Mr Welsby stops.

'We've always sworn never to share this,' says Mrs Welsby, 'as the man was already in another relationship.' She looks at her husband.

'We owe it to Madeline,' he says.

She continues. 'The man's partner travelled a lot to New York for work. Aaron would often stay on site long into the evening, spending more and more time with the owner. More often than not, they'd grab something to eat, share a late supper. They became close, in all honesty probably too close. The other man was married.'

'Who was the man?' I ask.

'It was the chef, East Mailer.'

Six

'He walks slowly towards her. When she wraps her arms around him, he begins to sob.'

He sat on the edge of his bed and looked at his empty room. Every day for the past four years, he'd wished he could escape. Now he was going, he couldn't stand the thought of leaving.

He heard the man's footsteps coming quickly up the stairs; always two at a time. A gentle tap and the door creaked open.

'All set?' he asked.

He didn't reply, simply stared at the floor and nodded.

'Only two bags?' The man crossed the room and picked up the red sports holdall. 'We can carry one each.' The man looked at the bag. 'Nice bag this, but I think my squash-playing days are behind me. Best you keep it.'

The holdall wasn't new, but he did think it looked cool. He'd stuffed all of his clothes inside. Still sitting on the edge of his bed, he hung his chin to his chest.

The man ruffled his hair. 'Come on, let's not make this any harder than it needs to be.'

When he got to his feet, he suddenly found himself wrapping his arms around the man's waist. He pressed his face into the man's side.

'It'll be okay.'

He bit his lip. He was determined not to cry. He kept telling himself he was better off without them. He let go of the man, wiped his hands across his eyes and picked up the rucksack he used for school.

'New school next term,' said the man. 'Keep trying your hardest, and one day you'll make it into space.'

He knew that wasn't true, but he smiled and threw the rucksack over his shoulder. Inside were his most precious possessions – his book on the stars, the photograph album of his family, and his secret notebook where he wrote about all the places he'd visited with his grandad.

The man put his arm around his shoulders and steered him towards the door. He looked at his room one last time, wondering if he'd ever have his own room again.

Carefully, he made his way down the stairs. He stopped outside Travis's door and looked into the room. His Spider-Man duvet long since replaced by one for his favourite football team. Every other Saturday afternoon, Travis went to watch the team play. He'd often wished he could join him, but whenever he'd dared mention it there was always a reason for him not to go.

At the top of the next flight of stairs he reached for the banister. He remembered how she'd stared up at him at the end of his very first week in the house. She'd hated him from the very beginning. After he'd pushed her, he'd seen that same expression on her face. Night after night he'd hear them arguing about him – her shouting at the man until she finally got her way. Once the plan was in place, she'd never spoken to him again.

The front door was open. Before he stepped outside, he looked towards the kitchen. She had her back to him. He waited to see if she would turn around. But she didn't, and he walked out into the driveway, where a car was waiting. A woman in a smart trouser suit climbed out and said hello. He didn't reply. The man opened the door and put his bag on the back seat.

'You can ride up front with me, if you like,' said the woman. She spoke to him as if it was a treat to sit up front. He wasn't a baby.

'Look after yourself,' said the man. He felt him squeeze his arm before he pressed something into his hand and closed the door.

The woman looked over her shoulder and reversed out of the drive. He opened his hand and saw the man had given him five twenty-pound notes. He'd never seen so much money. He pressed the button to open the window.

'Thank you!' he shouted to the man, who was standing in the middle of the driveway.

'Good luck, Billy!' he called in reply.

SATURDAY

CHAPTER 41

'I want you to stay away from my wife and my son.'

James Wright's angry voice reverberated around Will's kitchen. Sitting across from his father, Nathan tapped the mute button on his phone. 'All I'm trying to do is help,' he said to Will.

'I'd leave it for now,' replied his father. He could see the regret in his son's face and his ache to be with Sarah and Max, but at one in the morning there was nothing more to be done. 'James is with them now, so I think that means you have to leave it.'

'Are you still there?' James's voice emanated from the phone, which lay in front of them on the kitchen surface. Nathan unmuted his phone.

'As I said earlier, James, all I want to do is help.'

'Staying away from my wife and child is the best help you can be.' Will rolled his eyes at Nathan as James continued. 'If it wasn't for all your crazy social media stalkers, their lives wouldn't be at risk. Stay away!'

Nathan leaned forward, ready to argue with James but Will rested his hand on his son's shoulder. 'Don't.'

'I'll message Sarah in the morning,' was all Nathan said, quickly disconnecting his phone before James could reply.

'He's talking crap, but there's no point getting into an argument now,' said Will as his son picked up his phone and slipped it into his pocket. 'Everyone's exhausted and I'm sure that's especially true of Sarah. James is emotional but at least Sarah and Max are safe.'

On receiving a short message from Sarah after the police had left her home, Nathan had called her instantly. He'd been surprised when James Wright had answered his ex-wife's phone, immediately launching into an attack on Nathan. Will had seen how keen James was to use the opportunity to warn off his son.

'I still care for them both,' said Nathan, leaning back in his chair, his hands resting on his head.

'I know you do, but James is Max's father and Sarah's husband.'

'Ex.'

'Yes, but he's still Max's father. Give it time.'

'I feel so useless,' replied Nathan. 'I can't escape the feeling I created this whole effing mess.'

'Don't say that.'

'But what if I am the one who's put them in danger?'

'You haven't. You can't control social media, and for all we know this has nothing to do with you.'

Nathan was silent, and even though Will had less than a year's experience as a parent, he'd already learned sometimes it was better to say nothing more. He crossed the kitchen and poured himself a glass of water. 'Want some?'

'Thanks,' replied Nathan. 'Are you waiting up for East?' Will shrugged. 'Have you spoken to him today?' asked his son.

Will shook his head. 'I thought it best to keep my distance. I stayed home and finished my book.' He looked at his watch. 'He should be done clearing up at the restaurant by now.'

'Time for me to get going,' replied Nathan.

'Don't feel you have to rush off. Stay here tonight if you like.'

'I've still a few things to pack,' replied Nathan, before adding, 'And it's probably best I'm not here when he gets home.'

'Me and East were struggling long before you arrived. You do know that?'

Nathan drank a mouthful of water. 'Even so, I should head off. Leave from here around ten in the morning?'

Nathan remained determined to return home to Wales. Will had tried repeatedly to characterise the trip purely as a visit, but his son had refused to engage. 'Ten works for me,' he replied.

'Mum's looking forward to meeting you. She's making lunch.'

'Have you thought about when you might be back?'

Nathan's eyes widened when he heard the turn of a key in the front door. 'I'll slip out the back,' he said, avoiding Will's question. 'Thanks for an excellent dinner.'

'Don't let him hear you say that. Pasta sauce from a jar is sacrilege as far as he's concerned.'

'You're forgetting the gourmet garlic bread,' replied Nathan, as he opened the sliding door into the garden.

'Sneaking out?' called East, entering the kitchen. There was a bitterness in his tone.

'I'm heading home,' said Nathan, standing in the doorway. 'Goodbye, East.' He didn't wait for a response before disappearing into the dark night.

Will slid the door closed. He looked at his husband. His long, wet hair clung to his back, his beard was damp and matted, his face bloated and tired. 'You look a mess.'

'If you didn't know, it's raining outside. I had a walk around the village before coming in.' East turned back into the hallway.

'Where're you going?'

'To grab a shower.'

Will followed his husband upstairs. 'Perhaps if you told me what was wrong, I might be able to help. Is it the restaurant? If it is, honestly, there's no need to worry. I can put some more money in.'

Standing in the bathroom doorway, East pulled off his chef's whites and threw them on the floor. 'That's always your answer to everything: money. There are some things even your money can't solve.'

Will walked out onto the landing and sat on the top step of the winding marble staircase. He stared down on the vast entrance hall of his home, the walls decorated with artworks, each one chosen by East. In the past, his money had made East happy, but sitting alone on the cold floor he realised, never him.

Minutes later, East reappeared dressed in jeans and a T-shirt. Pulling on his jacket, he walked past Will.

'Where're you going?' he asked. 'It's one in the morning.'

'Out,' he replied, running down the stairs.

'But you've only just come in. And it's raining outside.'

'I need some air.' Opening the front door, he turned. 'Don't wait up,' he said, slamming the door behind him.

CHAPTER 42

A fine drizzle falls from the early morning sky. I open the car door and climb in beside Sam.

'Here you go,' I say, passing him a breakfast sandwich. 'They didn't have any bacon, so you've got sausage.'

'No bacon?' he replies, opening the bag. Looking inside the bread roll, he curls his lip. 'What kind of supermarket doesn't have bacon?'

'It was a café inside a supermarket. The bloke said it would be fifteen minutes for bacon, so I said not to bother.'

With his teeth, Sam tears open a packet of brown sauce and squirts its contents on his sandwich. 'Want some?' he asks.

I hold open my roll. 'Anything happen here?'

'Nada,' he replies. 'You don't think we've missed him, do you?'

We left the home of Mr and Mrs Welsby a little before one in the morning. Generously, they offered us both a bed for the night, but we explained we needed to be on our way. An atmosphere of deep sadness hung over the Welsbys. I could see how the loss of their son had drained away their former

210

spirit. I left the house thinking of my mum and the terrible suffering she endured after losing my brother.

From Winchcombe we drove directly to Wolverhampton. For the past six hours we have waited on a small, terraced street, outside the Old Gold chip shop. Above the shop is the bedsit rented by Ethan Harris, Billy Monroe's childhood friend. Both Sam and I have dozed on and off during the night, but as yet there has been no sign of life in the flat.

'We need to give him a bit longer,' I say to Sam. 'If he doesn't come off shift until eight, he'll not be back here much before nine.'

Sam bites into his sandwich. 'It's cold,' he says.

'I had to carry it from the shop.'

'At least the tea's hot,' he replies, taking a swig from a takeaway cup. 'Did you get a newspaper?'

'What do you think this is, room service?' I look out at the West Park newsagents, which neighbours the chip shop. 'You could always nip in there and buy one yourself.'

'Don't want to blow my cover,' he replies.

I smile before flipping open the ashtray where I always throw my loose change. 'Here you go,' I say, handing Sam three pound coins.

'Thanks, Dad.' Opening the car door, he takes another bite out of his sandwich before wrapping it in its bag and tossing it in the bin outside the newsagents. As I watch him disappear inside, my phone buzzes with a message from Min. She's forwarded me a photograph of Ethan Harris.

Can't find anything more recent, she tells me.

I look at the picture, taken outside a courthouse sixteen years earlier. I message her back, asking her to run a search on East Mailer.

What are you looking for?

Anything not food related, is my reply.

Sam reappears with a copy of *The Times* and a packet of crisps.

'Shove that in the bin,' I say, throwing him my sandwich wrapper when he opens the car door. When he climbs back into his seat, he's complaining about the weather. I tell him I've asked for a search on East.

'Maddy and East have been close since they were teenagers. There are very few secrets between them.'

Neither Sam nor I have any reason to doubt what the Welsbys told us. Aaron and East were in a relationship at the time of Aaron's murder. Every Christmas, the Welsbys receive a luxurious hamper courtesy of East Mailer and every year, on Aaron's birthday, an arrangement of flowers arrives.

I turn to Sam. 'What if East was with Aaron on the night he was killed?'

'Go on.'

'Aaron and East meet at Mailer's. They walk along the river path to St Marnham Bridge.' I imagine them following the path I took only two nights ago. 'They cross the bridge, following the steps down on the north side. Billy Monroe is hiding in the alcove.'

'But we know this from the trial?'

'No, from the trial we know Billy launched a random, hate-crime attack on Aaron. But if Aaron was walking with East, we know it wasn't a random attack. Aaron was a direct target.'

'How can you be so sure?' asks Sam.

'Because when Monroe ran towards him, he called Aaron's name.'

'And that wasn't Madeline embellishing for effect ...'

'East told her.'

CHAPTER 43

'East was Madeline's witness,' says Sam. We watch another empty red bus slow at the neighbouring stop before rolling past. 'He told her everything she needed to campaign for Billy Monroe's conviction.'

'Down to the smallest details.'

'But why didn't East come forward? Or do something on the night?'

'Hiding on the stairs gave Billy Monroe the element of surprise. He runs forward and stabs Aaron. East helps Aaron back up the stairs, but with a flailing knife Monroe is after them. If you're East, however desperate it might seem, does there come a point where you have to save your own life?'

'What about the police?'

'The world is a far from perfect place and fourteen years ago it was very different from how it is today. I think even Dame Elizabeth Jones would understand East not wanting to throw his lot in with the Met Police.'

Sam sniffs. 'And, of course, he did already have a partner. Perhaps sending flowers and luxury hampers to the

Welsbys helps assuage his guilt for fleeing the scene of their son's murder.'

I take one more sip from my overly milky coffee, open my car door and pour half a cup out onto the roadside. Sam passes me his empty teacup and I jump out to push our empties into an already overflowing bin.

'Right now, we can only speculate,' I say, sitting back behind the wheel. 'What I think we do know is East was with Aaron at the time of the killing. That tells us Aaron was a target as Billy Monroe called his name, but why?'

'Maybe Billy had a grudge. Or Aaron knew something, but who the hell knows what.'

'A secret Billy Monroe was willing to kill to protect?'

Sam rubs his hands across his face. 'That doesn't sound like the Billy Monroe we know. He was a simple kid. His own grandfather called him gullible.'

'Hiding a secret for somebody else?'

I lean forward and, resting on the steering wheel, look down the road in front of us. A double-decker bus, its windscreen wipers jerking from side to side, slows at a pedestrian crossing. A woman, pushing a baby in a buggy while trying to drag two other small children behind her, crosses in front. The bus moves forward but slows again almost immediately to pull into the bus stop. I open the picture of Ethan Harris and watch as, first, an older couple, both carrying empty shopping bags, step off the bus and head in the direction of the supermarket. After them, a man with curly dark hair and a receding hairline steps off and stands inside the bus shelter.

Sam glances at the image on my phone. 'That's him.'

CHAPTER 44

'Less hair and fatter around the waist, but he'd probably say the same about me,' says Sam. 'It's definitely him.'

Harris stops to light a cigarette and, hiding from the rain, remains inside the bus shelter. He rests against a plastic seat. 'We need to be careful,' I say to Sam, as together we cross in front of the Old Gold chip shop.

Sam enters the bus shelter and takes the seat next to Harris, while I walk to the far side and stand in the opposite opening.

'Bad for your health that,' says Sam, nodding towards the burning cigarette in Harris's right hand. Harris barely looks up. 'Are you Ethan Harris?'

'Who's asking?'

'Donald Duck, that's who.'

'Fuck off, grandad.' He sucks on his cigarette.

'We just want to ask you a couple of questions,' I say, moving forward to block the opening. Harris gauges his escape, shifting towards the opposite exit.

Sam rests his hand on Harris's arm. 'A couple of questions, that's all.'

'About what?'

'Billy Monroe,' I reply, sitting beside him. Pressed between Sam and me, he has little room for manoeuvre.

'I don't know any Billy Monroe,' he says, flicking ash onto Sam's shoes and smiling.

Sam knocks his feet together. 'Weren't you at school with him? And then bunked up for a couple of years in Winson Green prison?'

'I don't remember,' replies Harris, grinding his cigarette beneath his boot. 'I've left the likes of Billy Monroe long behind me.'

'Really?' I reply. 'That wasn't what we heard.'

Agitated, Harris faces me. 'What did you hear?'

'That Billy Monroe was here only last week.'

He sneers, before jumping to his feet and pushing past Sam. Sam throws out his leg and Harris stumbles forward. His shoulder crashes into the side of the bus shelter. Sam makes a grab for his collar, but Harris is quick to his feet. He darts out onto the pavement and, with the sound of car horns blaring, sprints across the road.

'After him, Ben,' shouts Sam, and I'm already chasing Harris along the main road. He dives down a narrow side street and, approaching the end of the road, I can see the tree-lined West Park. I charge after Harris, the cold morning air burning in my lungs, but he ducks through the park's open gates. Sprinting across the neatly maintained grass, behind me I can hear Sam shouting instructions. I keep running and when Harris turns towards the lake, I see him begin to slow. I sprint harder and, approaching the water's edge, I have him cornered. He turns to face me.

'Neither of us wants to take an early morning bath,' I say. I can hear him wheezing heavily. Still catching my own breath, I step slowly forwards. 'We're not interested in you or what you might or might not have done. We just want to find Billy.' I pause before adding, 'And Madeline Wilson.'

Harris cannot hide his instant recognition of Madeline's name. He takes a step towards me, and I can see him weighing up his escape options. Suddenly, he spins and jumps into the lake behind him.

'Fuck!' I plunge into the water after him. With three quick strokes, I have hold of him. I grab his arm, but he rolls and a punch lands on the side of my head. I'm knocked backwards but, with Sam now shouting from the bank, I jump up onto his back. Harris falls forward and together we crash beneath the surface. We wrestle under the water until I'm able to force him further down. When I come up for air, my hand grips his neck. I hold him under. After a moment, I drag him to the surface, and he desperately fills his lungs with air.

'Where's Madeline?' I yell. He says nothing and I plunge him back under the water. When I next drag him to the surface, he begins to gag, choking on the pond's muddy water.

'That's enough, Ben,' calls Sam.

I haul Harris to the side of the lake. He collapses onto the bank, gasping for air. Sam takes two steps down. When he stands on Harris's fingers, I hear the crunch.

'Where's my daughter?'

CHAPTER 45

Sam looks at me with raised eyebrows as I climb out of the water. 'I hope you brought a towel.'

I grimace before bending to drag Ethan Harris to his feet. 'Where's Billy?' I say, my face almost touching his.

'I don't know, honestly, I don't.'

I push him down onto a park bench. Still breathless, he shivers in his soaking wet clothes.

'Let me help. Not long after his release he came to see you.' Harris stares into the murky water. 'You can go back in if you like?' I say.

'All right, he came to see me.'

Sam moves to stand in front of Harris. 'He didn't come to see you. He came to stay in your shithole above the fish shop.'

'He said he needed somewhere to bunk for a few nights.' Harris slowly lifts his head. 'Billy somehow always got the rough end of the stick. What difference did a few days on my sofa make to me?'

'Madeline Wilson is my daughter.' I hear the frustration in Sam's voice. 'Tell me what you know.'

Harris's eyes dart quickly back to me before he jumps to his feet. I grab hold of him and push him back down onto the bench.

'You need to tell him everything you know,' I say, 'or I won't be responsible for his actions.'

Harris pulls his wet shirt away from his skin. 'Yes, we were at school together and then in Winson Green.'

'Did you know Aaron Welsby?'

'The bloke Billy stabbed? No, I was inside when he killed him.' Harris looks at Sam. 'He blamed your daughter for his conviction, said one day he'd get his revenge. I never thought he meant it. With Billy, you learn pretty quickly everything is talk. I went back to visit him a couple of times after I'd been released. I know it sounds stupid, but despite everything, he's a not a bad lad. Each time I saw him, he was still giving it the big talk, but . . .'

'But what?' asks Sam.

'But I never believed him, not until he was out, and he came to stay. From the minute he arrived, all he did was talk about your daughter and the plan he'd made for her.' I see Sam's body tense, but Harris continues. 'Somehow he did actually have a plan – he knew the restaurant where she ate, the spot where her driver parked up and always fell asleep, how to switch vehicles on the old sports ground before leaving along the river track to avoid traffic cameras.'

'And let me guess,' I say. 'Your driving experience made you the ideal candidate to help out?'

'It was the only reason he'd come to stay with me. I'd been

set up by Billy Monroe.' Harris laughs at himself. 'All I did was nick the van, respray it and then drive the car.'

'What happened to Madeline's driver?' I ask. 'Is he dead?'

'I never touched him,' Harris is quick to reply. 'That afternoon, Billy and I hung out by the river, did a few lines.' I think back to Thursday evening and the two men I saw at the back of the pub. 'When we got to the car, the keys were lying in the passenger seat,' continues Harris. 'I've no idea what happened to the driver.'

'Did Billy kill him?'

Harris shrugs. 'If he did, I never saw him do it.'

'You were there when he took Madeline?' says Sam.

'When she climbed into the car, Billy was waiting.'

Sam hesitates. 'Did he hurt her?' he asks, but Harris doesn't respond. Sam leans forward and yells at Harris. 'Did he hurt her?' From nowhere, Sam throws a punch, hitting Harris full in the face. Harris doesn't fight back, and Sam hits him again. Blood spurts from Harris's nose.

'I'm sure the police will be in touch,' says Sam, before turning and with his shoulders drooping, he walks away.

His hand pressed against his nose, Harris looks up at me. 'I guess I deserved that. She is his daughter.'

'Tell me what happened after Madeline was switched into the van.'

'I've no idea. At that point, Billy was on his own. All I knew is he was heading north. He never told me his plan after that, and I didn't want to know.'

'Billy's messaged Madeline's father, demanding a ransom. Is it a genuine exchange?'

'I've no idea, but I do know Billy wants the money. He kept telling me about the luxury camper van he planned on buying.'

'And you? Why did you get involved?'

'Same reason. Money.'

'How much?'

'Ten grand up front.'

'Where did Billy get that kind of cash?'

'I've no idea.'

'Somebody helped him?'

'I don't know,' replies Harris. 'I didn't want it to end like this. You have to believe me.'

'So, tell me who helped him.'

'I honestly don't know. The only person he ever mentioned was his brother. They lived together when they were kids. For a while we all went to the same school.'

'Are they still in touch?'

'Couple of things he said gave me that impression. Told me his brother had found him a girl. Billy never could keep his mouth shut.'

'What was his brother's name?'

Harris shakes his head. 'I don't remember. Something Scottish.'

'Think.'

Harris sighs. 'Travis. Travis Monroe.'

CHAPTER 46

Lesley Barnsdale turned off her screen and grabbed her jacket from the back of her chair. Seeing Dani Cash leaving through the exit at the back of the CID offices, she called to her.

'One second and I'll walk with you.'

Cash hit the exit button and held the doors open before the two women walked down the ramp and into the station car park.

'Done for the weekend?' asked Barnsdale.

'Hopefully,' replied Cash. 'I'm still working through the social media posts of the intruder's victims. Right now, there's not much more than posts about birthday gifts and parties.'

'How is Mrs Wright coping?'

'Her ex is spending a couple of nights at her house, but I can't believe the intruder will risk coming back a third time.'

Barnsdale searched distractedly in her bag for her car keys. Unable to find them, she unzipped two inside pockets but still found nothing. 'Damn,' she said, before hurriedly feeling in her jacket. 'Thank God for that,' she said, producing the keys.

'Anything on the body at the boathouse?' asked Cash.

'Nothing yet. I'm due up at the morgue this afternoon.' Barnsdale unlocked her car doors and paused. 'I meant to ask you if there was any update on the stolen van?' She felt her face flush. She was acting like a fourteen-year-old schoolgirl.

'The one from the delivery company?' asked Cash.

'That's the one.'

'I passed it on to uniform, but they haven't come back with anything yet, I'm afraid.'

Barnsdale nodded. 'Thanks anyway.'

'Much planned for the weekend?' said Cash.

Although only a throwaway question but having no real plans, Barnsdale somehow still somehow felt the sting.

'I think you know it's my birthday tomorrow,' she replied.

'I did hear you'd had a bit of a celebration on Thursday night.'

'I'm sorry you couldn't make it. We had fun.' Barnsdale's hand gripped hold of the top of her car door.

'Perhaps we could go for a drink after work next week? Raise a glass in your honour.'

Barnsdale was surprised, but pleasantly so. She'd worked with Cash for the past three years, and while never friends, she was one of the few officers she felt she could trust. 'That'd be nice.'

'Shall we try and fix something for the start of the week?'

She could see Cash was eager to talk. 'Is there something on your mind?'

'No, no, nothing in particular.' Cash changed the subject. 'Any special plans for tomorrow?'

Immediately, she worried Cash was fishing. She couldn't help but wonder if the station gossip had already caught up with her and Phil.

'A quiet one,' she replied. 'No more than a couple of drinks,' she added, finding herself suddenly hoping Phil might remember it was her birthday.

She climbed into her car and, before she'd even called *enjoy your weekend*, had firmly closed her door. Starting the engine, she hung her head over the steering wheel and let the car's cool air calm her blushing face.

CHAPTER 47

Sam stands outside the men's fitting-room curtain as I quickly change into a new pair of tracksuit trousers and a black-and-white striped sweater.

'You won't feature on the fashion page next week,' he says, pulling back the curtain. 'Here, this will warm you up,' he says, handing me a cup of coffee as I stuff my wet clothes into a plastic carrier bag. 'I got you an extra shot.'

'You always do spoil me,' I reply. I'm about to leave the fitting room when Sam steps inside and closes the curtain behind him. 'What are you doing?'

He sits on the small stool in the corner of the room. 'What's our next move?'

Ethan Harris has given us certainty around Billy Monroe's motives, but we're still no closer to finding Madeline. 'We need to track down Travis,' I say.

Sam searches in his pockets before passing me the scrap of paper given to him by Tosh Monroe.

'I don't think it's worth calling Billy again,' I say.

Sam shakes his head. 'Tosh wrote his own number

at the bottom. Why don't we ask him about his other grandson?'

I dial the number but the phone rings out. 'No answer,' I say, leaning back against the fitting-room wall. 'We could drive back to Nottingham?'

Sam shrugs. 'I think it's time for a backup plan.'

'You want me to call the police?'

'No,' replies Sam, opening his phone. I can hear a FaceTime dialling tone.

'Who are you calling?'

'Sam, what's wrong?' asks a voice, before he has chance to answer me.

'Annabel, lovely to see you too,' he replies, holding his phone in front of his face. I realise Sam is speaking to his ex-wife and Madeline's mother.

'Don't give me that, Sam. You never call me, and certainly not on video.'

'I don't want you to panic, Annabel.'

'Sam, I don't panic.'

'Our girl's in a bit of a bind.'

'What kind of bind?'

'You promise me you won't panic?'

'Sam!' snaps Annabel. 'Tell me now!'

'Madeline's been kidnapped.'

'What the bloody hell?'

I rest my head back against the wall as Sam recounts events from the past twenty-four hours.

'You're doing the right thing,' says Annabel. 'If he says no police, that's what we should do.'

227

Sam looks at me over the top of his phone.

'All we want is Madeline home safely,' Annabel continues. 'I'll meet you at your flat in Richmond. I'm on my way.'

CHAPTER 48

Saturday lunchtime traffic on Haddley Hill was heavy. Lesley Barnsdale drummed her fingers on the dashboard of her car and, as the digital clock flashed twelve, she cut across the traffic and turned down an empty side street. Passing through the residential area on the outskirts of the town, she followed the road over Haddley Heath and on into a small industrial park. The security barrier rose as she arrived at the gates for PDQ Deliveries, and she stopped in the visitors' parking area at the front of the warehouse. Only then did she hesitate. From nowhere, she was racing into a relationship with a man she hardly knew. Her job taught her to avoid risk and spontaneity. She'd spent her life being cautious, working hard and focusing on her career. And yet, this suddenly felt so right.

She walked quickly towards reception. As she approached, the doors opened. Leaving the building was Phil's business partner, Dom, accompanied by a teenage boy, whom she instantly assumed to be his son.

'Dom,' she called, eagerly, hoping he would remember her.

'Hello again, detective,' he replied.

'Lesley, please.'

'I take it you're not here on official business? Here was me hoping you might have found Phil's van.'

'Nothing yet,' she replied, 'but we're still looking.'

'This is my son, Ryan,' he said, introducing the boy, who managed a self-conscious half smile. He was wearing a bright orange shirt.

'Football this afternoon?' she asked.

'On our way now,' replied Dom, clicking open the doors of his BMW for his son before stepping back towards the building's front door. 'Here, let me buzz you in,' he continued, moving back inside and swiping his pass on the security gate. 'Phil's office is at the top of the stairs, second door on the left.'

'Thank you,' she called, hurrying inside. 'Hope you win!'

She followed the metal stairs up to the first floor of the warehouse. Standing outside Phil's office door, she could hear him speaking on the phone. While she waited, two women passed her in the narrow corridor. One of the women looked back over her shoulder, and Lesley shifted uncomfortably. She felt certain she was not the kind of woman Phil usually invited into his office. But something she only ever saw happening to other people was happening to her. And she felt happy.

On the other side of the door, she could hear Phil trying to persuade a driver to take on extra shifts this weekend. She realised that his call was in no way confidential, so she popped her head into the room. Seeing her, Phil immediately smiled and waved her in. While he finished his conversation, she crossed the office and stood at one of the four windows that looked down onto the warehouse floor. Hundreds of brown cardboard boxes were slowly journeying around a giant conveyor belt, an endless train of future deliveries.

'Very impressive,' she said, when Phil disconnected his phone.

'We're hardly Amazon,' he replied, standing behind her and slipping his arms around her waist, 'but it keeps us busy.' He pushed back her hair and kissed her on the neck. 'I wasn't expecting you so soon.'

'I'm sorry,' she replied. 'We'd said lunch and I wasn't sure what time that meant for you.'

'No problem.' He sat on the edge of his desk and pulled her towards him. 'I see you made it through our great security set up?'

'Dom let me in.'

'Off to his football.'

'Brentford?' she asked, their local London team.

Phil shook his head and reached across his desk for a photo frame. 'Luton Town,' he said, passing her the picture. 'Dom takes Ryan pretty much every week. He's from a village somewhere outside the town, always been his team. That's the three of us at a game last season. They made me wear the bobble hat!'

Lesley laughed before putting down the picture and taking hold of Phil's hand. She leaned forward and kissed him again.

'Not hungry?' he said, before getting up and closing the shutters across his office windows.

CHAPTER 49

'Annabel's your backup plan?' I ask Sam, as we walk across the Asda car park.

'I don't care what we have to do to get Madeline home, even if that means paying the ransom.' Now I realise why Sam called his ex-wife.

'Paying the ransom doesn't guarantee he'll free Madeline.'

'But it's what Monroe wants, and it might be our best shot.'

I think of the ten thousand pounds Billy Monroe paid Ethan Harris and the planning that went into Madeline's kidnapping.

'Somebody has to be helping Billy,' I say to Sam. 'No way he does all this alone. He's not smart enough. There are too many tiny details, right down to knowing where Madeline ate. Billy's been inside for the past twelve years.'

Pulling out of the car park, I click again on my phone. The call rings through on the car's speakers.

'Min, it's me,' I say, when the call connects.

'Where are you?' she asks.

'Leaving Wolverhampton. Billy has a brother, something

his grandfather absent-mindedly forgot to mention. I need anything you can find on Travis Monroe.'

'Ideally, where the hell he is,' adds Sam.

'I'll do my best.'

I slow as we approach a red light. 'It really is a case of anything you can find.'

'And quick!'

'Leave it with me, Sam, I'm on it now. I hope you're holding up okay,' she says. 'I'm praying for Madeline.'

Sam's struggles to reply.

'One way or another, we're getting closer,' I say before disconnecting the phone. I turn to Sam. 'I spoke to Min last night while you were sleeping,' I explain. 'I had to tell her what was happening. I'd trust her with my life.'

We head out of the city, towards the motorway. My phone buzzes and I look down at the screen. 'Fuck!'

Sam looks at the caller's name. 'I think you'd better answer it.'

I take a deep breath. 'Dani,' I say, 'I'm so sorry.'

'I've been sitting outside your house for the past hour. Where are you?'

I wince. 'I really am sorry,' I say. 'Something came up.'

'Something came up? What does that mean?'

'A story,' I say. 'One Madeline wanted me to do. I couldn't get out of it.'

'You didn't think to call me?'

I hesitate.

'Ben?' she continues. 'A quick call, that's all I'm asking.'

'It won't happen again, I promise.'

'How long until you're back?'

'I'm not one hundred per cent sure.'

'I thought we were going away for the night?'

Sam looks at me and grins.

'We were, we are,' I answer, quickly. 'We were,' I add, hesitating again. 'I'm sorry.'

'Ben, you're messing me about. I've told Mat I'm away for the night.'

'Why don't you stay at mine?' I say. 'I'll get home as soon as I can.' I move out of the fast lane to let a white van surge by. 'Dani, what do you think?'

There's a moment's silence. 'Whatever,' she replies. 'I could make us something to eat if you like.'

Realising I haven't thought that far ahead, I say, 'The story's very fluid.'

'Ben, what the hell does that mean? What time will you be back?'

'It's kind of difficult to say, but Holly, three doors down, can give you a key. Put your feet up, watch a bit of TV and I'll be home as soon as I can.'

'This is our exit!' cries Sam, as we are about to pass the junction with the M42. I swerve across the road.

'Who the hell was that?' asks Dani.

I turn to Sam. *Thanks,* I mouth. 'Sam, Madeline's dad. He's with me.'

'Is he working for you now?'

'Other way round,' replies Sam.

'Sam, be quiet,' I say, while trying simultaneously to follow my satnav. 'It's a story we've both got an interest in. Let me call you later. I'll have a better idea of timings by then.'

'Do what you like, Ben,' says Dani. 'I've better things to do than be messed around by you.'

CHAPTER 50

'She said she'd be here by nine,' says Sam, looking at his watch for the third time in the last five minutes.

'Sam, sit down,' I reply. Instead, he walks out of his living room and through to his spare bedroom. From there, he can see any cars turning into the driveway below. Seconds later, he's back pacing the living room.

'I'm sure we'd have heard something if there was a problem.'

'You don't know Annabel. She's spent her life thinking the whole world revolves around her. I can't remember when she was last on time for anything. She was even thirty minutes late for our wedding. She blamed her mother, but I should have learned then never to trust her.'

He hurries back out of the room. Before following him, I look briefly at my phone. I've called Tosh Monroe repeatedly during the afternoon and evening, but he's failed to return any of my calls. Still now, there's nothing. Walking into Sam's spare bedroom, I find him leaning over his desk, peering down at the driveway below. I place my hand on his shoulder.

'Come and have something to eat,' I say.

'I'm not hungry,' he replies, barking at me.

I take a deep breath. 'We've a long night ahead. You need to eat something.'

I wander back through to Sam's kitchen and open his fridge. Alongside a case of beer are two Melton Mowbray pork pies and a block of cheese. I reach for the pies.

'Here,' I say, returning to the bedroom and handing Sam a pie.

'Thanks,' he replies, slowly turning away from the window and perching on the leather-topped reporter's desk. I sit beside him and unwrap the other pie.

'If we don't make this exchange,' he says, 'I don't know what I will do. I won't be able to go on living without her.'

'Don't say that. We are going to make the exchange and Madeline is coming home tonight.'

Eating his pie, Sam reaches across and squeezes my arm. I stare straight ahead, my gaze focused on the framed edition of the *Richmond Times* Madeline gave Sam for his birthday. He's left it propped against the wall. I know if I look at Sam, I'll be in danger of breaking down.

Sam is quickly back at the window when he hears a car outside. 'It's her,' he tells me as an elegantly dressed woman, with smoky grey hair, steps out of the chauffeur-driven Mercedes.

'I don't know what she ever saw in you,' I say to Sam, smiling, as I try to lift his mood.

He looks at me and winks. 'Make them laugh, Ben. It works every time.' He steps away from the window. 'You'll have to go down and meet her.'

'Why me?'

'I haven't seen her face-to-face in more than ten years.'

'And?'

'Ben, just go.'

I decide it's easier not to argue and do as instructed. Outside, I introduce myself to Annabel Wilson. Grateful for my support, she is both calm and instantly focused. She wants to know our plan for the exchange, and I realise Madeline inherited her razor-like attention to detail from her mother. Annabel asks her chauffeur to wait at the rear of the apartment block, before together she and I ride up in the lift.

'How's Sam?' she asks.

'Holding it together, just,' I reply.

'From the minute she was born, he adored Madeline. We both did. She kept the two of us together for a long time. But there's a bond between the two of them, something I could never break into.'

'Something in the blood,' I say, as we exit the lift.

The door to Sam's apartment is open and, stepping inside, I call to him. He appears in the living-room doorway.

'You took your bloody time,' he says to Annabel.

She says nothing in reply, simply opening her arms. He walks slowly towards her. When she wraps her arms around him, he begins to sob. I step back into the hallway, allowing them time together.

Ten minutes later, I drag the first of two giant holdalls from the boot of Annabel's car up into Sam's flat.

'I cannot believe the weight of a million pounds,' I say.

Sam and Annabel are sat together at his glass dining table.

'How did you get the bags through security?' he asks.

She squeezes his hand. 'Sam, my darling, at private airfields, you don't line up as if you're catching an EasyJet to Alicante.'

I head back downstairs for the second bag and, when I return, Annabel is nursing a small glass of red wine.

'Why would he arrange the drop in the same stairwell?' she asks.

Instructions sent to Sam have told us to leave the money in the concealed space where Billy Monroe hid on the night of Aaron's murder.

'Bloody macabre if you ask me,' replies Sam.

'My guess is he knows it's a very quiet spot, and it's easy to get in and out of unseen.'

Billy's instructions have told us to drop the money at midnight on the Baron's Field side of the footbridge. Ten minutes later, on the St Marnham village side of the river, Madeline will be released. I'm concerned the release isn't simultaneous, but both Sam and Annabel are insistent we must go ahead.

'Our only interest is bringing Madeline home safely. I couldn't care less about the money.'

'As soon as Madeline is safe, we go to the police,' says Sam. 'They'll pick Monroe up in no time. We know exactly who we're dealing with.'

Increasingly, I have a nagging doubt if we really do.

CHAPTER 51

The clock on my dashboard tells me it's five minutes to midnight. As we cross Chiswick Bridge, a lone moped speeds past, ferrying a late-night curry to some hungry drinkers. Approaching the junction with Baron's Field, I slow. Waiting for the lights to change, I notice a police red-light camera positioned to capture any amber gamblers. Could the same camera have captured Billy Monroe entering and exiting Baron's Field? I can't help thinking it might, but I know it's now too late. Madeline's life rests with Sam and me.

We leave the main road and follow a narrowing trail towards the riverbank. We pass the last of the streetlamps and the dipped headlights on my car offer the only light under a heavy night sky. Sam points ahead to a close right turn, shielded by overgrown bushes. I slow to a crawl before taking the tight turn, tree branches scratching at my door. When we enter a small, unlit car park, my tyres groan as they roll across the stony track. At the farthest corner of the car park, I kill the engine. Sam and I sit in silence, our breathing slow and in unison. In the darkness, I'm only able to see the outline of his face.

'Are you ready?' I ask, my voice quiet.

'Yes,' he replies. 'And thank you, Ben. We couldn't have done this without you.' I feel him squeeze my hand.

'We're not there yet,' I reply.

When I open the car door, the light briefly lights his face. Beneath the sudden brightness he raises his hand, but not before I see the unease in his eyes.

'Let's get Madeline home,' I say. I step out into the darkness. Gently, I push my car door closed before clicking open the boot. A light illuminates the space and I lift the first of the two oversized holdalls. Tension grips my body. It's even heavier than I remember, but adrenaline kicks in and I haul the bag onto my shoulder and close the boot. Using only the light from the screen on my phone, I cross onto a muddy path that leads through a small copse of trees and on towards the footbridge. I chance a look over my shoulder and see Sam, illuminated by the light on his phone, sitting rigid in the front seat of my car.

Bending forward, I follow the path down to the water's edge. My legs move quickly under the weight on my back, and occasionally I stumble over knotted tree roots. The light from St Marnham village spills across the water. I trace my way along the winding path before arriving at the concrete stairs, which lead up onto the bridge.

I stop. Standing at the foot of the steps, all I can hear is the sound of water lapping on the shoreline. I drop the bag, walk to the side of the steps, and lower my head to peer beneath the bridge. When I light the torch on my phone, all I can see are broken beer bottles and empty lager cans mingled with debris washed up from the river. I return to the foot of the stairs, lift the bag and begin a slow climb. In the pitch-black alcove that concealed Billy Monroe on the night of Aaron Welsby's murder, I drop the bag.

Hearing a creak behind me, I spin around, but it's only the breeze blowing through the woods. I run down the steps and back through the trees, following the path back to the car. I emerge onto the car park, and I see Sam sitting static in the front seat of my car.

'See anyone?' I whisper, as he edges open the door.

'Not a soul. You?'

I shake my head and he pulls the door closed. I race around to the boot and lift the second bag. I retrace my steps, now quicker, more certain of my route, and am almost immediately back at the stairwell. I turn and look back at the trees. Is somebody watching me? I feel sure they are, but when I look across the river to the lights of St Marnham, my only thought is for Madeline's safety.

I hurry up the stairs and place the second bag on top of the first. I push them both deep into the alcove before turning and running back through the woods. I jump into the car and fire the engine.

I turn to Sam. 'Do we go?'

'We go,' he replies, and racing from the car park we leave behind any chance we had of seizing Billy Monroe. The money is now his to take.

Sam and I are silent as we accelerate back across Chiswick

Bridge. We speed through the traffic lights and fly along the deserted river road towards St Marnham. I slow as we enter the village. Neither Sam nor I can stop our eyes drifting towards the open courtyard in front of Mailer's restaurant. Oddly for a Saturday night, it is deserted, its usual bright lights eerily extinguished.

We exit a small roundabout on the edge of the village. I bump the car up onto the curb outside the White Hart pub, from where the evening's last drinkers are heading for home. Sam is instantly out of the car, and I have to run to catch him. We follow a short path down the side of the pub, leading to the water's edge. Annabel is waiting at a wooden outdoor table. She offers her hand to Sam, and he grasps hold of it.

'Any sign of Madeline?' he asks, urgently.

'Nothing yet,' she replies. 'All go okay with you?'

'Exactly as planned,' I reply. I follow the couple as they dash along the river path; a space normally shared by dog walkers and cyclists now carries the desperate hopes of two parents who will never stop loving their child. We climb up the path. Ahead of us, beneath the bridge's Victorian structure, I see a homeless man seeking a night's shelter. It's the same man I walked past only forty-eight hours earlier as I headed for dinner with Madeline and Sam.

Annabel and Sam stop at the top of the path, beneath the bright lamps that light the steps up to St Marnham Bridge. Each of us turns and turns again, scanning the space around us, our eyes searching desperately for any sign of Madeline.

'Where is she?' yells Sam.

I look at my phone. It's fourteen minutes after midnight. 'Let's give it a couple more minutes,' I say.

Annabel moves forward and looks down from our elevated position towards the water's edge. 'Down there,' she cries, pointing towards a body lying on the shoreline.

My heart is in my mouth. I jump down a flight of steps, scramble along a moss-covered path before charging across the pebbled shore. My feet slide in all directions, but I force myself forward until I reach the body.

The water laps over its legs. I haul the body out of the river and turn it over.

Staring up at me are the cold, dead eyes of Billy Monroe.

Seven

'If Aaron was a direct target, we're looking at a very different killing. Understanding what happened in the days before his murder becomes vital.'

He stood at the window and watched Billy go.

Billy's lip was quivering as he climbed into the front seat of the car, and he could see he was close to tears. Gratefully clutching his five twenty-pound notes and waving goodbye, he looked pitiful. But then Billy was always emotional; it never took much to set him off. Time and again, he'd watched him crawl upstairs to his attic room. It was that vulnerability that left him weak and malleable.

He waited at the window until the social worker reversed out of the drive. Then he walked down the hallway into the kitchen, where he knew his mother was sitting alone at the table. He wrapped his arms tightly around her. She smiled and kissed him on the forehead. They were both glad he was gone.

Upstairs, the empty attic room smelled damp. He'd visited the room only a handful of times over the last four years. Letting Billy come to his room was a far more powerful act. Whenever he'd had a use for him – taking the blame for a stolen bottle of wine or porn on his father's laptop – he'd invited him in. Offering occasional, unpredictable but intense attention, he'd learned he could get Billy to take the blame for almost anything.

Looking around the attic bedroom, he could see there was nothing worth taking. The furniture was cheap, bought from online discounters; the bedding rough to the touch. He pulled open the drawers of a collapsing cabinet, but they were empty

247

save for some dirty socks and moth-eaten T-shirts. He emptied a box of old board games onto the floor. Nothing of any interest to him. Then he lifted up the thin mattress and flipped it on its side. Hidden beneath was a notebook; Billy had scrawled his name across the front cover.

He sat on the bed frame and flicked through the book. Spidery letters covered each page. Most of it was rubbish, ramblings about space rockets and the moon. He turned to the back of the book. Letters to his grandfather, never sent. Reading them made him laugh. How much Billy loved his grandfather, remembering all the places they'd visited together, and believing one day they would visit them again. Always childlike in his faith, and endlessly gullible.

He'd keep the notebook.

SUNDAY

CHAPTER 52

I grab an old sweater off the sofa at the back of my kitchen and switch off my coffee machine before searching for the key to open the sliding door, which leads out into my small rear garden. Outside, my first sip of coffee eases the tension in my head.

A crack in the clouds lets the dawn light brighten the chill late February morning. Heavy rain has fallen during the night, and my feet sink into the square patch of grass I struggle to keep alive each summer. I cross the garden and sit on the narrow stone wall I built with my mum fifteen years ago. For a moment I can see my mum, wearing her green gardening gloves, hand mixing cement, while I race to haul bricks from the front of the house. She always faced life with a fierce independence. *How hard can it be to build a wall?* she asked. Harder than we ever imagined, it turned out, as we battled endlessly with runny concrete, but I smile at the thought of my mum's wall still proudly standing so many years later. That independence, coupled with a determination never to accept no for an answer, is something she instilled in me. At times, it can leave me up to my neck in very hot water, but the only thing I know how to do is keep going until I find answers.

The kitchen door slides open again. Wearing my grey fleece sweatshirt, Dani crosses the garden. She places a glass of water carefully on the wall before sitting beside me.

'Hi,' I say, quietly. 'You were sleeping.'

She runs her hands through her hair, her blonde curls always so unruly in the morning. 'Not quite the weekend away I'd imagined,' she replies.

Along with DS Lesley Barnsdale, Dani attended the discovery of Billy Monroe's body. Sam and Annabel are now working with the Met Police and the National Crime Agency as they desperately seek to discover Madeline's whereabouts. In the early hours of the morning, I waited by the river until Monroe's body was finally removed, and Dani was able to leave the scene. We walked, in virtual silence, back to my home in Haddley.

'I could make you some breakfast?' I say. 'My bacon sandwiches are better than anything you'll find in a fancy hotel.'

She shakes her head. 'I'm not hungry.' She lifts her eyes to mine. 'I thought you trusted me?'

'I do, absolutely, one hundred per cent,' I reply, far too quickly. I find myself stripped bare by Dani's sharp, blue eyes. 'I'm sorry,' I add.

'Act first, worry about the consequences later. I'm beginning to realise that's your mantra in life, except you never do take responsibility for the consequences.'

'I wanted to tell you, but Sam was adamant no police. I

had my doubts and tried to convince him, but it's what he and Annabel wanted. Madeline is their daughter.'

'That's not what I mean,' replies Dani, reaching for her glass. I bite my thumb, waiting for her to continue. 'I mean us, you and me, not the police. You told me I could trust you. And you said you would always trust in me, as someone you love.'

'Yes, always.'

'But not enough to talk to me, to confide in me, to tell me you're safe.'

I hesitate. Dani keeps her eyes fixed on me and I feel myself shrink. 'It was Sam—'

'Don't,' she interrupts. 'It was you, it's what you always do. You put Madeline's life at risk, Sam's, and your own. And you didn't want to talk to me.'

I swallow the last of my coffee. 'I'm sorry,' I say, 'but you are a serving police officer, and we decided no police. I didn't want to compromise you.' I can see the conflict between my life as a journalist and Dani's as a police officer laid bare before us.

'Above everything else, for me to end my marriage, you and I must be a team. I thought that was what you wanted?' Dani's voice drifts away. 'You promised me, Ben.'

I lace my fingers with hers, but she pulls her hand away. 'I spent my whole life building a wall around myself until I felt safe,' I tell her. 'It was the only way I could survive. I want to change. For you, I know I must change.'

She picks up her glass and I follow her back inside. She perches on a stool beside the kitchen island. 'You and me must come above everything else. You have to want that as much as I do. Whatever happens after that, we decide together. For us to have any kind of future, I have to be certain.'

There's a rap on the front door of my house. 'I'll try and get rid of them,' I say as Dani follows me out into the hall.

I open the front door and sigh. As I rub my hands across my face, from the back of the hall, I hear Dani whisper under her breath, 'Fuck,' at the sight of DS Barnsdale.

CHAPTER 53

'Here we are again, Mr Harper,' says DS Barnsdale, taking a seat opposite me and smoothing the creases in her black trousers, 'you withholding evidence from the police in a murder case.'

'That's not fair,' I reply. We're sitting in the living room at the front of my house. It's a room I rarely use as it's part of the house that always very much belonged to my mum when this was her home. Barnsdale is referring to events surrounding her murder. If I'd waited for Haddley Police, the identity of my mum's killer would still be unknown today. 'My one and only aim over the past forty-eight hours has been to find Madeline and bring her safely home.'

'Something you thought you were better equipped to do than specially trained police officers?' Barnsdale is angry and I glance towards Dani. Standing at the window, she pushes her hands through her hair. She refuses to catch my eye. I decide it's better not to argue with the detective.

'If I'd ever thought I was putting Madeline in more danger—'

'That's the problem, Mr Harper, you never do think,' interrupts Barnsdale, sitting on the edge of her chair. 'A kidnapped woman, a man throttled to death and his body dumped on the banks of the River Thames, and your friends seemingly two million pounds down. You have been busy.' Barnsdale looks towards the window. 'DC Cash, have you anything to add?'

'No, ma'am,' replies Dani, her face flushing as she casts her eyes down.

'No, indeed,' says Barnsdale, snapping at Dani.

'All of our focus now should be on finding Madeline Wilson,' I say. 'I'd give my life for her, so whatever help I can give you—'

'Due to your antics, we've lost the most important forty-eight hours in searching for Ms Wilson. With the death of Billy Monroe, we have to believe her life is in imminent danger. I suggest you start by very quickly telling me everything you know.'

I recount the story of Madeline's kidnap, in as much detail as I've been able to piece together. The demands sent to Sam, our tracking down of Tosh Monroe and the role played by Ethan Harris.

'After speaking to Ms Wilson's father, we arrested Harris in the early hours of this morning, attempting to board a ferry from Hull to Rotterdam,' Barnsdale replies. 'With the help of information received from him, officers are now searching Haddley Wood for Ms Wilson's car.'

I nod. 'I doubt there's much more he can give you, other than the fact Billy Monroe has a brother.'

'We are already aware of that,' Barnsdale tells me. 'We're speaking to his grandfather now.'

'I think finding Travis could be crucial.'

Barnsdale doesn't respond and when her phone rings, she looks at the screen. 'I have to take this,' she says, stepping out of the room.

'Is there anything else you haven't told her?' asks Dani, still standing by the window with her arms tightly folded.

I run my tongue around the inside of my mouth. 'The problem is, I know how she'll react.'

'Ben! You need to tell her everything,' says Dani. 'She's a good officer and I trust her.'

I don't reply and, in silence, we wait for Barnsdale to return to the room.

'A burned-out vehicle has been discovered at the far side of Haddley Woods. We believe it is the Mercedes belonging to Ms Wilson.' Barnsdale stands directly in front of me. 'And Mr Harper, you should also be aware of the discovery of an unidentified male body in the car park of the St Marnham boathouse on Friday evening. We now believe that to be the body of Ms Wilson's driver, Dennis Thackeray.'

I drop my head and run my hand through my hair. 'He was a nice guy,' I say, my voice cracking. 'He would do anything for anybody.'

Barnsdale sits on the sofa beside me. 'If you have anything more, I need it now.'

I inhale deeply. 'Sam and I met with Aaron Welsby's parents.'

'Go on,' says Barnsdale.

257

'Before his death, Aaron was involved in a brief relationship with East Mailer. We found nothing to link East to Billy's murder, but the Welsbys are in touch with him. It's quite possible East was aware of Billy's release.'

Barnsdale gets to her feet. 'I hope from this point forward, Mr Harper, you will leave all elements of this investigation to the police.' She stops at the door and turns to Dani. 'DC Cash, I'll wait for you in the car while you finish getting dressed.'

CHAPTER 54

I stand at the foot of my stairs. Moments later, Dani appears dressed in jeans and a white sweater, taken from the few clothes she keeps at my house.

'Barnsdale's right. We've lost the most important forty-eight hours in finding Madeline. If she's in the hands of whoever killed Monroe . . . '

'I should've called you. I realise that now,' I say, pressing my hand on the back of my neck. She snatches her jacket from beside the front door. 'Can we talk tonight?' I ask.

She shakes her head. 'I don't know. At some point I need to go home. I'll phone you later.' She briefly kisses me on the cheek.

I watch her walk down the path at the front of my house. 'Dani, wait,' I say, calling after her. I take two quick steps and she turns. 'Billy Monroe didn't plan Madeline's kidnapping on his own. And I don't believe he acted alone in killing Aaron Welsby.'

'What makes you say that?' she asks.

'The Met Police, and Madeline in her reporting, always

assumed Aaron's death to be a random hate crime.' Dani listens intently and I hurriedly explain Billy calling Aaron's name on the night of the murder. 'If Aaron was a direct target, we're looking at a very different killing. Understanding what happened in the days before his murder becomes vital.' Dani nods and I continue. 'Aaron's father told us his son met East while he was still working on a project designing the sports pavilion at Haddley Grammar School. What happened while he was there? And at the same time, Billy Monroe was working as a labourer on various building sites across town.'

'There's no evidence of them ever working on the same construction project.'

'But what if their paths did somehow cross? If we can understand why Billy killed Aaron Welsby, we'll know who killed Billy.'

Dani says nothing, but a fleeting smile crosses her face before she turns and walks away. I stand and watch Barnsdale's car head towards the Lower Haddley Road and find myself desperately hoping the detective will find a way to bring Madeline home.

Very much in need of a second cup of coffee, I'm about to return to my kitchen when a dark red Mercedes sports car accelerates rapidly along the lower common. Directly in front of my house, the car comes to a sharp stop and the driver's window lowers.

'Ben, get in,' calls Annabel Wilson, issuing a rapid instruction in the same manner as her daughter. 'Sam's onto something.'

For a split second I hesitate. 'Annabel, what's going on? Surely, it's the police who need to find Madeline now? Specialist officers are searching for her. Shouldn't we leave it to them?'

'From what Madeline told me about you, you don't believe a word of that.' I can't help smiling and she continues. 'Sam and I have given the police everything we can. They've told us all we can do now is wait for any further contact from whoever is holding Madeline. But, Ben, while there's still chance of finding our daughter alive, why would we stop now?'

Thinking of my own mum's determination never to take no for an answer, I grab my keys and slam the front door closed behind me.

'Sam's waiting for us on the high street,' Annabel tells me as I climb into a car that will have cost considerably more than I can ever hope to earn in a year. 'He's got a line into Travis Monroe.'

'You're sure about this?' I ask as Annabel rests her foot on the accelerator.

Annabel's eyebrows furrow. 'Whoever killed Billy Monroe, and took my two million quid, might be the only person alive who knows where Madeline is. That's the person we must find.'

On the Lower Haddley Road, Annabel races past two delivery vans out making early morning drop-offs. Approaching the traffic lights, I find myself closing my eyes as she defies a changing red light and sprints up the high street.

'Nice car,' I say, smiling nervously as we pass in front of the police station. Suddenly, we come to a shuddering stop.

'Jump out and let them in,' says Annabel, pointing towards Sam, who is standing inside the entrance of a local charity shop. Beside him is Tosh Monroe.

'Mr Monroe,' I say, surprised by his presence in Haddley. 'Whatever he did, I'm sorry your grandson's life ended in such a brutal way.' I can see him slightly wrongfooted by my condolences.

'No time for that now,' replies Sam, his energy renewed in his determination to find his daughter. 'Ben, you squeeze in the back with me,' he says, pulling forward the car's front seat and wedging himself in. I climb in beside him and tuck my knees beneath my chin.

'Tosh, you get in the front,' he calls. As we accelerate away, I find it impossible to judge if a genuine connection has developed between the two septuagenarian men, or if Sam simply found a way to get through to Tosh that I couldn't. In our cramped space, I turn to Sam, and he reads the puzzled look on my face,

'I got word the police brought Tosh down to Haddley last night, to identify Billy's body,' Sam says to me.

'You got word?'

'You're not the only one with contacts.' Sam reaches forward and presses his hand on Tosh Monroe's shoulder.

'The police came to the warehouse where I work in Leicester at two this morning, brought me down to London in a car.'

'Tosh has agreed to talk to us and help in any way he can.'

'I don't want any harm to come to Madeline. And whoever did that to Billy needs to pay.'

Annabel pulls up outside the artisan coffee shop on the
Upper Haddley Road. Inside, we find a small table for four.
Holding my coffee cup closely, I lean towards Tosh Monroe.
'Billy and Ethan Harris kidnapped Madeline. We know
from Ethan, Billy planned to take Madeline north, out of
London. Have you any idea where he might go?'

'I wish I did.' Monroe scratches his unshaven face. 'There's
so much about Billy's life I simply don't know. At the age
of nine, the authorities placed Billy for adoption. The first
Christmas he was away from me, I received a letter along
with a couple of photographs. The letter came from his adoptive parents to tell me how he was fairing in school, what
sports he liked, that kind of stuff. He had his own bedroom
at the top of their house where he liked to spend much of
his time. After the second year the letters stopped. At that
point, I lost touch with Billy for almost five years.'

Sam dunks a ginger biscuit in his coffee and sucks it
between his teeth. 'Tosh, you need to tell us about the rest
of your family.'

CHAPTER 55

The waitress clears our table before returning with a fresh round of coffees. Tosh hesitates but Annabel puts her hand on his and says, 'Why don't you tell us about your daughter?'

'Mairi,' he replies. A brief smile crosses his face but fades almost immediately. 'From soon after her seventh birthday, it was just her and me. Her mum disappeared with the bloke who came to fix the roof. I was more upset for Mairi than for me; a little girl needs her mum. I did try to track her mum down, persuade her to come home, if only for Mairi's sake, but she always found an excuse, didn't even visit. She did stick with the roofer. Last I'd heard they were living in Finland; good a place as any, I suppose. Mairi never saw her mother again.'

'And what happened to Mairi?' asks Annabel.

'I thought I was doing a half-decent job. Her teachers always said how attentive she was. At the end of each term, always a nice school report – I kept one or two of them, the ones saying she was destined for great things – and then at fifteen she was pregnant. We rowed, a lot. She wanted to keep the baby, but she was still a child herself. I had no idea how to handle her, and all that did was make me more stubborn. Perhaps if I'd acted differently, who knows? Mairi moved out and into a squat with the laddie she was desperately in love with. Of course, three weeks later he was gone. That's blokes for you. I asked her to come home, but she was as stubborn as me. And I wasn't going to beg. After that she fell in with the *wrong crowd*. Isn't that always the way? She took some stuff while she was pregnant with Billy; stupid, but what did she know? Once she'd had him, she got herself a council flat on the Meadows estate, in Nottingham. I hate to think what she did for money. At twenty she was pregnant again, and that's when I swallowed my pride and, this time, I begged her to come home. She wanted nothing of it. She was determined she could take care of herself. I started giving her money and she did let me spend some time with Billy. You'll hate me for saying it, but he was the sweetest kid. There were days you'd have thought there was nothing wrong with him, other than being a bit slow.'

'Tell us about the second child,' says Annabel.

'Travis. He was a bright boy; had both Mairi and Billy wrapped around his little finger. God knows who his father was, but two little kiddies proved too much for Mairi. She started taking things again. At twenty-four she was dead.'

'I'm sorry,' says Annabel, the fear for her own daughter etched across her face.

'And did the boys come to live with you?' I ask, quietly.

Tosh nods. 'I tried, but so often I'd find myself thinking

265

about what had happened to Mairi. Had all of that been down to me?'

'I'm sure you can't take all the blame,' says Annabel.

'Who knows?' replies Tosh, blowing out his cheeks. 'Not long after, the doctors diagnosed me with emphysema; they gave me five years. I proved them wrong,' he tells us, a bitterness in his laugh. 'The boys were still young enough that somebody else could do a better job than me. My only request was for them to stay together.'

'And did they?' asks Sam.

'There was a couple desperate to adopt, living somewhere near Welwyn Garden City. Nice house with lots of outside space. It sounded perfect. I always knew Travis would find his way. He was bright, people liked him, and he knew it. Billy was a lot for anybody to take on, and so it proved.'

'What happened?' I ask.

'The couple who adopted him kept him for four years,' replies Tosh. 'Then, like a second-hand car, they simply gave him back.'

CHAPTER 56

Will Andrews sat behind his husband's desk in the small office at the back of Mailer's restaurant. He scrolled down the computer screen showing reservations for Sunday lunch and dialled the next number. Mrs Pitt, of East Sheen, was the twenty-first guest he'd called that morning. She was quick to answer and once again he explained that, regrettably, today Mailer's would be closed for lunch. He hoped to open the restaurant later in the week. As he said the words, he had no idea if they were true. Like all the other restaurant guests he'd called, Mrs Pitt was terribly understanding. She'd heard about the discovery of the body on the banks of the Thames, only yards from Mailer's outdoor terrace, and of course, out of respect, they must close for the day.

Will clicked off his phone and breathed a brief sigh of relief. Mrs Pitt's was the last call he had to make, for today at least. In reality, closing the restaurant had nothing to do with the dead body washing up on the banks of the river. Mailer's was closed as its eponymous owner and head chef had walked out of his home early on Saturday morning, and hadn't been seen since.

Pushing back the desk chair, Will ran his fingers across the kitchen's spotless surfaces. Yesterday afternoon he'd received a call from one of East's team telling him his husband had not arrived at the restaurant. Left with no other option, he'd made his excuses to Nathan's parents and raced back to London. An introductory lunch, which had been going badly, ended disastrously. He wasn't sure what he'd expected, but Nathan's mother had struggled with his presence in her home. Speaking of Nathan's birth mother or of his adoption was, of course, impossible, but even polite conversation about his son's childhood appeared out of reach. Leaving the lunch before the main course hadn't helped. As he showed his father out of his family home, Nathan had hugged him and whispered, 'It was a first meeting. It was always going to be a bit tricky, but it could have gone worse.'

Will had smiled at his son. 'I think they'd probably prefer it if I didn't exist.'

'If you didn't exist, then neither would I,' Nathan had replied. 'It'll take a bit of time. They always knew this day might come. Any adopted child can choose to discover their birth parents.'

'Just unfortunate who yours are.'

'Neither of us can change that, even if we wanted to.'

'And I guess you probably do.' With that comment, Will had left. Immediately he'd regretted it. It was stupid and self-pitying. Nathan had asked for none of the attention forced upon him. He'd been more open to Will than he might even have dreamed possible or deserved. Driving back to London he'd felt annoyed with himself, but since returning home had become distracted in tracking down East. He'd spent Saturday evening turning away disgruntled diners while multiple calls to East throughout the night had proved fruitless. In the early hours he called all the local hospitals, but now, as the morning wore on, he found he cared less and less about where his husband was.

He wandered through to the cocktail bar and stood looking at the cut-glass crystal shimmering alongside costly bottles of spirits. He reached for a bottle of Hibiki whisky and poured himself a generous shot. Taking a seat at the bar, he picked up a beer mat and flicked it through his fingers. He folded it neatly in half, before ripping it in two and tearing the pieces again. Then he scattered the pieces across the bar, and leaving his drink untouched, drifted through to the main restaurant. At the sound of a car entering the front courtyard, he turned, and watched in horror as a police car slowed to a halt outside the restaurant.

CHAPTER 57

Lesley Barnsdale pulled into the courtyard at the front of Mailer's. She climbed out of her car, briefly imagining herself walking with Phil Doorley towards the stone building, both eagerly anticipating dinner at East Mailer's restaurant. Today was her fortieth birthday, but instead of celebrating she was investigating the chef's links to a double murder and kidnapping.

At the entrance to the restaurant, she stopped and waited for DC Cash. They'd travelled in silence from Ben Harper's home on Haddley Common. 'Your private life is your own,' she said to the junior officer as she walked towards her. 'And you can be certain nobody at the station will learn anything from me.'

'Thank you, ma'am,' replied Cash, keeping her eyes turned towards the river road.

'But Dani, you need to be careful. I'm happy to be convinced he's a decent guy, but so often I find myself feeling he's competing with us. As a serving officer, is a future with an investigative journalist realistic?' Cash didn't reply.

'Let's get some time together next week to talk,' added Barnsdale.

'I'd appreciate that,' Dani replied, looking across the restaurant courtyard towards the padlocked iron gates that led through to the rear of St Marnham boathouse.

'Dennis Thackeray's body was found on the other side of those gates,' said Barnsdale. 'Nobody at the boathouse has a key for the lock.'

'Perhaps that's something else Mr Mailer can help with?'

'Indeed.' Barnsdale opened the door and stepped inside the restaurant's cool interior. It was strangely quiet. A man walked towards them and, after the officers had introduced themselves, he explained he was East Mailer's husband.

'Is Mr Mailer available?' asked Barnsdale.

'Can I ask what this is concerning?' replied Will Andrews.

'You may be aware of the discovery of a body on the banks of the river last night. We've a number of follow-up questions for potential witnesses who were in the vicinity at the time.'

'Anything I can help with?'

'You were at the restaurant last night?'

'Only briefly. We closed early. I was back home at my house in the village a little after nine.'

'With Mr Mailer?'

He hesitated. 'I'd had a long day, decided to have an early night.'

'But was Mr Mailer with you or not?' pressed Barnsdale.

'Shall we sit down?' he replied.

'If you prefer.' Walking through the restaurant, Barnsdale's eye followed the spectacular river views, while inside, beneath the polished bronze lights, she noticed how precisely each table was set for lunch. Sitting opposite the restaurant's owner, she found herself running her fingers across the soft linen tablecloth. She caught his eye and she clasped her hands tightly together in her lap.

'Was Mr Mailer with you last night?' she said, repeating her question. Will Andrews leaned back in his green leather chair and folded his arms. 'It's a simple question,' she added.

'I think he was home, but I didn't see him.'

'Really?' she replied, allowing her voice to illustrate her disbelief. 'You didn't see him in the house all evening?'

'It's a big house.'

Barnsdale raises her eyebrows. 'Mr Andrews, we're investigating a murder. I need answers, honest answers. Was Mr Mailer at your home last night?'

His shoulders dropped. 'No,' he replied.

'And is he here now?'

'No.'

'Thank you,' replied Barnsdale. 'That wasn't too difficult, was it? When did you last see him?'

'One-thirty Saturday morning.'

'And not since?'

He shook his head, but as he did the warehouse-style door at the far end of the restaurant slid open. 'East!' he called.

Barnsdale was quick to her feet, meeting the highly recognisable chef as he walked into the cocktail bar. When she introduced herself, he took an immediate step back, but seeing his husband already seated with the police, he grudgingly agreed to join them.

'If you'd prefer,' said Barnsdale, 'we can speak to you alone.'

As he took the seat next to him, Will looked at his husband. 'East?'

'No,' he replied, 'I think it's time you heard this.'

CHAPTER 58

'No wonder Billy was fucked up,' says Annabel.

'Returning to care is never going to be a great experience for a kid,' replies Tosh.

'He didn't come back to you?' she asks.

'Doesn't work like that.' I can hear the weight of Tosh's broken family in his voice. 'Legally, they remained his parents.'

'But yours was the only real home he'd ever known.'

Tosh rubs his strawberry nose. 'He went back into the system. First, a children's home, then a couple of foster homes, but of course he knew where I lived. Each time social services placed him with a family, a couple of weeks later and he'd be climbing out of his bedroom window and hitch-hiking a ride back to mine. He'd stay for a few days until the authorities caught up with him and then off he'd go again.'

'How old was he?' asks Annabel.

'Fourteen, but by the time he turned fifteen social services pretty much gave up. At that point, I was happy to welcome him home and for two or three years all was well. When he was sixteen, I found him a job at the warehouse I was running, and then for his eighteenth birthday I bought him a car. Only an old banger, but he was convinced with his new wheels he'd have the pick of the girls. I can still see him now, waving madly, as he drove away from my house.' Tosh struggles. 'I watched him drive away on that day, so happy, and I thought, yes, he's going to be okay. And then I didn't see him again for another two years.'

'What happened?' I ask.

'Just like his mother, he got mixed up with the *wrong crowd*.' Tosh pauses to drain his coffee cup. 'Petty crime, nicking from shops, breaking into a warehouse.' He stops, placing his cup down on the table. 'He still had access to the warehouse I ran. Not a huge place; a family business shipping education supplies to schools across the country. Billy spent a Sunday afternoon drinking in a nearby pub. Got caught up with some lads, and just like Billy, desperate to be liked, told them he had access to the warehouse. The three lads got away with ten grand's worth of kit. The owners were fair. I explained about Billy, said he was a bit naive, and I'd pay them back the money. They agreed but it cost me my job. After that, Billy knocked around different towns, mostly getting jobs as a builder's labourer. He was a big lad and always useful on site. I've no idea where he actually lived but a couple of times a year he'd turn up at my front door. And then at Christmas, he'd be there again, looking for a nice gift. He suckered me in every time.'

I ask Tosh another question. 'In the months between the killing of Aaron Welsby and Billy's arrest, did you see him?'

'Never,' replies Tosh, 'not once, not even at Christmas.'

'Where did he go?' asks Sam.

'I don't know, but he wasn't with me.'

I look at Sam. Even back then, somebody was helping Billy.

'Tosh,' I say, 'time's running out for Madeline. Where do we find Travis?'

'I've not seen him since the day of his adoption. Like Billy, a couple of letters and some photos in the first two years, but after that nothing.'

'How old was he then?'

'Last picture I have of him, he's seven years old. He'd be ...' Tosh pauses, working out his grandson's age, '... thirty-three now. Hard to believe.'

'When you did see Billy, did he ever talk about his brother?'

'Never,' replies Tosh, shaking his head. 'But he never talked about anybody, except for Ethan Harris. I wish I could tell you more.'

'Travis Monroe can't be a common name,' I say to Tosh, 'but even after a full search, we've turned up nothing.'

Tosh reaches inside his coat pocket. 'To Billy, his brother would always be Travis, but right from the start, for his new parents the name didn't fit. In the last letter I received from them, they told me they'd changed his name.'

'Could they do that?' asks Sam.

'I didn't like it, but there was nothing I could do. I can't understand how overnight you give a five-year-old kid a brand new name.'

'They dropped Travis?'

'Completely,' he replies. 'Never gave me a reason, other

than to say they were his legal parents and could do what they liked.' He unfolds the crumpled sheet of paper he's pulled from his pocket. 'It's all here,' he says, pointing at the handwritten note. 'Travis was renamed Sebastian Elliot-Taylor-Chapman.'

CHAPTER 59

Barnsdale looked across the table at East Mailer. Unshaven with his long, dark hair hanging lank over his shoulders, he was some way from the man she'd imagined.

'Mr Mailer,' she said, looking at his giant frame, 'the body discovered last night was that of Billy Monroe.' He raised his eyes to hers. 'He was strangled,' she continued, 'and after that thrown from St Marnham Bridge. An act of some considerable strength.'

Mailer nodded slowly, and for one brief moment she thought he was about to confess. 'There's no point me saying anything other than I'm glad.'

Will Andrews looked at his husband. 'Who's Billy Monroe?' East was silent.

'The Aaron Welsby murder,' said Dani, quietly.

'East, what's that got to do with you?'

'Mr Andrews, please,' said Barnsdale, resenting the interruption. 'I've questions I need to ask Mr Mailer.' She turned her gaze back to the chef. 'Why don't you start by telling me about you and Aaron Welsby? Am I right in thinking you did know him?' A call to Welsby's parents had confirmed what Ben Harper had told her. Mailer rubbed his finger along a deep scar that ran across the length of his thumb. 'I need answers, Mr Mailer.'

Mailer looked at his husband, his partner for the past fifteen years. 'I'm sorry, Will.' He turned back to Barnsdale. 'Yes, I knew Aaron Welsby. He was employed as an architect in the design of this restaurant. And we became close. I loved him.'

Barnsdale could see this was the first time Will Andrews had heard this, but she needed information, so she pressed on. 'The night of Aaron's murder. Where were you?'

Mailer's breathing slowed. 'Aaron and I were together. That morning, Will had come home from a business trip to New York, so we knew we couldn't meet at our house. I cooked for us here in the restaurant. We were the first to ever eat here. I doubt the kitchen would have been installed for more than a week.' East paused.

'Mr Mailer, after you'd eaten?' said Barnsdale. 'What happened then?'

'Aaron and I had fallen into the habit of going for a walk most evenings, pretty much always the same route, around the village pond and over the bridge. We were deep in conversation; I don't remember about what. On the Baron's Field side of the bridge, we started down the steps. It was a miserable night, and as the rain fell harder Aaron pulled up the hood on his coat. The hood covered most of his face. It made us laugh. When Monroe ran towards us, out of the alcove, we were distracted. He called Aaron's name. In his hand he had a knife and before we realised what was happening, he'd stabbed Aaron in the stomach. Twice. Aaron was so brave. I half carried him back up onto the bridge. I could see he was fading and begged him to hold on. When I turned, Monroe was on us again. He stabbed Aaron a third time, this time in the chest. Aaron was dead. I hated myself for it, but I ran. I had no other choice. Monroe would've killed me.'

'Why didn't you come forward?' asked Dani.

'Monroe had seen my face. I was terrified he'd come after me.'

'The police would have protected you,' said Barnsdale.

'A gay hate crime?' he replied. 'How seriously would the Met Police have taken the threat to my safety?'

Barnsdale found herself unable to answer.

'More than anything else, I wanted him punished,' continued Mailer, 'but there were other ways to achieve that.'

'Madeline Wilson?' said Dani.

'Yes,' he replied. 'I'd trust her with my life. I shared with her all the information I had. I'd watched him flee along the railway tracks and over time, she identified Billy Monroe. Soon after, she began the campaign for his arrest.'

Barnsdale picked up a polished fork from the table in front of her and, feeling its weight, turned it over in her fingers. 'Returning to Mr Welsby's death,' she said. 'On the night of the killing, did you believe Monroe had directly targeted him?'

'Undoubtedly. Monroe was waiting for Aaron.'

'Why?' asked Barnsdale, putting the fork precisely back in its place.

'As I said, a hate crime.'

Barnsdale felt uncertain. 'Prior to the attack, had Mr Welsby expressed any specific concerns to you over his safety?'

'No.'

'Or had he received any threats?'

'Nothing that I was aware of.'

'Mr Mailer,' said Dani, 'while he was working for you, Mr Welsby was also working on a project for Haddley Grammar School?'

'Yes, the sports pavilion.'

'Did he talk much about the school?'

'He was proud of the work he'd done. It was the first major project for his new firm.'

'And the staff at the school? Did he meet many of them?'

'He'd been there off and on for almost two years, so yes, he knew a few.'

'Well enough to socialise?' asked Dani.

'There might have been the odd drink. I don't really know.'

Barnsdale leaned forward, resting her arms on the table. 'Mr Mailer,' she said, 'this is a murder case. Did something happen at the school?'

'A week before his death, Aaron arrived at the restaurant late one evening. His face was bruised. The restaurant was still to open, and I remember desperately searching for ice. We sat at the bar drinking gin because it was the only alcohol we had. He told me he'd argued with one of the teachers. Aaron never went back to the school again.'

CHAPTER 60

The double shot of Hibiki whisky stood untouched on the cocktail bar. Will downed it in one.

Across the restaurant, East sat alone at the corner dining table. On leaving the restaurant, the two officers had asked him to attend Haddley police station later in the day in order to make a full statement.

'I don't think you should go alone,' said Will. He didn't look at his husband. 'I can make a couple of calls and find you a good solicitor.'

'I don't need a solicitor,' replied East, his voice filling the empty restaurant. 'I haven't done anything wrong.'

'At the very least, you didn't come forward after witnessing a murder.'

'If I hadn't worked with Madeline, Billy Monroe would never have been convicted.'

'Whatever you did, you withheld evidence. Both of you. You might want to call her.'

'Later,' he replied, dismissively.

'You could go to prison.'

'I don't care.'

'Now you're being ridiculous.' When his phone began to ring Will briefly caught sight of a Cowbridge number, before he silenced the call.

East walked slowly across the restaurant. 'I'd do anything to bring Aaron back,' he said.

Staring vacantly at the glass bottles lined up in front of him, Will kept his gaze from his husband. 'You knew Billy Monroe had been released?'

'Yes, from Aaron's parents. They're good people. I became convinced Monroe would come after me. I was terrified.'

'That's why you became obsessed with social media and with Nathan? Because you were afraid it would lead Monroe to you?'

'To all of us.'

Will bit his lip. 'Where were you last night?' he asked.

'Why?'

'Because someone killed Billy Monroe a hundred yards from your restaurant.'

'Do you think I killed him? Is that why you want to buy me a solicitor?'

Will saw his phone ring again from the same Cowbridge number. He wondered why Nathan wasn't calling from his mobile but still tapped to reject the call. His son could leave him a voicemail. 'You said yourself you were terrified. I know your temper. I'm only asking now what the police will ask you later.'

'Aaron's buried in St Mary's churchyard in Richmond. I've sat with him for the past two nights. Talking to him made me feel safe.'

'Rather than talking to me?'

'I can't lie to you any more. I miss him every single day.'

Will stepped down from the bar and crossed to the terrace exit. He stopped and looked at East. 'Message me if you want a solicitor.'

Will stood for a while outside, staring blankly at the river until he felt his phone ring again. Once the call had disconnected, he dialled in to his voicemail. What was so urgent on a Sunday morning? Listening to the messages, it wasn't his son's voice he heard but that of Nathan's mother, Rosanna.

'Fuck,' he said to himself. He pushed his phone in his pocket, felt for his car keys and ran.

CHAPTER 61

Dani Cash sat on the corner of her desk as Chief Inspector Bridget Freeman called for quiet across the packed unit. Instantly the room fell silent.

'I'm sure on a Sunday morning we've all got far better places to be,' Freeman began, 'but we've got a woman kidnapped from outside a restaurant in St Marnham, a murderer most likely hiding somewhere locally, and two million quid in ransom money hauled off to God knows where.' Dani remained silent but there was an audible hum of condemnation among her colleagues who filled the room. 'I know, I know, people do stupid things, but I don't want to hear it,' said Freeman, and Dani saw how quickly her team responded to the chief inspector's authority. 'Add to that, we've got a pervert stalking women in their bedrooms. We need results. Now, I recognise a good number of you will have worked on the original Aaron Welsby murder case and I get that you might not be too sad at the passing of Billy Monroe.'

'God rest his bloody soul,' said a voice from the side of the room.

'I said I don't want to hear it. Monroe's killer throttled him to death before throwing him into the Thames. In my book, whoever the victim might be, that's murder. DS Barnsdale,' continued the station's commanding officer, turning towards the detective sergeant, 'is going to tell us what we need to know.'

'Billy Monroe was released from Winson Green just over two weeks ago,' said Barnsdale. 'A revenge attack upon Monroe, for the killing of Aaron Welsby, is not impossible but, taking into account the kidnapping, does appear unlikely. Both of Welsby's parents are in their eighties and he had no other discernible family. The only other person he was known to be close to was the chef, East Mailer. Mailer has reason to want Monroe dead but between him and his husband, two million quid seems largely irrelevant. Them setting up the whole kidnap scam appears very unlikely.'

'I'd have throttled him for two million.'

'And PC Higgins, I'll throttle you if you can't keep your mouth shut.' A burst of laughter filled the room before the chief inspector continued. 'I do have to admit it must be nice to be in a position where two million quid isn't worth the effort, but even so, DS Barnsdale is right. With what we've got right now, this isn't shaping up as a revenge attack.' She turned back to Barnsdale.

'What we need to understand is: did Billy Monroe have an accomplice from the very start?'

'Who's now two million quid to the good?' said Mat Moore.

'Indeed,' replied Barnsdale. 'We're tracking down any

CCTV taken from the bridge last night but there's nothing in the immediate vicinity of the cash drop. We're also trying to track down Billy's brother, Travis Monroe, but he was adopted at a young age and as yet he's proving elusive.'

Freeman picked up the thread. 'We have to be open to the idea that whoever killed Billy was also an accomplice to the original murder.'

An audible groan filled the room. 'We had Billy Monroe bang to rights,' called an older voice from the back of the room.

'Nobody's saying he wasn't guilty,' replied Freeman, 'but he may not have acted alone. It's quite possible Aaron Welsby was directly targeted, and we need to understand why. DC Cash, what can you tell us about the final weeks of Welsby's life?'

'Aaron Welsby worked on a building project at Haddley Grammar School. Somehow it ended badly. I've just come off the phone from . . . ' she looked down at her notes, ' . . . a call with a Mr Łukasz Nowak, who as a school governor was involved in the project fourteen years ago. Mr Nowak owns the mini market on Haddley Hill, and we can speak with him this afternoon.'

'DS Barnsdale, that's with you. Take a uniformed officer,' said Freeman. 'Turning to our intruder, DC Cash is leading with my support, but every single person in this room is responsible for stopping this man. I will not have another violent crime here in Haddley. Something must link these six women. DC Cash?'

'We're looking for any kind of connection between the

women, and social media is our main focus. On the man himself, the only thing we do know for certain is he's becoming more brazen.'

Freeman turned to DS Moore. 'Mat, you're leading for us on the Madeline Wilson kidnapping.'

'Yes, ma'am,' replied Moore. 'The National Crime Agency now have the lead, and if there is any contact from a *second* kidnapper, the NCA will take that conversation. Despite the efforts of her parents, and our very own local superhero, Ben Harper,' Moore raised his voice above jeers from the room, 'Madeline Wilson was not released upon the payment of ransom money. Time is now obviously of the essence. From the driver, Ethan Harris, we know he was the one who stole the van from PDQ Deliveries, and then switched the plates. He also provided a second set of plates for Monroe to switch again at some point on his journey. We've picked up an unmarked white van, heading north on the M1 from Staples Corner, late on Thursday night. We think it's Monroe. What we don't know is how far he went. Traffic at that time of night is light and we're hopeful we'll have something later this afternoon. Monroe's childhood was split between a village outside Welwyn Garden City and a town on the outskirts of Nottingham. They have to be our immediate areas of focus, but even with a number plate and using ANPR, we're still some way off knowing where Monroe might've been holding Madeline Wilson.'

'Thanks, Mat,' replied Freeman. 'We're all up against it, but the one thing I know about this team is it always delivers results. Number one, find the woman. Whatever NCA need, we get it for them. Number two, find the killer. In all like-lihood, whoever killed Billy Monroe also murdered Dennis Thackeray.' Freeman paused and looked directly at Dani. 'And number three, stop the intruder before it's too late.'

CHAPTER 62

With PC Karen Cooke beside her, Lesley Barnsdale crossed at the lights at the top of Haddley high street. They walked the short distance up the hill before stopping outside Nowak's Mini Market.

'Go ahead, constable,' said Barnsdale, standing aside to allow the uniformed officer to lead. The automatic doors slid open, and the pair stepped inside.

A pungent smell of fresh spices filled the well-stocked store. Cooke introduced herself to the young assistant sitting at the small checkout and asked if Łukasz Nowak was available.

'He owns the shop,' replied the woman.

'We're aware of that,' said Cooke, 'but is he here now?'

The young woman looked at Cooke as if she was stupid. 'He's here every single hour we're open, and I'd imagine a whole lot more beside. He never bloody leaves.'

'Where is he now?'

'In the stockroom.' The woman nodded in the direction of the back of the store. 'I think he goes in there to count his money.'

Barnsdale smiled. 'Thank you,' she said, as she walked past the checkout and followed Cooke towards a door at the back of the shop.

'What is it?' called a voice, after Cooke tapped on the door. 'I'm busy.'

'Police,' she replied.

Instantly, the door opened. 'My apologies, officer, you caught me red-handed,' said a man, holding up a vape cartridge.

'No law against vaping indoors,' said Cooke.

'There is in my store,' replied the man, pressing his finger to his lips. 'I tell my staff I'm reviewing stock.'

Cooke smiled. 'It's Mr Nowak, isn't it?'

'Łukasz Nowak,' he replied, offering his hand. 'Very pleased to meet you.'

Cooke introduced herself and Barnsdale before Nowak invited them through to his small office at the back of the stockroom.

'Sit, please,' he said, while still standing himself. 'You came sooner than I imagined. Let me make you both some tea. And I have some delicious Bahlsen biscuits in the shop. We will share them together.'

'Thank you, that's very kind but we're fine,' said Barnsdale, holding up her hand. 'We don't want to take up too much of your time.'

'Please, I insist. The police here in Haddley are part of our wonderful community. This year, I have been here for twenty-five years, and I've never known a home like it.'

'That's good to hear,' said Barnsdale, before adding, with

a firmness in her tone, 'but we really are fine. We only have a couple of questions for you. Please sit,' she continued, and Mr Nowak followed her instructions by pulling up a chair next to hers.

Cooke looked to her superior before continuing. 'I understand you spoke earlier with one of our colleagues?'

'I did.'

'In regard to your time on the board of governors of Haddley Grammar School?'

'Absolutely,' he replied. 'We must all find ways to give back to the community. I have two British daughters; one is a newly qualified GP working in Kent and the other is at Oxford University. Oxford! Can you believe that? My daughter studying economics at Oxford. I tell her she'll learn all about the economy right here in my shop!' Mr Nowak laughed, and both Barnsdale and Cooke couldn't help smiling.

'The school board of governors?' said Barnsdale.

'Ah, yes. Twenty years. Both of my girls attended Haddley Grammar. I couldn't be more proud. And this year I am to be vice chair of the board.'

'Congratulations,' replied Barnsdale. 'Mr Nowak, I understand your position involves you reviewing many of the school's procurement projects?'

'That's right, always the economy for me. From purchasing cheaper notebooks to building the sixth-form block, I've run the numbers on them all.'

Barnsdale pushed on. 'We're interested in the construction of the sports pavilion, perhaps fourteen or fifteen years ago.'

Barnsdale watched as Nowak leaned back and gripped the arms of his chair.

'Oh, yes,' he replied.

'You were involved with that project?' she asked.

'It was a very difficult time for both our school and the whole community.' He leaned forward, dropping his voice. 'You both know of the murder of Aaron Welsby?' The two officers nodded. 'Then you will understand. He was the architect. Such a very sad time. Mr Welsby was a lovely man, so very clever. I met with him on numerous occasions to review costings and plans. Nothing ever too much trouble. Then to be killed in such circumstances. All so very sad.'

'Before the murder,' said Barnsdale, 'while Mr Welsby was still working at the school, were you aware of any incidents, confrontations, he may have been involved in?'

'Mr Welsby? No, never. I was never aware of anything with Mr Welsby. That's why what happened came as such a surprise to all of us.'

Barnsdale edged her chair closer to Nowak. 'You referred to a difficult time for the school. Do you mean beyond the murder of Aaron Welsby?'

Mr Nowak raised his eyebrows, nodding.

'Might you be able to tell us more?' she asked.

He moved his chair so close to hers she saw their knees were almost touching. 'As governors,' he said, his voice deeply conspiratorial, 'we're asked to oversee all areas in the running of the school.'

'Of course,' said Barnsdale.

'Two weeks before the murder, one of the younger

members of staff, but one with a very great career ahead of him, was regrettably asked to resign. He had also been working on the sports pavilion.'

'And that's why he was asked to resign?'

'No, no. I confuse you.' Mr Nowak paused before leaning closer to Barnsdale. Even in the very small room, glancing at Cooke, Barnsdale could see she was straining to hear. 'A most unfortunate occurrence,' he said. 'It came to light the teacher concerned had been involved in relations of a sexual nature with a sixth-form pupil. The head was quite right in asking for his immediate resignation.'

'Do you recall the name of the teacher?' asked Barnsdale.

'Indeed, I do. He was named Philip Doorley.'

Eight

'Approaching slowly, he looked for any signs of life. There was none.'

He made it a rule never to leave the house without hugging her close.

He stood in the doorway and waited for her to come to him. When she did, he wrapped his arms around her. After a brief goodbye, he walked down the driveway and looked back over his shoulder. He knew she'd still be lingering, hoping for a final farewell. A simple smile and a brief wave, such futile gestures, but he'd learned each tiny detail helped to build his control over her. Occasionally, at the end of the driveway he'd stop and blow her an air kiss – how she loved that – but he'd also learned the power of scarcity. Today, he simply waved and walked away.

He'd told her he was leaving early to avoid the yobs seeking trouble. He saw no value in football violence. His train pulled into Nottingham station late morning. On a sunny day, a few early arrivals had already planted themselves outside the local pubs. Wrapped in partisan flags, pints in hand, he ignored them all. He hurried over the bridge, passed the football ground, and kept walking. From Billy's notebook, he'd memorised the scrawled address and followed the tree-lined streets until he stood outside the house. He could see no signs of life, but he'd taught himself to be patient. He'd already decided the meeting must appear spontaneous. If it meant missing the match, he'd do that.

He wandered back down the street to the sandwich shop on

the corner. He pulled out one of the two twenty-pound notes he'd taken from his mother's purse. Surely, she noticed him taking her money? She never said, so why would he stop? He ordered a ham and cheese sandwich, then perched on the wall at the end of the road to wait.

For almost two hours he sat until, finally, his patience was rewarded. When Billy left the house, he followed him at a short distance. Outside the Co-op he waited until he emerged with a packet of bread rolls and a can of Coke.

He acted quickly. With his head down, appearing to text on his phone, he barged into him. Rapid apologies followed and then he saw the surprised look of recognition. All it took was an easy smile and feigned interest in Billy's pitiful life. A shared recollection of times spent together. He'd made the connection.

A loose arrangement was made for a drink sometime soon. As brothers, they swore this was their secret.

All too easy.

At some point, Billy would be useful.

CHAPTER 63

'This Sebastian-Elliot?' says Sam, now sat beside Annabel in the front of her Mercedes sports car. We're edging our way through central London in heavy lunchtime traffic. 'He's Billy Monroe's brother?'

I catch Annabel's eye in her mirror. 'Yes, it looks like it,' I reply to Sam, 'but his name isn't Sebastian-Elliot, it's Sebastian.'

Sam turns around in his seat. 'But Tosh told us his parents changed his name to Sebastian-Elliot. Bit of a mouthful if you ask me. I'd have stuck with Travis.'

I laugh. 'His first name is Sebastian.'

'That's what I just said.'

'No,' replies Annabel, 'you said Sebastian-Elliot.' She dives between two black cabs, and we race up the inside lane of Marylebone Road.

'Elliot's his middle name?'

'No!' replies Annabel.

'Elliot-Taylor-Chapman was the surname of Billy and Travis's adopted family,' I explain.

'Three surnames?'

'Triple barrelled,' says Annabel.

'Ridiculous.'

'It's more common than you think, Sam,' I reply, 'especially these days. Lots of people like to keep their own names when they get married.'

Sam looks at Annabel. 'Some always did.'

'I'd have had no issue with you becoming Sam Hardy-Wilson,' says Annabel.

'Wilson-Hardy,' he replies.

Annabel cuts across the traffic and turns onto Baker Street. After seeing Tosh Monroe onto a Nottingham-bound train at St Pancras station, I messaged Min and asked her to locate Sebastian Elliot-Taylor-Chapman. An initial search suggested Billy's younger brother didn't exist in the digital world, with Min unable to find any evidence of the triple-barrelled name. With no obvious evidence of Sebastian surviving into adulthood, I began to wonder if we'd reached the end of the road. Ultimately, Min's persistence paid off. The man formerly known as Travis Monroe now goes by the name of Sebastian Chapman.

'The obvious question we have to ask,' I say, as Annabel drives past Regent's Park before turning north onto Finchley Road, 'is why did he change his name for a second time?'

'Because he didn't want to be found,' replies Sam.

We stop at yet another set of traffic lights and Annabel lifts her eyes to her mirror. 'Ben, are we absolutely certain the man Min's found is Billy's brother?'

I open my phone and reread my last message from Min.

'According to the register of births, Travis Monroe was born in Nottingham thirty-three years ago. After his adoption at the age of five, there is no further record of Travis but months later a five-year-old boy named Sebastian Elliot-Taylor-Chapman entered the school system in Welwyn Garden City. At the age of eighteen he left school with four A levels. After university he made a legal name change to Sebastian Chapman and has stayed that way for the past twelve years.'

'If you ask me,' says Sam, 'someone who constantly changes their name has something to hide.'

'I think we do have to accept the first name change, from Travis to Sebastian, was nothing to do with him,' replies Annabel. The lights turn green, and she accelerates away. 'Did you believe Tosh when he told us he'd never had any contact with Sebastian?' she asks Sam.

'Unless he's protecting him, I don't see why he'd lie.'

Annabel agrees. 'How then did Sebastian find Billy? The grandfather is their only link.'

'When Billy was returned to the care system, Sebastian would have been around ten?' I reply. 'Not impossible the two brothers found their own way to keep in touch.'

'Or Sebastian simply sought him out years later,' adds Sam. 'According to Ethan Harris, Billy was in contact with his brother while he was in Winson Green.'

'So, if Sebastian was involved in the killing of Aaron Welsby,' I reply, 'as long as Billy was inside, he posed him no threat. Only after Billy's release did he become a problem.'

'Sebastian always had Billy wrapped around his little

finger, and together they come up with a plan to kidnap Madeline. Problem is, for his kid brother, blabbermouth Billy is too much of a loose cannon.'

Traffic moving across the North Circular Road is stop–start, and, inside the warm car, I see Sam's eyes beginning to drop. We pass the entrance to Finchley Central Underground station before turning into the residential streets of North Finchley. A late-winter sun breaks through the cloud and Sunday afternoon dog walkers are out in force in the local park. We follow a maze of Edwardian side streets, where parked cars line the roads and neatly trimmed hedges conceal uniform gardens. Chislehurst Avenue is a tree-lined street of 1930s semis; many now converted into sizeable flats well out of the price range of the average first-time home buyer. Outside the address Min gave us for Sebastian Chapman, Annabel stops.

'Is this the place?' asks Sam, rousing himself. 'Not quite what I'd imagined.'

I point to a first-floor flat on the opposite side of the road. 'That's the one, with the blinds closed.' Like Sam, I'm surprised this is the home of Billy Monroe's brother.

'Do you think he's inside?' asks Annabel.

Sam opens his door and stands on the pavement. He looks at the house. 'If he is inside, he doesn't want to be seen.'

302

CHAPTER 64

Lesley Barnsdale walked deliberately down Haddley Hill, away from Nowak's Mini Market. At the junction with the high street, she stopped and waited for the lights to change. She felt numb. Still trying to comprehend what she'd heard, she told herself to focus on her work. It was the one thing she knew how to do and the only thing that might give her solace.

Billy Monroe was dead, murdered. Murdered by somebody who had been with him from the very beginning, perhaps somebody who'd helped him kill Aaron Welsby. East Mailer had told her of a direct confrontation between Aaron Welsby and a teacher at Haddley Grammar. She told herself not to jump to conclusions and to follow process, but when she closed her eyes all she could see was herself lying naked in Phil's immaculate bedroom. And then, an image of a teenage schoolgirl lying naked in the same bed.

She took a deep breath and caught a taste of the heavy car fumes that filled the air. Beside her, PC Cooke remained silent. She'd said nothing since leaving Mr Nowak's office.

What was she thinking? Barnsdale knew her junior colleague's reputation for station gossip. Today, all her Christmases had come at once. Focus on process, she told herself. A serious accusation had been made against him, and Phil deserved a fair hearing. She had no choice but to question him.

The lights turned and the traffic stopped. She crossed quickly, PC Cooke following one step behind. The pair walked past the bargain clothes shop that filled a giant space at the end of the high street, before cutting down a narrow road that led into Haddley's Victorian side streets. A late Sunday lunch awaited those making their way into the River Head pub. Drinkers packed the outdoor terrace, gathering around giant screens to watch the latest live football match. Her only time inside the pub was after a scuffle broke out between two sets of local supporters. The pub's nautical theme and cosy fireplace had surprised her. After appeasing the intoxicated fans, she'd briefly glanced at the dinner menu. Its Thai theme had appealed to her, but she'd never been back.

Passing the pub's entrance, she saw Cooke half raise her hand to a young couple entering the beer garden. Somehow, she imagined Cooke as a regular at the pub. Always first to suggest a drink with colleagues at the end of her shift, Cooke was at the heart of all the station's social activities. Never finding small talk easy, she herself rarely joined in.

'Ma'am,' said Cooke, as they followed another winding road through lower Haddley's residential streets, 'I'm sorry this has happened today.' She paused. 'On your birthday, I mean. It can't be easy for you.'

'No need to be sorry,' she replied, widening her step, and moving quickly on, 'not when we've work to do.'

'Of course not, ma'am.'

The pair turned onto Stanthorpe Street. Seeing a PDQ van parked outside Phil's house made her swallow hard. She thought of the disappearance of Phil's own van on the day of the kidnapping. 'As a member of the sports department, Phil Doorley worked closely with Aaron Welsby. The week before Welsby's murder, Doorley was fired for having sexual relations with a sixth-form pupil. From East Mailer, we know of a physical altercation between Aaron Welsby and a Haddley schoolteacher. It's our job to establish if there is a link.' Approaching Phil's home, she realised everything she'd said was designed to reassure herself as much as it was to lead Cooke. Why had she been so quick to let her guard down with him?

Barnsdale walked ahead, and she was first to arrive at the house. She rang the doorbell, and almost immediately pressed for a second time. With no reply, she reached for her phone. She felt Cooke looking over her shoulder.

'Ma'am,' said Cooke, hesitantly. 'I wonder if it might be easier if I call him?'

She stared at the contact name on her phone. 'Maybe that would make more sense.' She spoke with a clipped tone, forcing herself to slow down. Confronting Phil outside his home was irrational. Her emotions were clouding her judgement. 'We should head back to the station,' she continued, trying to calm her voice, 'and you can make the call from there. Probably best if you arrange a time for him to come in for an interview.'

She turned away from the house but, at the end of the short garden pathway, came to an abrupt stop. Walking directly towards her, alongside another man she couldn't quite place, was Phil. She froze.

'Ma'am?' said Cooke.

'I'm fine,' she replied, quickly regaining her composure and stepping onto the roadside.

'Lesley,' called Phil, as he neared. 'I wasn't expecting to see you so early. You've caught us in the act – on our way home from a cheeky lunchtime pint. If we'd known you were free, you could've joined us. Have you got news on my van?'

She didn't reply and was relieved when Cooke stepped forward.

'Mr Wright,' said Cooke, speaking to the second man.

'Look out, James, you're personally known to the local constabulary.'

'We met at the home of his former wife,' said Cooke.

Wright was quick to move away. He fumbled in his jacket pocket until he found his car keys. The headlights on a black Range Rover, parked across from the PDQ van, flashed. 'I should get going,' he said, slapping Phil on the back before quickly jogging over the road.

'Just one pint, I hope, Mr Wright?' called Cooke, as he opened his car door.

Wright stopped and glanced back towards Cooke and then up at the brightening sky. 'Such a beautiful afternoon,' he said. 'You know what, I think I might take a walk along the river and enjoy a burst of sunshine.'

'Why don't you do that,' replied Cooke, as Wright hurried away.

'We only had a couple of pints,' said Phil, laughing. He gently placed his hand at the bottom of Barnsdale's back. She flinched and took a sideways step. Before she'd time to react further, he was walking up the pathway to his home with his key in his hand. With the door open, he called. 'Are you coming in for coffee?'

Barnsdale took two steps up the path. 'Phil, we need to talk to you, on a police matter.' She stopped. Looking through the open front door, her heart sank. Floating in the hallway were two gold fortieth birthday balloons.

CHAPTER 65

Three giant wheelie bins fill the narrow pathway that leads to Sebastian Chapman's home. In single file, we approach the bright yellow door. Peering through one of the small panels of glass I can see a tiny hallway, almost filled by a child's buggy. At the back of the hallway are two wooden interior doors, one leading to each of the two flats. It doesn't strike me as the home of a killer but, as Madeline always taught me, assume nothing.

'First thing we do is find out if he's here,' I say, 'and then we'll see if he's willing to talk. Right now, all we're asking for is his help in finding Madeline, nothing more than that. We don't want to spook him.'

Flat B is on the first floor, and I go to press the buzzer. Annabel reaches past me and takes hold of my hand. 'Let me do this,' she says. 'A late middle-aged woman is far less confrontational than a six-foot brute with a bruised lip.'

Behind me, I hear Sam chuckle. 'Late middle-aged?' he says. 'Six-foot brute? What is this, *The Twilight Zone*?'

'Sam, be quiet,' replies Annabel.

'Be careful,' I say, striking a note of caution. 'We don't know what we're going to find.'

'This is about Madeline.' Annabel's wide eyes remind me of her daughter. 'I'll take whatever chance we have.' She presses the buzzer. 'And anyway, you're right behind me,' she adds, glancing over her shoulder, 'along with Old Father Time by the gate.'

'I'm keeping lookout,' says Sam.

Hearing the inner door open, Annabel moves a step forward. 'Here we go,' she says.

A tall man with neatly parted blond hair quickly opens the door. He's dressed in a Hugo Boss sweatshirt and trousers. A young child, perhaps six months old, nestles in his arms.

'I'm going to stop you straight away,' he says, smiling, but with an unwavering tone. 'I'm on daddy day-care today, so I'm not signing up for any charity or any religion, even though I'm sure you're all asking for a very good cause.' He starts to close the door.

'We're not Jehovah's or Methodists, or any other religious denomination,' replies Annabel, placing her hand on the door. 'And rest assured we don't want your money. We're looking for a man named Sebastian Chapman. Have you any idea where we might find him?'

'You already have,' he replies.

'Oh, I see, I'm sorry,' says Annabel, and I realise she has made the same assumption as me. The man standing in front of us bears no resemblance to the man I imagined to be Billy Monroe's brother. 'My name is Annabel Wilson and hiding by the gate is my former husband Sam Hardy. And we desperately need your help.'

'I wish you all the best, but I think you've probably got the wrong man,' replies Chapman, politely, as again he begins to close the front door.

'No, really we haven't,' says Sam, hurrying down the path. 'Our daughter has been kidnapped and her kidnapper is now dead.'

Annabel looks at Sam and raises her eyebrows. 'I can manage, thank you,' she says as a baffled-looking Chapman continues to push the door closed.

'I should get Noah back upstairs,' he says, raising his son up in his arms. Noah begins to investigate his father's ear.

'No, please,' says Annabel, again reaching forward. 'Our daughter was kidnapped by a man named Billy Monroe—'

A flash of recognition crosses Chapman's face. I tense but his hand slowly drops from the door before he wraps his arms tightly around his smiling son.

'That's why we're here,' adds Annabel, her voice soft.

Chapman takes a step back into the small entrance hall. 'My girlfriend's out at lunch with mates from our NCT group.'

'I promise we won't take up much of your time,' I say, quickly introducing myself. 'Time is running out for us to find Madeline alive.'

Chapman pauses, considering what we've said. 'You'd better come in,' he replies, moving aside. We follow him up a narrow staircase and onto a small landing. 'Apologies for the closed blinds, Noah's just up from his nap.' A passageway leads us through to a freshly decorated living room, filled with afternoon sunlight. Chapman lays his son down on a colourful play mat, from where the child grabs hold of a bright orange monkey.

'He seems very chilled,' I say. I look around the room, dotted with toys and blankets. On the walls hang photographs of Chapman and his girlfriend, together with their young son.

'We're lucky,' replies Chapman, before offering us refreshments, which we politely decline. 'He even pretty much sleeps through the night; that certainly helps me get up for work in a morning.'

'Where's that?' asks Annabel.

'I'm a graphic designer at a gaming company, just up the road in Whetstone.' He stops before adding, 'But you didn't come here to talk about my career.'

Annabel shakes her head. Briefly, she tells him the details of Madeline's kidnap and Monroe's murder. Chapman listens intently.

'Billy was my brother,' he says, 'but I haven't seen him since I was ten years old. The last time I saw him was the day he left our adopted family home.'

'Do you know what happened to him?' asks Annabel.

'He was returned to care.' He pauses. 'Even as a ten-year-old kid, I could see that was a shocking thing to do.' Chapman gently squeezes his young son's hand. The little boy lets out a gurgling giggle. 'It was a miserable time. He was my brother and we'd always been together. He'd been the only constant in my life. Like all little brothers, I'm sure occasionally I was a pest, but I hated it when he left.' He looks at Annabel. 'Billy had a kind heart. When I was small, we spent every waking hour together. He looked after me. As I got older, I realised he needed someone to take care of him.'

'And he never found that?' she asks.

He shakes his head. 'Not with my parents. Billy struggled with some stuff. Even when I was small, I could see things took him one or two beats longer. He needed someone to give him time, to show him patience. That was in short supply with my parents, especially my mother.'

'Your adoptive mother?' I ask.

'Yes. She wanted the perfect family. A brood of children doing well in school to make her proud. Billy needed more, and from the very beginning it was obvious she had little interest in giving him what he needed. Billy was never happy there.'

'And you?'

Chapman shrugs. 'I was younger, and they were all I really knew. I don't remember my birth mother.'

'Or your grandfather?' asks Sam.

'Not really.'

'After Billy left, did you try and keep in touch with him?'

Chapman shakes his head. 'I missed him, but I was only ten. I didn't know where he'd gone.'

'And as you got older?' I ask.

'It sounds harsh, but I had my own life. I was at university at the time of the Aaron Welsby murder. With all the media campaigning around Billy's arrest, I felt embarrassed. I read about his trial, but I never told anyone he was my brother.'

'Did you visit him when he was in prison?' asks Sam.

'No, never. After Billy went back into care, I've honestly no idea what happened to him. I didn't even know he was out of prison. I'm sorry how his life ended, but for me it's all a very long time ago.'

I lean back in my chair, desperately wanting to find a connection between the brothers. 'Your adopted parents,' I say. 'Did they keep in touch with him?'

'Not once, from the moment he left our house.'

'Where are they now?'

'They were killed in a car crash, three years ago.'

'I'm sorry,' I say.

'Don't be, not on my behalf,' he replies. 'Once I went to university, I drifted away from them.'

'How come?'

'I'm surprised you need to ask. This was a couple who gave their son back to social services because he didn't fit their profile of the perfect family. That probably tells you all you need to know.'

'Is that why you changed your name?' asks Sam.

'That bloody mouthful,' he replies. 'My mother certainly didn't like it when I did that.' Missing his father, the baby starts to whimper. 'Hey Noah, what's that all about?' Chapman picks up his son and sits him on his knee. The boy's face lights up with a toothless grin.

'Is there anything more you can tell us?' asks Annabel.

'I wish there was. Billy was a people pleaser, always doing things to make people laugh, to make them like him. That left him vulnerable. My guess is somebody got to him.'

Chapman carries his son downstairs and shows us out of the front of the house. Stepping out onto the pathway, Sam stops. 'I don't want to offend, but I have to ask you what you were doing last night?'

'No offence taken,' replies Chapman. 'Noah might be a good sleeper but he's still pretty exhausting. I think we were all in bed by nine.'

Chapman steps back inside his home while Annabel and Sam walk slowly back across the road. Their steps are heavy and slow, and I feel certain they are thinking the same as me. Sebastian Chapman didn't kill Billy Monroe. And he didn't kidnap Madeline.

Have we finally reached a dead end?

CHAPTER 66

The sign on the door for Interview Room 1 read *occupied*. Barnsdale gripped the door handle, inhaled a sharp breath, and stepped inside the windowless room. Phil Doorley raised his eyes to hers but taking a seat opposite him and his solicitor, she refused to engage. She turned briefly towards DC Cash, who she'd asked to join the interview. The detective constable activated the recording equipment before Barnsdale officially informed Mr Doorley his interview was under caution, pursuant to the Sexual Offences Act 2003.

Phil responded by locking his eyes on hers. Fighting to stop a shake in her hand, she opened the folder lying in front of her on the table. She stared blankly at the first page, desperately trying to compose her thoughts.

'Mr Doorley,' she began, 'fourteen years ago you were employed at Haddley Grammar School?'

'Yes,' he replied.

'And that was for a period of three years?'

'Yes.'

'And during that time, you were part of the team involved in overseeing the construction of a new sports pavilion?'

'I think overseeing is a stretch. My involvement was purely in a practical sense, advising on the location of sports equipment and the like.'

'But you were involved?'

'Yes.'

'Despite your involvement, you left the school directly before the completion of the project?'

'It was pretty much done.'

Barnsdale looked down at the notes in front of her. Her hand wavered as she turned the page. 'Why did your employment cease?' Doorley laced his fingers together, before resting his hands on the table in front of him. Looking down, she saw his knuckles were white. 'Mr Doorley, why did your employment cease?'

He leaned back in his chair and briefly consulted with his solicitor. Folding his arms, he answered Barnsdale's question. 'I resigned.'

'It's our understanding,' continued Barnsdale, 'from speaking to a long-serving school governor, the headmaster in fact asked you to resign. Is that correct?'

'I made the decision to resign.'

'You made the decision to resign, giving up a promising career with no other job to go to. Why would you do that?'

'I made the decision to resign,' repeated Doorley.

'I'm aware your marriage broke down at a similar time.'

'Detective, really?' said Doorley's solicitor.

Barnsdale cast her eyes down. She rested her hands on

top of her papers. Slowly, she lifted her eyes to Phil's. 'Were you asked to resign by the headmaster after you had sexual relations with a sixth-form school pupil?'

Doorley's mouth tightened and he made no attempt to hide his contempt for her. 'I made the decision to resign.'

'Mr Doorley, are you denying you resigned from your teaching position at Haddley Grammar School after you had sexual relations with a sixth-form pupil?'

Doorley whispered to his solicitor, and she leaned forward to answer the detective's question. 'My client has answered this question on multiple occasions. He took the decision to resign, and that decision is recorded in all official paperwork with the school.'

'Did you agree that as a settlement with the headmaster?'

'Detective, Mr Doorley resigned. I suggest you go and read the school documents for yourself.'

Barnsdale smoothed a crease in her trousers with her palms. 'Returning to the construction of the sports pavilion,' she said. 'Aaron Welsby designed and managed the project. Were you associated with him?'

'I met him, if that's what you mean; probably on half a dozen occasions. At most, seven or eight. As I said, I was involved with the planning of the sporting facilities. The bulk of the responsibility sat with the board of governors.'

'At any time, did you come into conflict with Mr Welsby?'
He shook his head. 'No.'

'A week prior to his death, Mr Welsby became involved in a physical altercation with a teacher from Haddley Grammar. Was that you?'

Touching away the moisture on his forehead, Doorley edged back in his chair. He didn't answer the question.

'Mr Doorley?' said Barnsdale. 'Did you become involved in a physical altercation with Aaron Welsby? Did he somehow become aware of you conducting sexual relations with other pupils at the school?'

'No!' Doorley slammed his fist on the table. Barnsdale flinched, and took in a sharp breath.

'No, you weren't involved in an altercation with Mr Welsby, or no you weren't involved in further sexual relations?'

'No to both.'

Barnsdale turned the page in her notes. 'Last night, Mr Welsby's killer, Billy Monroe, was himself killed in St Marnham. Where were you between nine and midnight?'

'I worked late into the evening. As you're aware, Detective, I have my own delivery business and we're short of drivers. I made some drop-offs myself. I can give you the addresses.'

'We'd appreciate that,' Barnsdale replied. 'What time did you finish?'

'I'm not sure, sometime around ten. That's our last delivery slot.'

'And after that?'

'I had a quick pint at the River Head pub before closing and then walked home.'

'Alone?'

'Yes, alone.'

Barnsdale briefly tapped her fingers on the table. 'You hadn't arranged to meet Billy Monroe in St Marnham?'

'No,' he replied, his voice rising, 'absolutely not.'

CHAPTER 67

Phil Doorley's solicitor moved quickly to refute any suggestion of her client's involvement in the killing of Billy Monroe. A rapid termination of the interview followed, with the detective sergeant escorting Doorley and his solicitor out of Interview Room 1. Outside the room, Doorley moved towards the station exit, briefly shaking hands with his solicitor as he went. Then he stopped and suddenly headed back towards Barnsdale as she opened the door to the station's CID office.

'Phil, wait! Don't!' called his solicitor, but it was too late.

'Happy?' said Doorley, chasing after Barnsdale.

Barnsdale baulked. She pushed open the CID office door, only to feel Doorley's hand land on her shoulder.

'Don't you dare run away from me,' he said, his voice echoing in the narrow hallway.

She turned sharply, and as she did Doorley's solicitor grabbed hold of his hand. 'Mr Doorley,' said Barnsdale, 'the interview is concluded. I suggest you leave the building, now.'

Doorley's solicitor pulled at his arm, attempting to lead

her client back down the corridor. 'Phil, let's go,' she said, but shaking his arm free he waved her away.

Doorley leaned forward. With his face almost touching Barnsdale's, for a moment she thought he might kiss her. Then, his lips close to her ear, he dropped his voice to a whisper.

'I was at a party, drinking too much cheap wine. On my walk home, I stopped at a pub. I got chatting to a group of girls. I was twenty-six, she was eighteen and studying drama. I'd never seen her before in my life. I went back to her flat. It was a stupid mistake. When I left in the early hours of Sunday morning, she said she'd see me at school on Monday. Immediately, I realised what she meant. I was devastated.' Barnsdale edged a step back, but Doorley moved forward. He took hold of her arm. 'On the Sunday night, I went to see the headmaster at his home. I told him everything. There was no crime, but for the sake of the school I knew I had to resign, and I did. Right there and then.' Doorley stepped back. 'Is that what you wanted to hear?'

Barnsdale saw his face was red, his eyes wide with anger. 'We'll be in touch if we have any further questions,' she said, a break in her voice betraying her.

Doorley's solicitor led him away towards the exit. About to leave, Doorley turned and called back down the hall, 'Enjoy your birthday.'

CHAPTER 68

Under a heavy, grey sky, the train edged slowly forward into the deserted commuter station on the outskirts of Nottingham. Tosh Monroe remained seated until his carriage pulled alongside the platform and the train came to a complete stop. He looked out at the miserable afternoon, zipped up his anorak and pulled his hood over his head.

A cold wind blew across the open station and the corrugated roof offered little shelter. He hurried down the platform before slowing as he began to clamber up the steep flight of steps. Halfway up, he stopped to catch his breath and found himself wishing he'd made the effort to find the lift. A young couple walked past him, each only interested in themselves, and then an older woman with a small child he presumed to be her grandson. The woman took hold of the child's hand and kept moving, but as he climbed the next step the little boy turned and waved. Tosh lifted his hand and waved back. Then he gripped hold of the handrail and slowly followed them up the stairs.

By the time he reached the small station hall, his chest was unbearably tight. He needed to sit down. Across the hall, he saw a passport photo booth. Fighting for each breath, he inched forward. Reaching the booth, he yanked back the curtain and slumped down onto the small stool inside. He struggled with the zip on his anorak, but finally he was able to reach into his inside pocket and feel for his inhaler. He sucked air through the mouthpiece, staring at his reflection on the screen in front of him as he did. A moment later he inhaled again, and gradually he began to feel the positive effects of his medication.

Resting his head against the side of the booth, he found his mind drifting back to a time when Billy was not much older than the little boy he'd seen on the stairs. One evening, as he'd left Mairi's tiny flat, Billy had begged him not to go, gripping hold of his leg, tears streaming down his face. Tosh had needed to peel away his grandson's arms before hurrying away, hating himself. Climbing into his car, he'd looked up to see Billy still standing in the outdoor passageway, frantically waving goodbye. That little boy had grown so quickly into an eighteen-year-old, still frantically waving, as he drove himself away from Tosh's own home. Now, as he stared at the weary face reflected back at him, he couldn't help but wonder if he should have done more to bring Billy home.

Feeling strong enough to stand, he pushed himself up onto his feet and shuffled out through the curtain. He paused, finding his bearings. A woman hurried past, rushing for a train.

'I think the photographs come out at the other end,' she called, smiling at Tosh as she passed.

He smiled back and moved in the direction she'd suggested, although he didn't really know why. 'Thank you,' he replied, before walking away. At the exit to the car park, rain blew across the vast open space. One of only a handful of cars remaining, his battered old Honda was at least close to the door; one of the few privileges of being old and sick. He turned on the ignition, revved the engine and pushed the heater up to five. He was happy to wait for the condensation to clear from the windscreen before he finally pulled away.

Leaving the car park, he followed the side road before navigating a small roundabout. At a second, larger roundabout, he stopped. He stared at the road in front of him, the fast-flowing traffic speeding towards the city. From behind, a car horn blared, and under his breath he swore at the young driver. He moved forward, but, at the last second, instead of turning for home he followed the side road that led out into the surrounding countryside.

The car's wipers raced against the falling rain, squeaking as they swung from side to side. The air inside the car became stifling. He unzipped his anorak and cracked open the window. Meandering along the winding country roads, he enjoyed the open space, the lush green fields surrounding the outskirts of the city. He followed a signpost towards the small village of Gotham. The name of the village always made him smile. He thought of those weekends many years ago, taking his two young grandsons for Sunday lunch and telling them their favourite superhero lived upstairs at the local pub. At an age where they believed everything their grandfather said was true, Billy and his brother would peek up the wooden stairs in the hope of catching a glimpse of Batman.

He stopped outside the Sun Inn and wandered inside. Little had changed. He sat at a small corner table and, savouring a pint of Beacon Hill ale, he remembered those times he'd shared with his young grandsons as the happiest of his life.

About to leave the village he slowed, pulling over to the side of the road. Off to his right was the narrow farm track he'd travelled so many times. After every lunch out, he'd take the boys to run in the neighbouring fields. In his rear-view mirror, he caught sight of an excited seven-year-old Billy keeping a tight hold of his bright red kite. He followed the narrow track, passed the deserted farm buildings, and stopped on the overgrown grass verge. With the rain clearing, he opened his door and climbed out. Although only a few miles from his home, the air here was clean and fresh. He walked a few paces along the track towards the old cowsheds and abandoned brick buildings. Looking across the vast open fields, he imagined the red kite fluttering in the wind as his two grandsons chased behind it.

Feeling the chill of the wind, he turned back towards his car. Only then did the roof of a white transit van, hidden alongside one of the abandoned buildings, catch his eye. Approaching slowly, he looked for any signs of life. There were none. On the back of the van, he could see where a bad paint job had failed to obscure the letters, PDQ.

'Billy,' he muttered, with a sad shake of his head. 'What have you done?'

CHAPTER 69

At the entrance gates to PDQ Deliveries, the woman in the gatehouse was taking a bite out of what looked like a thick-cut, ham and cheese sandwich. Turning the page of her tabloid newspaper, she was oblivious to Dani Cash's car waiting at the entrance barrier.

Dani touched her horn. The woman slowly lifted her eyes before she saw Dani's warrant card and quickly raised the barrier. Driving past, Dani mouthed a *thank you*, just as the woman opened a large bag of barbecue-flavoured Hula Hoops and returned to her newspaper.

From reception, Dani was shown upstairs and found the door to Phil Doorley's office standing open. With his back to her, he was looking down onto the warehouse floor.

'Mr Doorley,' she said, half knocking on the open door. She stepped into the room. 'I was hoping . . . '

He turned. 'For Christ's sake, what more do you people want?'

'I'm sorry to disturb you again so soon,' she replied, 'but I'm afraid we need access to your delivery logs from Saturday evening.' She paused. 'To confirm you were out making deliveries.'

Doorley laughed. 'Lesley isn't letting this go.' Dani didn't reply. He sat at his desk and typed on his keyboard. 'She wouldn't take my word for it? Did she think I was making it up?'

'The sooner we can confirm your whereabouts for last night the better. The delivery records should help us do that.'

An old inkjet printer, balanced precariously on top of a wooden cupboard, whirred into life. Doorley got to his feet, grabbed three sheets of paper off the printer and thrust them in Dani's direction.

'Here,' he said. 'You'll see my initials next to the delivery addresses.'

'Thank you,' she replied, glancing down at the series of timestamped deliveries. 'We'll speak to a number of these households to confirm it was you making the drop-offs.'

'Fill your boots,' he replied. 'And while you're wasting your time doing that, whoever killed Billy Monroe is wandering around St Marnham.'

'Our job is to rule out as many people as possible.'

Doorley sat on the edge of his desk. 'You can give your boss a message from me if you like.'

'I should probably get going,' she replied, stepping backwards.

'I liked her, liked her a lot. I thought she trusted me, might give me at least some benefit of the doubt.'

'Like I said, I should get going.'

'You run along.' Doorley's laugh was a bitter one. 'I even

prepared a birthday dinner, with balloons and an ice-cream cake. She's got quite a sweet tooth, your boss.' Dani smiled uncomfortably but he continued. 'Everything I said at the station was true.'

'We have to investigate all possibilities.'

'I've regretted that night for the rest of my life. It cost me my job and my marriage, although that was probably already done for. A house party where, surprise, surprise, people like me and Aaron Welsby drank too much and ended up doing stupid things. The kind of stupid things that happen every weekend, but here I am fourteen years later still paying the price.'

Dani took a step back inside Doorley's office. 'Aaron Welsby was at the party?' Doorley nodded. 'When exactly was this?' she asked.

He shrugged and said nothing.

'Mr Doorley, when was this party?'

Doorley met her gaze. 'A week before the murder,' he said, after a moment. 'I've never given it much thought.'

'Why was Aaron Welsby at the party?'

'He'd been working at the school for a couple of years, made a few friends. Even so, I was still a bit surprised to see him there.'

'Why?'

'Other than him, it was all staff.'

'Teachers?'

'They are allowed to socialise outside of school.'

'Did Aaron come with someone in particular?'

Doorley sat back at his desk and rattled his keyboard. 'It

was a long time ago,' he replied. 'I've regretted that night ever since. I don't want to get involved. I shouldn't have said anything.'

'Mr Doorley, if you have any information, any information at all on Aaron Welsby, you should share it with me now.' He stared at his computer screen, but Dani moved to stand directly in front of him. 'Mr Doorley, please.'

He lifted his eyes to Dani. 'I'd seen him in the pub a couple of times, chatting to the new chemistry teacher, Harry Eden. Only a young guy, science geek, but handsome if you like that kind of thing.'

'He went to the party with Aaron?'

Doorley shook his head. 'I can't say that. They were both at the party, but not necessarily together. I've no idea if Aaron was even interested in Eden.' He leaned forward on his desk. 'It's very easy to misread signals.'

'What happened at the party?' asked Dani.

'As I said, there was a lot of drinking. Late in the evening I went into the kitchen to refill my glass.' He ran his fingers across the back of his neck. 'I found Aaron with his head over the sink. At first, I thought he was throwing up, but then I saw blood coming from his mouth. All he'd tell me was he'd been in an argument, but he claimed it was nothing. I drank one more glass of wine and decided I'd had enough. When I left, Aaron followed me out. He told me he was going for a walk round the park to clear his head.'

'And that's what he did?'

'He set off in that direction, so I guess so. I stopped outside for a minute as there were a dozen or so school kids hanging around at the front of the house, often the way if they get wind of a teacher's party. Usual suspects, passing around a plastic bottle of cheap cider. All of them were year ten. I told them to clear off home. When I walked back past the house, Harry Eden, the chemistry teacher, was leaving.'

'Did you see where he was going?'

'He was heading in the direction of the park.'

CHAPTER 70

Through the narrow cracks in the boarded-up window, Madeline watched the last of the fading daylight disappear from the bare room. Her head ached and, through her broken nose, her breathing was laboured. For three nights she'd barely slept, only occasionally drifting in and out of consciousness. There was no heating and for much of the time she'd shivered in the darkness. The merest sound, a gust of wind, a creak on the stairs, and she was instantly alert to her surroundings back inside her brick prison cell. Tonight would be her second night without a visit from Billy Monroe. On the first morning of her captivity, she'd realised who her captor was. However much she'd hated it, she'd had to win his trust. Her only hope of staying alive had been to convince him she posed him no threat. But increasingly, she felt certain the ransom collection, of which he'd spoken with such belief, had not gone to plan.

Her mouth felt dry, and she reached for the plastic bottle lying on the floor beside her. The water was warm and did little to quench her thirst. After her third sip, she stopped drinking. It was impossible to know how long she might remain captive. She needed to save what water she had left.

Leaning back, she jerked the handcuff chaining her to the wall. In a brief flash of anger, she yanked her arm forward; the water pipes rattled around the abandoned building. She closed her eyes. However long it might take, she had to keep believing help would come. She was still alive.

Her thoughts began to wander. In the chaos outside the Old Bailey following Billy Monroe's conviction, it was her father who'd stood beside her. She could still see the pride in his eyes – a guilty man convicted because of the work she'd done. Her love of discovering the very best stories coupled with her passion for the truth both came from Sam. His determination became hers. She wouldn't have enjoyed one ounce of the success she had without everything he'd taught her. And if she had her time over, she would do exactly the same again.

She drifted in and out of sleep, stirring at the slightest sound. But then the faint clanking of the outer door caused her to shudder. Soon after, the unmistakable sound of the second door opening followed. Billy's footsteps climbing the stairs, now quicker than before, hurriedly approaching the third padlocked door. Pushing back her tangled hair, she tried to focus her eyes. She listened as he unlocked the door to the room, praying she was about to be free.

The door opened. A torchlight dazzled her, and she raised her hand to her eyes.

'Billy, put the light down, please.'

From behind his pig-face mask, his voice was almost inaudible. 'I can see you.'

Her body twitched, and she pressed herself back against the cold brick wall. 'I thought we were done with the mask,' she said. Hesitantly, she asked, 'Did you get what you hoped for?'

He lowered the light to the floor. 'Almost everything.' When he moved towards her, she noticed he was wearing different shoes. Gone were his battered old boots, replaced now with designer trainers.

She picked up her plastic bottle. 'I'm almost out of water,' she said, 'but perhaps I won't need it?'

He snatched the bottle and tossed it through the open door. The sound of the bottle slowly tumbling down the stairs seemed never-ending. He knelt beside her, and when he reached for her chained-up arm, her heart raced. The keys rattled and then suddenly the padlock, which had kept her imprisoned, was gone.

'Billy' she said, quietly, still unsure if he was releasing her. 'Have you got your money?'

With his full weight, he leaned forward and trapped her against the wall. The rubbery mask pressed against her cheek. She couldn't breathe. Panic raced through her body as he forced his hand between her legs. 'Billy, no, please,' she yelled.

Through the pig's nostrils, his warm breath filled her ear. 'It's not Billy any more.'

CHAPTER 71

He traced his dry fingers down her cheek and across her lips. His hand gripped her throat, pinning her to the floor. Madeline screamed, only for him to stuff a greasy cloth inside her open mouth. He jammed his knee between her legs, holding her down and forcing her arms above her head.

'I'm going to kill you,' he said, pushing the pig's nose into her ear, 'but not before I've rutted you like a feral sow.' He laughed. 'One last time for Billy to take the blame.'

She kicked her legs and violently jerked her body, frantically trying to throw him off. She fought with every sinew, but all he did was laugh. His strength was simply too great, crushing her into submission. With one hand, he held her arms; with his other, he ripped open the button on her trousers.

A surge of rage crashed through her body. She arched her back and twisted away. With her legs free, she kicked his stomach and scrambled towards the open door. He leaped forward, slamming his weight on top of her. Her face pressed against the floor, he lay on her back.

'I like a fighter,' he said.

She stared vainly towards the open door. The wooden flight of steps to freedom; they were beyond her reach. When he flipped her over, all she could do was stare vacantly down the stairs, only for a scream to again surge through her as a pair of muddied boots began to slowly climb upwards.

An explosion ripped through the room. The reverberating sound deafened Madeline. Suddenly, the man's weight fell away. Crawling across the floor, only the muddied boots stood in her way.

'Get out!' yelled a voice, and then the path to the stairs was clear. Half bent, she stumbled before tumbling down. At the foot of the stairs, dazed, she staggered to her feet and stepped outside. For a split second, she stood beneath the moonlit sky and inhaled the fresh air. Then she began to run down a muddy track, ahead of her the lights of a small village. As she ran, a second explosion, now instantly recognisable as the blast of a shotgun, erupted behind her.

Nine

'When he told us he hadn't seen Billy for the past two decades, I believed him. But somebody is lying.'

The voice of the television quiz show host squealed with excitement. The audience erupted into rapturous applause while a giant cheque for one hundred and twenty-five thousand pounds was carried onto the stage. The contestant beamed, her delight overwhelming and surpassed only by that of the host.

'His teeth are so white,' said his mother, 'they can't be natural.'

He sat beside her on the sofa. 'I bet he has someone to polish them for him.'

His mother agreed. 'He probably takes them out to have them cleaned.'

They both laughed.

'Programmes like this only make people more greedy,' she continued. 'One million pounds is too much money for anybody to win out of the blue.' She looked at the woman on television, still clutching her cheque. 'A woman like that will have no idea what to do with the money. She won't know how to invest it. You mark my words, in a few weeks it'll all be gone – squandered on fast cars and package holidays to Magaluf.' She ran her hand through his hair. 'Your education is more valuable than any amount of money won on a game show. Always earn your money. You'll find it far more rewarding.'

He smiled at her and told her how much he loved her.

He didn't love her.

He'd never been enough for her. Somehow, she'd still wanted something more.

'You'll make your own million,' she said. 'I know you will. That'll make me so proud.'

He nestled close to his mother.

She was right, he would have his own million and more, but he didn't care how he got it.

CHAPTER 72

Will Andrews felt a hand rest upon his shoulder. He looked up at Nathan's mother and placed his hand upon hers.

After hearing Rosanna's message, Will had run from Mailer's outdoor terrace across to his car. From there, he'd raced the two hundred miles back to Cowbridge. Throughout the journey, his hands tightly gripping the steering wheel, all he could think of was the recent suffering his son had endured. The brutal abuse inflicted upon him following the revelation of his birth mother's identity. The guilt by association, the unhinged theories given credence in the online world. Pure poison poured over him by the keyboard warriors. The fleeting happiness he'd found with Sarah Wright, suffocated by an all-consuming commentary, and choked by the barrage of her ex-husband.

Arriving at the Royal Glamorgan Hospital, he'd abandoned his car, sprinted inside and received directions to Ward 3. There he'd found Rosanna, sitting silently at her son's bedside, pain etched across her face. Uncertain, Will had stepped back, until Rosanna came to him. She'd taken hold of his hand and led him to his son. Nathan's face was sallow and pale, and when Will held him all the strength appeared to have drained out of him.

Will and Rosanna had exchanged only a few words in the hours that followed, but a solidarity existed between them, unified in their determination for Nathan to live. After Will had left Nathan's family home the previous lunchtime, Nathan had joined a small group of friends. The group had grown throughout the afternoon with one drink following another. At some point in the evening, Nathan had taken some pills and then drunk some more. In the early hours, his sister had found him collapsed on the lawn at the front of their home.

A stupid accident, Rosanna had said. Will had agreed and they'd said nothing more, but still, he couldn't banish his own selfishness from his mind. His eager acquisition of a son, only to place him at the centre of his own marriage breakdown. He refused to admit what it might all mean. His thoughts must only be for Nathan.

Rosanna pulled a chair forward and sat beside Will. She took hold of Nathan's hand, holding it between her own. All around, monitors bleeped as nurses moved swiftly from patient to patient, while Will and Rosanna watched desperately for any flicker of life from the son they now so painfully shared.

CHAPTER 73

Floodlights illuminated the car park at the rear of Haddley police station. Her head full of her conversation with Phil Doorley, Dani hurried inside, swiping her security pass to take her directly into the CID office. Never had she seen such a buzz of activity on a Sunday evening. She dropped her jacket on the back of her chair and crossed quickly to Barnsdale.

'Ma'am, can I grab two minutes?' she said. 'I think I might have something.'

Barnsdale indicated the seat beside her desk, but as Dani sat down the door at the top of the room burst open.

'We've got her and she's safe!' called Chief Inspector Freeman. A cheer swept across the room, more in relief than celebration. 'Ten minutes ago, Madeline Wilson staggered into the Sun Inn, a small pub in a tiny village outside Nottingham. Bruised and beaten, she collapsed on the floor but staff in the pub were able to bring her around pretty quickly. Paramedics have now taken her into the ...' Freeman checked her iPad for the details, '... the Queen's

Medical Centre where she'll stay for the next few days, largely for observation. Family can attend and I've spoken with her parents who, needless to say, are beyond thrilled. I'm heading up to Nottingham now.'

'Any news on where she was held, ma'am?' asked Mat Moore.

'Abandoned farm buildings, on the edge of the village. I'm still waiting on more details, but Nottinghamshire Police have discovered a dead body at the scene, apparently killed by gunshot wounds. Right now, we've no idea if that was her captor, or how her escape played out. All our focus must remain on apprehending the killer of Billy Monroe and Dennis Thackeray. Until we hear otherwise, we work on the basis that, whoever they are, they're still on our patch with two million quid of ransom money in tow.'

Dani watched Freeman exit the room. It was impossible not to be impressed by her command of the case and the manner in which she led her team.

'She thrives under pressure,' said Dani, turning back to Barnsdale.

'I guess that's why she runs the station.'

Dani agreed and tried to dismiss the thoughts bouncing around her mind. Why would Freeman put at risk everything she'd built?

'Something on your mind?' asked Barnsdale.

'Nothing, ma'am, but it'd be nice to get together next week.'

'I'm sure we could both do with a drink.'

Dani smiled, seeing the human side to her senior officer,

which Mat always refused to acknowledge. 'Shall we talk outside?'

'Agreed,' said Barnsdale. 'You can be sure in here somebody'll be bloody listening.'

At the back of the station car park was an old bus shelter, still used by a few colleagues for an occasional cigarette.

'I'm sorry the way your birthday's turned out,' said Dani, sitting beside Barnsdale in the nicotine-stained shelter.

Barnsdale shook her head. 'Can't be helped.'

'I wanted to say, ma'am, what you said to me outside Mailer's, about my private life being my own and nobody at the station learning anything from you, well, the same goes for me.'

'Thank you,' replied Barnsdale, 'I appreciate that, although I'd imagine with PC Cooke the cat is well and truly out of the bag.'

Dani smiled. 'Karen does have a reputation.' She paused. 'Any thought of giving Phil Doorley the benefit of the doubt? Talking to him, just now, I'm sure he is telling the truth, if that's any comfort.'

Barnsdale shifted in her seat. 'At the very best he committed an enormous error of judgement.'

'Perhaps he did, but it was fourteen years ago. Surely, that's worth a conversation.'

'I doubt we'll be speaking again.'

'He cares about you.'

Barnsdale held her hand to her face. 'Our job is to follow process,' was all she said.

'Yes, ma'am,' replied Dani. She reported her conversation

with Doorley, the party a week before Welsby's death and Welsby's altercation with the chemistry teacher, Harry Eden.

'That's good work,' said Barnsdale. 'You believe all Phil told you?'

'I've no reason not to.'

'Seven days after that party, Aaron Welsby was dead. I need to speak to Harry Eden.'

CHAPTER 74

Barnsdale pulled into a small 1980s cul-de-sac of carefully maintained homes. Windows were polished clean and bright, while plastic window frames ensured there was no unsightly peeling paintwork. She stopped against the curb and followed the narrow pavement to number five. The house number was clearly visible, painted on a large, grey stone, which nestled in a small flowerbed. Bright green ivy clambered up the side of the neat link house, where window boxes and a hanging basket completed the floral array.

Standing outside the home's wooden front door, its metal handle brilliantly polished, Barnsdale heard bright voices chattering inside. She leaned forward, peering through the front window's half-drawn blinds. Warmly lit, the room felt safe and secure. Two children, both under ten, sat together on a small sofa, transfixed by the cartoons playing on television. A third child, perhaps two years old, no more than three, eagerly ate pieces of fruit carefully handed to her by her mother. Unconsciously, Barnsdale touched the palm of her hand to the window. The entrance into the room by a tall, curly haired man caused her to step back quickly. She stood at the front door, smoothed her hair, pulling it tight at the back of her head, and knocked firmly. It was the man who opened the door.

'Mr Eden? Mr Harry Eden?' she enquired of the bespectacled man she'd seen enter the living room. He nodded and in response she briefly introduced herself. 'I was hoping I might be able to have a quick word,' she continued.

Uncertain, he took a step forward. A look of fear and dread covered his face. It was a look she'd seen a thousand times before.

'It shouldn't take long,' she added, 'just a few brief enquiries.'

'Has something happened at the school?' he asked. 'I had no idea I was on call – the heads of department rotate the responsibility of being the weekend contact, but I lose track. It's not one of the boys, is it?'

She saw the concern on his face. 'No, nothing like that, sir,' she reassured him.

'That's a relief,' he replied. 'It's chemistry I'm head of, at Twickenham Dukes school.' It was something of which she was already fully aware.

'I can assure you it's not related to your current school,' she replied. 'In fact, I'm investigating an incident related to your former school.'

He shook his head. 'It'll be more than a decade since I left Haddley Grammar. I doubt I can be of any use to you.' He took a step back inside his house.

'The incident I'm investigating is a historic one. Perhaps it might be easier if we speak inside?'

346

'My wife,' he said, hesitantly. 'My wife and three children,' he continued, gesturing towards the living room.

'Perhaps we could speak in the kitchen?'

'I'm not sure.'

'Harry, what is it?' came a faint voice from inside the house.

He turned his head. 'It's nothing to worry about,' he replied, 'a school matter. I won't be more than a couple of minutes.'

'Mr Eden, I need to speak with you now,' said Barnsdale, adopting a firmer tone. 'If you prefer, we can speak out here, but I will need some answers.'

Eden pulled his front door closed. 'Let's walk over the road,' he said.

Barnsdale followed him until they stood outside a single-storey garage, its door painted royal blue.

'I saw on the news about Billy Monroe's murder.'

She was surprised by his directness. 'You knew him?'

'No.'

'But you did know Aaron Welsby?' She looked at his face, now illuminated by the security light attached to the garage. When the front door of a neighbouring house slammed closed, his eyes darted sideways. 'We can talk here, or we can move to an interview room at Haddley police station?' It was a phrase Barnsdale knew nearly always guaranteed the response she desired.

'Yes, I knew Aaron.'

'And you left Haddley Grammar soon after his death?'

'I left more than a year later.' She could hear the dryness in his throat.

'But you left because of Aaron?'

'No.'

She said nothing and waited.

'A new opportunity arose, one which was too good for me to turn down. And yes, maybe I was looking for a fresh start.'

'Mr Eden, can you tell me what happened between you and Mr Welsby?'

'Detective, my wife is the new minister at St Stephen's Church on Haddley Common. We're moving into the vicarage in a couple of weeks' time.'

A child's eyes briefly peeked through the blinds at the front of the Eden house, before rapidly disappearing again. Only now did Barnsdale notice the *sold* sign standing in the garden.

'Mr Eden, I'm investigating a double murder. I need to understand Aaron Welsby's state of mind directly before his death.'

Eden remained silent.

'Perhaps I can help you. You were pursuing Aaron Welsby.'

'Hardly,' he replied.

'You were lovers?'

'We were friends. There was very little more to it than that.'

'Tell me about the party, a week before Aaron was killed.'

Eden sighed. 'Yes, there was a party. We argued and I pushed him. He cut his lip. But it was a stupid quarrel about something and nothing. You can't think because of that—'

'Why don't you tell me what happened after you pushed Mr Welsby?'

'He left, walked up to Haddley Hill Park to clear his head.

I followed him. It was a foolish argument and I wanted to apologise.'

'And did you, apologise?'

'I caught up with him in the park.' He paused. 'I persuaded him to come back to my place.'

'And after that?

'Aaron had left his jacket at the party. He said there was no point us both going back. It would take him no more than ten minutes and then he'd come on to mine.'

Under the garage light, Eden turned his eyes to Barnsdale's. 'He never showed.'

CHAPTER 75

In the tiny kitchen, tucked away at the far end of the CID room, Dani brewed herself a mug of tea. She took two biscuits from the barrel the officers shared and thought she must put some money into the collection pot.

Back at her desk, she logged into the social media accounts of the five women she believed the intruder had definitely targeted. With the sixth, Sarah Wright, Dani still remained unsure. Posts on Facebook by the first two victims did share some similarity. The first boasted of a new pair of Jimmy Choos. The second bemoaned her husband's lack of romance in sending her a pizza oven for her fortieth birthday. Neither was short of money, or possessions, but she couldn't find any other link. The next three women each had Facebook accounts, but one was dormant and the other two posted very rarely. Only one of the five women used Twitter, and all she ever did was share the comments of other people. Trawling through hundreds of images on Insta, she found nothing to tie the women together.

Sipping on her tea, she absent-mindedly flicked through

pictures taking her back almost three years. Among the random assortment of photos, she had no idea what she was looking for until an image posted by the fourth woman to fall victim of the intruder jumped out at her. Fifteen months earlier, the woman had posted pictures of her new Beauty Box subscription. Facial oils, butter hand cream and shower foam. All now delivered monthly. And on the same date each month.

She looked up from her desk and saw Karen Cooke walking towards the kitchen.

'Karen,' she called. 'Four of the victims received deliveries to their homes directly before the intruder break-ins.'

'How near?' she replied, coming to stand beside Dani's desk.

'From what I can see, one or two days at most.'

'Opening their front door, receiving a parcel; an absent-minded and unguarded conversation.'

'Very quickly, he has all the information he needs.'

'Without them ever realising,' said Cooke.

'But I can find nothing to link last week's victim, Shannon Lancaster. She rarely posts on social. Can you call her and find out if she received any deliveries in the two days before her attack?'

'I'll do it now.'

Dani reached for her car keys. 'I'm going to see Sarah Wright. After you've spoken to Shannon Lancaster, can you call the four other victims? Confirm they received a delivery in the forty-eight hours before the break-in. And ask who the delivery firm was.'

CHAPTER 76

Harry Eden walked quickly across the road before stopping in the garden at the front of his home.

'Mr Eden, we're not done,' said Barnsdale.

'I've told you all I know. I didn't see Aaron again.'

'Not at all?' asked Barnsdale, standing beside him.

'Detective, it's Sunday evening. My kids have school in the morning.' He turned and glanced towards his home. 'I should be helping my wife get them into bed.'

'Your evening will be much longer if you have to spend it in a police interview room.'

Eden sighed. 'The following week I saw Aaron in town. We only spoke very briefly. He told me the sports pavilion was built. He was moving on to a new project in St Marnham, a restaurant, I think.'

Barnsdale nodded. 'What else did you say?'

'I asked him what had happened on Saturday night, why didn't he show. All he did was shrug and walk away.'

'That was it? You didn't go after him?'

'No, it wasn't that kind of relationship. If he was done, so was I.'

'And after that?'

'A couple of days later, I saw him again, standing outside the school gates. He caught my attention as he was talking to a girl from year ten. It seemed an odd thing for him to be doing. It wasn't as if he was on the teaching staff.'

'Did you recognise the girl?'

'When I left the party to follow Aaron up to the park, there was a group of kids hanging around outside. Phil Doorley packed most of them off home, but a few laughed it off and stayed.'

'And the girl you saw Aaron with at the school gates was one from outside the party?'

'Yes.'

'I need her name.'

Eden shook his head and pushed his hands deep into his pockets.

'On the night of the party, after he left you in the park, I must understand what happened when Aaron went back to the house. I need a name.'

Eden brought his hand to his mouth. 'My grandmother lived her whole life in Limerick. I spent my childhood summers chasing along the banks of the River Shannon. The girl's name always stuck with me – Shannon Lancaster.'

CHAPTER 77

Hearing the news of Madeline's escape, Sam and Annabel were suddenly thirty years younger. Passers-by must have thought we were drunk; the three of us hugging and crying in the street. For me, the sense of relief felt so intoxicating, it was almost as if we were. Together, Sam and Annabel hurried back to her red Mercedes, their faces alight with pure joy, before racing away to be at their daughter's side.

Exhilarated, I walk through Finchley's Victoria Park. I've promised to join Sam and Annabel in Nottingham tomorrow. Madeline is safe but somebody worked with Billy Monroe, before killing both him and Dennis Thackeray. Something Ethan Harris told me yesterday, in Wolverhampton, keeps bouncing around my head.

His brother found him a girl.

Said to me in such a matter-of-fact manner, it's something I'm struggling to dismiss. Sebastian Chapman was nothing if not convincing this afternoon. When he told us he hadn't seen Billy for the past two decades, I believed him. But somebody is lying.

I message Min.

I need another favour.

Why wouldn't you? It's past seven o'clock on a Sunday evening.

Sorry. Can you find the names of all Billy Monroe's visitors while he was in Winson Green?

As I said, it's Sunday night.

Please!

Leave it with me.

I owe you.

You already do!

Leaving the park, I'm delighted to find a local Indian restaurant happy to serve me with a cup of coffee on a quiet Sunday evening. A waiter brings me a double espresso. He tells me his restaurant serves the best chilli paneer in London, before trying to persuade me to order a serving, along with a mushroom bhaji. Although briefly tempted, I politely decline.

My phone buzzes. I grab hold of it and as the waiter steps away, I answer without looking at the screen.

'Min, you're amazing.'

'It's me,' replies Dani.

'Hey, I'm sorry,' I say. 'I was waiting for some information.'

'I don't think I want to know.'

'Brilliant news about Madeline,' I say.

'You were lucky, Ben.'

'Let's be happy she's safe,' I reply. 'Where are you?'

'Outside your house.'

'Really? Can you stay tonight?'

'I definitely should go home at some point, but as there are no lights on, I'm guessing you're not home?'

'Are you checking up on me?'

'I'm on my way to see Sarah Wright.' Dani tells me of her breakthrough in the intruder case.

'Be careful,' I say.

'Always am,' she replies, adopting the phrase I often use with her. 'I thought you might have headed up to Nottingham?'

'I'll go tomorrow. I thought it'd be nice for Sam and Annabel to see her first. Everything I did was for them, and Madeline.'

'I know,' she replies. 'I should ask you what you're up to now, but I'm afraid of what your answer might be.'

There's a nervousness in my laugh. 'Who says I'm up to anything?'

'I've just come off a call with Barnsdale,' Dani tells me. 'During Madeline's escape, a man was killed. Nottinghamshire Police have identified him as Tosh Monroe.'

She explains to me how Tosh Monroe's arrival at the

deserted farm buildings allowed Madeline to flee. On entering the room where she was held, Monroe became embroiled in a struggle with her captor. 'He was shot in the face with his own gun.'

'God, no,' I reply, thinking of the lifetime of sadness the old man had endured.

'Whoever killed him fled the scene,' she tells me.

'That was what, two, three hours ago? Did he leave with the gun?' I ask.

'Yes.' Dani pauses. 'Whatever you're doing, Ben, promise me you'll be careful.'

'Always am,' I reply. 'I love you,' I say, but she's already disconnected the line.

I look down at my phone and see a message from Min. Billy's list of visitors has proved easier to access than she expected. The list is short, but I still have to read the names twice over.

CHAPTER 78

Dani Cash sat in Sarah Wright's makeshift living room and watched her flop down into her cushioned sofa.

'This time, I think he really is down,' said Sarah, after putting her son Max to bed for a third time.

'Does he ever stop?' asked Dani.

'Never, but I wouldn't have it any other way.'

Dani smiled. 'It must get tough on your own?'

'All I've ever really known. James left me during the first year of our marriage to set up home with a twenty-two-year-old law student. Now she's thrown him out, he's decided he wants to take more of an interest in Max.'

'Are you and James in a better place?'

'I hated him when we split, but then I realised it's pointless being angry for ever. Now, I simply don't care. But I'm pleased for Max.'

'Any hope of a future reconciliation?'

'God no, not a chance in hell.' From beside her on the sofa, Sarah reached for her iPad. 'You wanted me to check for deliveries?'

'Anything in the forty-eight hours before your first break-in.'

'Tuesday or Wednesday last week?' replied Sarah, flicking through her screen. 'Nothing. Both days I worked late as I had to prep for a court hearing. After school, Max stayed with friends across the common.'

'And in the week before?'

'There's sure to have been the odd thing. Max always needs something. I bought him a new football shirt, but it didn't fit properly. Any deliveries to the house, though, the builders would have signed for. If I'm honest, it's pretty rare for me to be at home during the day.'

Dani's phone rang. 'Can I take this?'

'Go ahead,' replied Sarah, and Dani stepped out onto the landing.

'Karen, hi,' she said, answering her phone, while keeping her voice low so as not to wake Max.

'All five women, including Shannon Lancaster, received a delivery in the twenty-four hours before the intruder break-in,' said Cooke. 'And the delivery was from the same firm.'

'PDQ?' asked Dani.

'Every time.'

'Thanks for your help,' she replied, before adding, 'That's great work.'

Sarah Wright appeared on the landing and Dani followed her downstairs, stopping at her front door.

'Are you absolutely certain you haven't signed for a delivery from PDQ in the last week?'

'One hundred per cent. James was at school with Phil

359

Doorley. I think they were in the same class. They're still friends now. If something came from PDQ, I'd remember. Phil came to our wedding.'

Dani asked Sarah to remain vigilant in the days ahead but as she walked down the steps at the front of the house, she felt certain the intruder was in her sights. Crossing the narrow lane that ran between the row of Victorian villas and the common, she stopped. At the far end of the lane, in an unlit corner where the road petered out into a footpath, she saw a familiar black Range Rover. Walking towards the vehicle, she could see the driver still sat inside. She approached the car and tapped on the window.

'Good evening, sir,' she said to James Wright as he lowered the window. 'Is there any reason you're waiting here?'

'Free country.' Dani raised her eyebrows before Wright continued. 'I saw your car parked outside my wife's house, so I thought it best if I wait.'

'Would you mind stepping out of the car?'

'Why?'

'Mr Wright, please step out of the car.'

He did as requested, leaning back against his vehicle.

'Of course, she isn't your wife,' said Dani, picking up on his previous comment.

'You know what I mean.'

'No, I don't. Why don't you explain?'

'Detective, we might be divorced but we're still close.'

'Really?' replied Dani. 'I wonder if that's more in your imagination.'

'What the hell's that to do with you?'

'It has everything to do with me if, as I suspect, you broke into your former wife's home.' When Wright turned away and reached for the car door, Dani caught hold of his wrist. 'I could arrest you now.'

'And I'd have my legal team on you for wrongful arrest before you made it back to the station.'

'After both break-ins at your ex-wife's property, you appeared on the scene incredibly fast.'

'I've no idea what you're talking about, and even if I did enter the house, I can see my son whenever I choose.'

'That's Mrs Wright's home, not yours. You're divorced.' She watched Wright edge nervously away from her. 'This is not a domestic. This is you breaking and entering. You used the spate of intruder break-ins to carry out a copycat crime against your ex-wife.' He offered no response, but feeling certain she was right, Dani pressed on. 'You set out to ter-rify your former wife, creating maximum fear to give you the opportunity to come riding to the rescue. My guess is somehow you thought you'd worm your way back into her life as some half-baked hero.' He opened his car door, but she slammed it closed. 'You deliberately scared your own son. What kind of father are you? You make me sick.'

'You can't prove any of that.'

'I don't need to,' replied Dani. 'All I have to do is tell Mrs Wright that you're scum.'

CHAPTER 79

The only money I have in my pocket is a twenty-pound note. I throw it down onto the table and run out of the door of the Indian restaurant. I sprint through the gates at the front of Victoria Park, race past the tennis courts and approach the trees at the back of the park. There, I light my phone and make my way through to the exit. On the far side of the park, residential streetlamps start to guide my way. Only when I stand at the end of Chislehurst Avenue do I slow to catch my breath.

I walk up the road and stop again outside the home of Sebastian Chapman. When I look up at his first-floor flat, I see a dim light illuminating the small kitchen. With the blind now open, I stand and watch him feed a bottle to his young son. Chapman turns in my direction. For a fleeting moment I think he might see me, but his young child quickly recaptures his attention. I cross onto the pathway at the front of his home and press the doorbell. Impatiently, I ring a second time, holding the button down. When I hear the door from his flat open, I take a step forward.

Still holding his son, his greeting does not attempt to hide his surprise at my rapid return. I explain that Madeline's safe, but I have more questions to which I urgently need answers. He invites me inside and I follow him back upstairs. Once again, we sit in his living room, his son feeding contentedly in his father's arms.

Suddenly it strikes me that the man sitting opposite me has no knowledge of his grandfather's death. At some point the police will track him down, but I need him to know the truth now.

'Tosh saved Madeline's life,' I conclude, after telling him of her escape from the farm buildings.

His son dozes contentedly in his arms. 'There is so little I can remember of him,' he says, 'but I can remember Gotham. He'd take us most Sundays for lunch, and we'd look for Batman upstairs at the pub. After lunch, we'd run in the farmer's fields. Billy had a kite.' He pauses. 'Because of what Billy did, I was ashamed of him. Ashamed of Billy, and somehow ashamed of my grandfather. I saw photographs of him at Billy's trial. I hate to admit it, but I wanted no part of him. I could've reached out later, told him about Noah, but I never did.'

'You've got your own family now,' I reply, feeling the need to offer some reassurance.

'Even so, I'd like to arrange his funeral, when his body's released. I owe him that much.'

I lean forward, sitting on the edge of the blue striped sofa. 'I still need to understand more about your family,' I say. Sebastian waits for my question. 'You and Billy were your mother's only children?'

363

'Yes,' he replies.

'You're absolutely certain?'

'Billy was born when she was very young, then it was me and she died not long after. It definitely was just me and Billy.'

'And soon after your mother's death, you were both adopted by the Elliot-Taylor-Chapmans?'

'Yes, until Billy was returned to social services.'

'Did your adoptive parents have any other children?' I ask.

'Yes, our other *brother* was their natural son.'

I exhale. 'Of course.'

'We were adopted once they'd learned they couldn't have any more kids. My mother suffered multiple miscarriages.'

'Your other brother? Did you get on well with him?'

'I was the little kid his mother fussed over. From the moment we arrived, he made a point of taking very little interest in me. Our worlds never really collided. We ate our meals together and that was about it. For a long time, he had the bedroom at the end of the hallway. When I arrived at the house, we had to share a bathroom. He'd make me wait outside even when I was desperate to pee. I hated him for that and thought he was weird, but then again, I was only five years old.'

'And Billy?'

'He was three years older than Billy. Any time they spent together was very much on his terms, never Billy's. Like I said, Billy would do anything to make people like him. That cost him from the start. He ended up in all kinds of trouble that wasn't his making.'

'Could he and Billy have stayed in contact, after your parents gave Billy up?'

Sebastian shrugs. 'I can't see how, but I guess it's not impossible. Billy didn't have many friends. He was easily taken in.'

'When did you last see him, your other brother?'

'At my parents' funeral. He gave the eulogy. We chatted for a few minutes. The last I'd heard he'd been working as a geography teacher in a south London school, but by the time I saw him at the funeral he had his own business, some kind of delivery firm. I think he's doing well.'

I flick on my phone and look again at my last message from Min. 'Do you know if he changed his name?'

'We laughed about that at the funeral. We'd both done the same thing. He told me as a teacher with a name like our parents', his life wouldn't have been worth living. He'd made the change before he started work. Hating our name was about the only thing we had in common.'

I glance down at my phone before looking back at Sebastian. 'Your brother is Dominic Taylor.'

CHAPTER 80

Lesley Barnsdale sat in a cramped, steam-filled kitchen in East Haddley.

'You don't mind if I don't sit down?' said Shannon Lancaster, straining a pan of pasta before running it under the cold tap. 'I've my mother-in-law coming for dinner in twenty minutes, and I need to get this in the oven.' She looked over her shoulder at Barnsdale. 'Ex-mother-in-law, I should say.'

'No, you carry on,' she replied. Shannon Lancaster had proved surprisingly easy to track down. A resident of Haddley her whole life, she'd never taken her former husband's surname. 'Were you married long?' she asked.

'Divorced longer,' replied Shannon. 'Two kids before I was twenty, and then we separated the following year. That was eight years ago. Mother-in-law's the only thing of his I kept. She takes my two girls every other weekend as well as cooking for them here most nights, when I'm working. Most days she's here more than me. Sometimes you'd think she bloody lived here. You married?' she asks.

'No,' replied Barnsdale.

'My advice is stay that way.' She opened the fridge and grabbed two packets of bacon. 'I'm assuming you're here about the intruder? Have to say you're all very keen. I only just got off the phone from another one of your lot.'

'Really?' said Barnsdale, puzzled by the woman's comment.

'Asking if I'd had a delivery or something. I told her I probably did but it would have been my mother-in-law who answered the door. I gave the officer her number.'

'Oh, no, sorry,' replied Barnsdale, trying to piece together what the woman was telling her, and only now remembering the woman's name as the last victim of the intruder. 'I'm not here about the intruder,' she said. 'He broke into your house last weekend?'

'Woke up with that freak standing over my bed,' said Shannon, 'when the girls were away at their grandma's for the night. Your officer thought he must have known I was home alone. I said the way my mother-in-law talks he'd have known my bloody life story.' The hot oil in her frying pan began to spit and Shannon tossed in the chopped bacon. 'I flew at him and when I grabbed at his mask, he made a run for the door. Even so, I'm sleeping with a carving knife under my bed until you catch him.'

'I can assure you we are making progress. We're very grateful for all of the information you've shared, but I actually came to talk to you about something very different.' Getting to her feet, she stood by the sink.

'Please, not one of the girls?' replied Shannon. 'Jess is twelve this year and she's already turning into a right little bugger.'

'No, nothing like that. Actually, it's something from when you were much younger.'

'Bloody hell, you're not doing me for nicking sweets from Mr Nowak's Mini Market?' She reached for the glass of wine she kept topped up on the windowsill. 'If you are, it's Jason Brearley you should be after, not me. He lifted a packet of fags while Alan Powell distracted the girl on the checkout by dropping his trousers.' Barnsdale couldn't help but laugh. Shannon smiled and said, 'Perhaps Alan Powell's your intruder. He never could keep his pants on.'

Shannon continued to busy herself with dinner preparations. Feeling as if she was getting in her way, Barnsdale sat back at the table.

'Do you remember the case of Aaron Welsby?' she asked.

'The murdered gay guy?'

'Yes,' she replied.

'Horrible.'

'He worked on a project at Haddley Grammar School. I'm guessing you'd have been a pupil there at the time?' Shannon nodded. 'Did you ever meet him?'

'No reason I would.' She stole a glance in Barnsdale's direction before quickly turning back to stir her pans.

'No, but I think you might have at least spoken to him.'

The woman said nothing and crossed back to the fridge. Barnsdale watched her open the door and stare inside. Shannon reached for a carton of milk that she didn't seem to need.

'It was all a long time ago,' she said. From a cupboard above the washing machine, she pulled out a stack of plates.

'Billy Monroe, the man convicted of killing Aaron Welsby is dead. Murdered.'

Shannon put the plates down on the table. 'He killed that poor bloke. If you ask me, it's good news if he's dead.'

'We don't think Billy Monroe acted alone. We think somebody else wanted Aaron dead.'

Shannon went back to the hob and turned off the heat. 'I guess dinner can be a few minutes late,' she said, before pulling out a chair from beneath the small table.

'Seven days before Aaron's murder, there was a party,' said Barnsdale.

Shannon leaned back in her chair, dropping her head back and staring at the ceiling. 'Bloody cracks,' she said, sighing.

'You were outside the party, drinking.'

'Me, Jason Brearley, Alan Powell and my best mate Kaitlin. A few others but they all scattered when Mr Doorley told them to scram.' She smiled at Barnsdale. 'Even now, whenever I see him out delivering, I still call him Mr Doorley.'

'What happened at the party?'

'Mr Taylor, although he liked us to call him Dominic, came outside when almost everyone else had gone home.'

Barnsdale squeezed her hands together. 'Dominic Taylor who works at PDQ?'

'Yes,' she replied. 'It was his party, his house.'

'He was a teacher at Haddley Grammar?'

'Yes, geography, same as Mr Doorley. That's how they met. His wife was away, staying at her parents for the weekend. I saw her not long afterwards, outside Tesco. She was heavily pregnant, poor cow. The four of us went inside with Dominic. There was a load of leftover beer in the kitchen.'

'How old were you?' asked Barnsdale.

'Fourteen. One of the boys might've been fifteen. Kaitlin and I, we'd no interest in drinking beer. I couldn't stomach the taste, still can't if I'm honest. Dominic said he'd find something else for us; orange juice, with a load of bloody vodka.'

'And then what happened?'

'One of the boys, Alan I think, threw up in the sink. Always the boys who couldn't hold their drink. Jason took him out into the backyard for some air. The kitchen stank so Dominic suggested we move into another room. Kaitlin and I could barely stand. We followed him upstairs.' Leaning forward, Shannon crossed her legs and ran her hand up and down her shin.

'I need to know what happened,' said Barnsdale, dropping her voice.

Shannon shook her head. 'I can't,' she replied.

'You were children.' Shannon folded her arms on the table and rested her head. Barnsdale gently touched her arm. 'Please,' she said. 'You can help me stop him.'

'He had a pill. I don't know what it was, acid or MDMA. He broke it in two and gave us half each. He undressed us. We were naked in bed when Aaron Welsby walked in. He was looking for his jacket.' She lifted her face and held it in her hands. 'Can you believe that? Our clothes were in a pile on the floor and all I can remember thinking is, *you won't find your bloody jacket in there.* Dominic jumped off the bed, grabbed him around the throat and rammed him up against the wardrobe. He said he was a fucking queer and if he ever told anyone what he'd seen, he'd kill him.'

'And you never told anyone?'

'Kaitlin and I were both terrified. We'd done drugs and a whole lot more with a teacher. We felt certain we'd be expelled if anyone ever found out.'

'The following week, a witness observed you talking to Aaron Welsby. What did he say?'

'He told me none of what'd happened was our fault, that he'd do everything he could to keep our names out if it, but he had no choice but to report what he'd seen.'

'What did you do?'

'I begged him not to say anything. And then I told Dominic.'

CHAPTER 81

Sitting in her car at the side of Haddley Common, Dani Cash waited until she saw James Wright disappear into the traffic on the Lower Haddley Road. The man had used fear in an attempt to coerce his ex-wife back into a relationship with him. He repulsed Dani. He was, however, right in the fact she lacked any direct evidence to arrest him. All she could do was return in the morning and speak to Sarah. She hoped, after that, James Wright's perverse grasp on family life would crumble around him.

She drove away from the common and weaved her way through Haddley's side streets before emerging on Haddley Hill. The late Sunday evening traffic was light and, minutes after driving across the heath, she approached the barrier at the entrance to the PDQ warehouse. This time the woman in the gatehouse recognised her instantly and Dani drove straight through. On the far side of the barrier, she stopped. About to walk back to the security hut, she saw her phone buzz on the passenger seat. It was Ben. The day, which had started with her sitting on his garden wall, felt endless. How she wished she was curled up with him on his sofa, sipping a glass of her favourite Gavi Italian wine. But she pushed away her fatigue. The intruder was within her reach. She leaned across and clicked off her phone.

'I wonder if you can help me,' she said to the security guard, who opened the gatehouse door as soon as she approached. 'I need information on a number of deliveries made in Haddley over the past three years.'

'Dispatch is your best bet, but they'll be gone for the night. It is Sunday evening, you know.'

Dani smiled. 'You and I are still working.'

The woman laughed. 'Too bloody right.'

'There isn't anyone else inside who might be able to help me? It is quite urgent.'

The woman pinched her lips. 'Well, Mr Taylor came in not much more than fifteen minutes ago. You say it's important?'

'Yes,' she replied.

'I bet he could do something.'

'That would be great if he could.'

The woman handed her a swipe card. 'Take this. It'll get you into the building. I'll message Mr Taylor and let him know you're on your way up. His office is up the stairs, first door on the left.'

Waving a quick thank you, Dani walked briskly up to the main building and found her way inside. At the top of the metal staircase, she stopped outside Dominic Taylor's office before tapping on the door.

'Mr Taylor,' she called, pushing open the door.

Wearing a bright red sweatshirt with the letters PDQ emblazoned across his chest, Taylor sat behind his desk. She introduced herself and, apologising for the late hour, explained the information she was looking for.

'Shouldn't be too difficult,' he replied.

Dani looked around the windowless room. The office was very different from Phil Doorley's. With no expansive rear windows, it felt claustrophobic. At the back of the room was a metal door, which she presumed led directly down onto the warehouse floor.

'Do you have the customer names and addresses?' he asked.

Dani confirmed she did.

'Let me log on here,' he said, using one hand to type his password. 'I have to head downstairs, make certain everything's secure for the night, but use this screen for as long as you need. If you enter the customer's surname and the first line of their address, it'll bring up the delivery time, date and the driver's initials. It's a simple system. If I can use it, anyone can.' Smiling, he stepped around his desk before opening the door at the back of the room. 'I'll leave you to it,' he said, letting the door swing closed behind him.

She sat down in front of Taylor's screen and, behind her, she heard him run down a metal staircase. She looked at the flashing cursor before finding the first name on her phone. She typed the woman's name followed by the first line of her address and hit enter.

Nothing.

She hit the escape key and, realising she'd entered both the woman's Christian and surname, typed only her last name and then her address. Instantly displayed was a list of deliveries to the woman's home. Alongside each was a set of dates and driver initials. She scanned the list, looking for the delivery date directly before the very first intruder attack. She noted the initials and typed the second victim's name. Then she typed the third and with a rush of adrenaline, the fourth and finally the fifth. The same initials for each delivery.

DTa.

Dani stood behind the desk, but rather than follow Taylor directly into the warehouse, she stepped out into the corridor and entered Phil Doorley's neighbouring office. From the rear window, she could look directly down onto the warehouse floor. She watched Taylor as he hauled two large black holdalls from the back of the warehouse, dragging them into the dispatch area. He opened a side door where she saw his car backed up to the exit.

Her mind racing, she moved away from the window and walked back into Taylor's office. Silently she followed the steps down into the warehouse. As she walked beside the winding conveyor belt, she felt the cool night air rushing in through the open door. Still keeping a distance from Taylor, she stood between three pallets of boxes and watched. Clearly in discomfort, he dragged the first holdall towards his open car. Audibly wincing, he lifted the bag into the boot and, when he turned, she moved forward.

'Mr Taylor,' she called, stepping out of the shadows. 'Can I have a word, please, sir?'

Ignoring her, he hurried back and grabbed the second bag.

'Mr Taylor,' she called, again.

He struggled to lift the bag into his car. Dani walked quickly forward. 'Looking at your records, it would appear a single driver made each of the five deliveries I'm investigating.'

His back to Dani, his attention remained on the boot of his car, pushing one holdall forward to make room for the second.

'According to your system, the initials of that driver are DTa.' Dani stepped inside the dispatch area. 'Unless you have another employee with the same initials, I'm going to need you to come to the station with me to answer some questions.'

Taylor stopped. Dani took a step back but as she did, he turned to face her. Gripped tight in his hands was a shotgun, his finger pressed against the trigger.

Ten

*'And a deadly sound reverberates
throughout the warehouse.'*

Four days after the death of his parents, he employed a house-clearance company to dispose of their lifetime's possessions. There was little of real worth, and not a single item of sentimental value, so he wanted it done quickly. If it wasn't for the need to engage an estate agent, he would never have returned to his childhood home.

The second agent he saw quoted the highest price and he employed him instantly. He promised him a cash bonus if he disposed of the house in under eight weeks. He was desperate for the money.

Alone, he roamed through the empty building. He discovered few, if any, fond memories. He followed the stairs up to the loft room, and it was here he recalled his greatest pleasures. The year after Billy's departure, his parents converted the space for him. His reward for doing well at school. With its own bathroom, new windows and sliding door out onto a small balcony, the room was unrecognisable to the one occupied by Billy.

He slid the door open and stood outside. Although the oak trees at the end of the garden were more mature, he could still see into each of the neighbouring houses. Night after night, unseen, he would stand naked on the balcony watching the woman in the house at the back of the garden undressing. When she'd laid silently in her bed, he'd felt as if he could almost *reach out and touch her. The power had been all his. It was a sensation he couldn't shake. And leaving the house, Dominic knew he had to feel it again.*

CHAPTER 82

'Mr Taylor, I want you to lower the gun and place it on the ground in front of you.'

He laughed. 'Detective, you're not in a position to be giving me instructions.' He flicked the shotgun in the direction of the open warehouse door. 'Outside,' he said, an eerie calm in his voice.

Dani steeled herself. 'I'm going to ask you again,' she said. 'Lower your weapon, place it on the ground in front of you and slide it in my direction.'

'Fucking move!' he screamed. Taylor took two quick steps forwards, waving the shotgun erratically. Unarmed, Dani had no other choice. She edged slowly towards the open door, her eyes fixed on his. She knew Taylor was more than simply the intruder she'd been pursuing.

He moved behind her. 'Keep going,' he said. 'Out to the car.'

She felt a bead of sweat trickle down her spine. 'Mr Taylor, none of this is going to help you. I saw your initials against the deliveries to the five Haddley women. You broke into their homes and entered their bedrooms.'

'Shut up!' he replied. 'Those were for fun. Who cares about a few bloody break-ins? Are you really that stupid?'

'You killed Billy Monroe, didn't you?'

She felt the barrel of the shotgun press against her back. 'I said outside!'

Edging forward, ahead of her she saw the open boot of Taylor's car. Inside, she could see the first of the two large holdalls.

'Move that bag, all the way to the back.'

With the gun still held against her spine, she leaned into the car and pushed the bag deep inside the boot.

'Now the second one,' he said, kicking the black holdall with his trainer. Dani bent to pick it up.

'I can't lift it,' she said, feeling its weight. 'You'll have to help me.'

'Try harder,' he replied. She felt him drive the barrel of the gun deep into her lower back. She crouched down and using both hands was able to turn the bag onto its side. Then she pushed it upwards and somehow managed to wrestle the bag into the boot.

'Shove it back as far as you can,' he said. 'That's if you want to leave yourself some room for when you climb in.'

Terror flooded her body, but she told herself to remain calm. Pushing the bag further into the boot, she tried desperately to think. If he forced her inside, she was unlikely to come out alive.

'That's far enough,' he said. 'Plenty of room now. Stay where you are and put your hands behind your back.'

Leaning into the boot, Dani hesitated. She thought of

the handcuffs Taylor had dropped at the home of Shannon Lancaster.

'Now!' he yelled.

As she clasped her hands behind her back, Dani made her decision. She wasn't getting into the boot.

'Try anything stupid, and I'll kill you now.'

Taylor propped the shotgun up against the side of the car. He grabbed hold of her left wrist.

She had only one chance. She span around and crashed her boot into his knee. His leg buckled and he staggered backwards. He lunged for the gun.

Dani darted back inside. Running through the dispatch area, she re-entered the warehouse. Row upon row of pallets, each stacked with packages, helped fill the vast space. Scrambling along the floor, she ducked behind a pallet of parcels tagged for delivery the following day. She stayed low and kept moving, scampering behind a second pallet. She held her breath.

Then the shotgun exploded.

CHAPTER 83

I speed along the Chelsea Embankment, thankful for the quiet Sunday-evening traffic. Driving Sebastian Chapman's car, I race up the inside of a dawdling night bus before cutting through the industrial waterfront, long since converted into overpriced warehouse apartments. I reach again for my phone. For a third time, I hit Dani's number. Again, it goes straight to her voicemail. I leave another message, this time more desperate, begging her to call me. On the King's Road, vast furniture shops remain illuminated long into the night. I take any route, again diving up the inside of traffic, weaving between cars, to get me back to Haddley in the shortest time possible.

A red light slows my approach to Haddley Bridge, but seeing the road is clear I accelerate through. Across the bridge, even on a Sunday night, traffic on the high street is slow. I veer into a side street and zigzag my way up Haddley Hill. Finally, the PDQ warehouse comes into view. At the entry barrier I'm forced to stop. With the gatehouse deserted, I pull the car to one side and grab my phone. Ahead of me,

I can see Dani's car. I call her number again, but when I look through her car window, I see her phone flashing on the passenger seat.

I slip my phone back in my pocket and move towards the pitch-black warehouse. At the main entrance, the sliding glass doors are locked for the night. I try to force them open, but they remain fast. Unable to find another way in, I follow the dimly illuminated path to the side of the building. I turn a corner and see a distant light shining through an open door. Backed up to the warehouse door is a black BMW, but I can see no signs of life. I'm about to follow the path to the door, when behind me car headlights appear at the warehouse entry barrier.

CHAPTER 84

'I've got to go, Mum,' said Lesley Barnsdale as she approached the barrier at the front of the PDQ warehouse. 'I promise I'll come up in the next couple of weeks and we'll have a proper celebration together.'

'You work too hard,' replied her mother.

'I know, Mum, I know. But I really do have to go now. I'll call you during the week. And thanks again for the lovely gift.'

Barnsdale killed her engine and reached for the torch she kept in her glove compartment. Crossing to the warehouse entrance, she saw a figure approaching from the side of the building. As he neared, she immediately recognised Ben Harper.

'Dani's inside the warehouse,' he said. 'There's a black BMW pulled up at the side of the building.'

'That's Dominic Taylor.'

'You think he killed Billy Monroe?'

'It's an ongoing investigation,' she replied.

'He's Monroe's brother.'

She tried to hide her surprise, but if Dani was inside with him, she knew her colleague was in danger. 'I'm calling for armed support,' she said. 'I'd ask you to move away from the building and return to the safety of your own vehicle.'

Harper took two steps back towards the building. She was about to stop him when the sound of an exploding shotgun echoed around the warehouse.

CHAPTER 85

When I hear the shotgun fire, I don't hesitate. I turn and sprint back towards the side of the building.

'Mr Harper, wait,' I hear Barnsdale call behind me.

I pass the corner of the warehouse and hurry down the side of the building. Light spills from the open door and I slow as I approach the black BMW. In the boot of the car, I see the two giant holdalls I dropped in the stairwell of St Marnham Bridge.

'Dani!' I shout through the open door. There is no reply. I step inside the entrance, and behind me, I hear Barnsdale's footsteps,

'Wait,' she says.

'Dani needs our help,' I reply, leaning forward and peering into the main warehouse.

Standing opposite me in the dispatch area, she nods.

'Can you see anyone?' she asks.

I shake my head.

Suddenly, inside the warehouse, a pallet of boxes tumbles

to the ground. Our eyes turn quickly, and we see a figure race across the floor.

Barnsdale takes a step forward, her hand outstretched towards me, telling me to stay where I am. 'Please,' she says, 'do as I say.'

Slowly, she walks into the warehouse. 'Mr Taylor,' she calls, 'this is Detective Sergeant Barnsdale of the Haddley Police.' She keeps moving forward until she stands in the centre of the warehouse, beside the snaking conveyor belt. She's exposed on all sides, and I can only admire her enormous bravery. 'Mr Taylor, put down your gun and show yourself.' I see her eyes dancing in every direction, searching for any sign of movement. There is no reply.

Barnsdale moves back towards the elevated office area at the far end of the warehouse. 'Mr Taylor,' she calls again. 'An armed response unit is on its way. Give yourself up now.'

Footsteps echo on the far side of the warehouse. Barnsdale darts to cover herself behind a row of pallets. 'DC Cash, are you hurt?' she calls into the open space.

'Not badly, ma'am,' shouts Dani in reply. My heart skips.

'Stay where you are,' replies Barnsdale.

A fleeting movement, halfway across the warehouse, catches my eye. I turn towards Barnsdale and raise my arm, pointing to a row of pallets. She presses her palm firmly in my direction and I remain still.

Barnsdale stays concealed behind a pallet stacked high with cardboard packages. Again, she calls Taylor's name but receives no response.

Another movement catches my eye. I slide sideways along

the warehouse wall. Looking down a third aisle, I see Dani crouched low, nursing her bloodied arm.

A crash echoes around the warehouse. Both Dani and I wheel around, desperately trying to understand the source. I turn quickly and see the metal door, leading from Dominic Taylor's office, thrown open. Standing at the top of the stairs, a security officer behind him, is Phil Doorley.

'Dom, this is crazy,' he yells. 'Give yourself up.'

CHAPTER 86

'Phil, no!' screams Barnsdale as he stands at the top of the stairs, hastily scanning the warehouse floor.

With all eyes drawn towards Doorley, I scramble along the row of pallets towards Dani.

'Dom, give yourself up. If you don't, you'll end up dead,' yells Doorley. He begins a slow descent of the stairs, his eyes searching for any sign of his business partner.

'Phil, stop, please,' calls Barnsdale, her arm raised, moving hurriedly towards him.

'Thank God, you're safe,' I whisper to Dani as I crouch beside her. 'Did you get hit?'

'Hardly a graze,' she replies. 'His shot ricocheted off the conveyor.'

'Where is he?'

In silence, she points to the far side of the warehouse, behind a giant sorting machine. I let go of her hand and press my finger to my lips. Staying hunched, I keep moving slowly forward.

'Ben, no,' she says, her voice quiet. 'Please wait for the armed support.'

'We need to stop him before he hurts anyone else.'

I crawl away, now moving faster, with the aim of positioning myself behind Taylor. When I creep to the back of the warehouse, for the first time I can see him. Hiding behind the metal sorter, he has what must be Tosh Monroe's shotgun trained in front of him. With one quick move I could be on his back but, holding my breath, I wait. If I jump forward now, both Dani and Barnsdale will be in his direct line of sight.

I slide backwards. Dani is looking down the narrow aisle, between stacked pallets. I lower my hand and in response she again crouches down. I point to Barnsdale and Dani turns, indicating to Barnsdale she should squat down. But Barnsdale's attention remains focused on Doorley.

'Phil, get down, please,' she says, but instead he leaps forward and vaults over the side of the staircase.

'He's there,' he shouts, pointing to the side of the warehouse where Taylor stays hidden. 'At the side of the sorter,' he shouts, before running towards him.

Barnsdale is quick to react. 'Phil, no,' she screams, throwing herself forward and knocking him to the ground.

Taylor fires the shotgun.

And a deadly sound reverberates throughout the warehouse.

THREE WEEKS LATER

CHAPTER 87

I snap a loose thread hanging from a button on my white shirt, and hastily run an iron over the sleeves and collar. For the third time in as many weeks I'm standing in front of my hallway mirror, knotting my tie and fastening the tight top button on my shirt. Yet it still feels strange. I reach for my suit jacket, left hanging at the foot of my stairs for the past week. I hope after today I can put my black suit away for a very long time.

Outside, a warm sun drenches the common on a bright spring morning. Colourful crocuses mix with a wash of daisies, covering the grass. I follow the footpath where daffodils stand sentry, forming a brilliant yellow corridor. I wait for a car to pass before I cross the narrow lane on the south side of the common. When I climb the steps at the front of Sarah Wright's home, I feel my black leather shoes rub against my heels.

'Morning,' says Sarah, opening her front door. She's dressed in a black paisley print dress. 'Are you still getting ready?'

With my shoes off, I'm sitting on the wall outside her door. 'My feet are bloody killing me,' I reply, rubbing my heels. 'It feels like I only ever wear these shoes for funerals.' She sits beside me on the wall as I loosen my laces. 'How are you doing?' I ask.

'I'm okay,' she replies, and her smile is warm.

'How's things with James?'

'Not easy, but I've decided he's still Max's father and I want them to have some kind of relationship, however limited that might be. If I was being generous, I'd say James is in a bad place. If I was being less generous, I'd say he was an absolute twat.' I smile and she continues. 'But I guess I knew that already and that's why I divorced him.' Haddley Police informed Sarah of the charges raised against Dominic Taylor for entering the homes of five women. However, there is no evidence to show he was responsible for the break-ins at her home. 'I cannot understand what was going through his head.'

'You spoke to him?' I ask, slipping on my shoes.

'For the first thirty seconds he tried to deny it. After that, he became super contrite and a bit pathetic. I'll never forgive him.'

'The police won't charge him?'

'Not without my support.' Fastening my laces, I raise my eyebrows, but Sarah shakes her head. 'In an ideal world he'd fuck off and I'd never see him again. But he's Max's father and, as Max gets older, he needs some kind of relationship with him. If he wants to keep seeing Max, James knows this is his last chance, but I don't want to create years of animosity between them. That would be no good for Max. I've tried to convince myself this was a supercharged midlife crisis.'

'I hope James knows how lucky he is. You could have ended his legal career.'

'I know,' she replies, shrugging, 'but what benefit would that have been to me?' I'm surprised how conciliatory Sarah is towards her ex-husband. She looks at me. 'Families are complicated, Ben. My job is to make sure his influence on Max's life is as good as it possibly can be.'

'How is Max?' I ask as we follow the steps down from the front of Sarah's house.

'Full of energy and a never-ending chatterbox. Thanks for spending time with him.'

'Chasing after the football is good exercise for me.' Along with my goddaughter, Alice, who lives with her mother, Holly, three doors away from mine, I spent much of Sunday afternoon playing football with Max on the common. Ending the game to visit the ice-cream van by the river was as much an excuse for me to have a rest as it was a treat for them. 'How was Nathan?'

'Doing well, really well,' she replies. Sarah travelled to Cowbridge at the weekend with Will. 'He's in a positive place and it's sure to be a big adventure for them both. It was nice to get the chance to say a proper goodbye.' At the end of the month, Nathan and Will are travelling to America, with Nathan enrolling at the law school of the University of Virginia. 'Whether I'd advise him to follow James and me into the legal profession I'm not sure, but I hope he has a wonderful time.'

'And Will?'

'From what he said to me, I doubt he'll be back this year. He wants to see Nathan settled, ensure he has the support he needs, and then he plans to travel. I think his marriage is over.'

Ahead of us, a new bell tower stands proudly above St Stephen's Church. In the last week, the removal of scaffolding revealed a restored structure and a gleaming new bell. Sarah and I cross the Lower Haddley Road and pass through the stone gates at the front of the church. The car park is already full, and with cars still arriving, drivers seek out spots in the narrow lane that neighbours the churchyard.

Outside the church, small groups congregate for fleeting conversations in hushed voices. Gradually, people drift inside, but Sarah and I wait until a chauffeur-driven black Mercedes stops at the front of the gates. The door to the front passenger seat opens immediately and Sam is climbing out almost before the car's come to a stop.

'Thank God you're here, Ben,' he says as we embrace with a hug and a slap on the back. 'She never shuts up. Ten days straight, it's all I've had. Sam, will you fetch this? Sam, why don't you walk down to the shops? Sam, do you really think that's wise? Sam, I'm not sure I'd do that. Sam, are you having *another* beer? Sam, Sam, Sam!'

'Only one more day,' I whisper in his ear. The last time I saw Sam was ten days ago at the funeral of Tosh Monroe in Nottingham. Sebastian Chapman was good to his word, arranging his grandfather's cremation as well as speaking briefly at the service of his own very earliest family memories. We shared a drink with him afterwards, all of us aware Madeline would not be alive today were it not for Tosh's actions. Two days later, following the funeral of Dennis Thackeray, Madeline's parents spirited her away on a family trip to Italy to aid her recovery. Before she left, we laughed when she told me of her dread of seven days trapped with Sam and Annabel. I told her all resistance was futile and to enjoy the fuss.

The rear door of the car opens and Annabel steps out. 'Sam, are you standing there chatting or are you helping Madeline?'

'Bite your tongue,' I say, quietly.

'On my way,' he replies, before hurrying around to the opposite rear door.

Annabel greets me with an air kiss and a brief hug. 'Ben, good to see you.' I briefly introduce Sarah.

'How was Lake Como?' she asks.

'Wonderful, and so good for Madeline to have a real break. Every time she tried to look at her phone, I was onto her. *No news!* I said, *Not here.*' Listening to Annabel, I smile and think how much my boss will have hated that. 'Of course, half the time she was scribbling away in her bloody notebook, but perhaps that might have been cathartic.' I know Madeline intends to write a feature article following Dominic Taylor's sentencing.

Madeline gently rests on her father's arm, her blonde curls scraped back from her face, sunglasses covering her eyes. When she walks through the churchyard gates, I hug her close and she whispers to me, 'I need to get back to the office. These two are driving me around the bloody bend.'

Grinning, I say, 'We can't wait to have you back.'

'Here, take my arm,' says Annabel.

'Mum, honestly, I'm fine.'

'Sam, can you grab my bag off the back seat?' says Annabel, dispatching her former husband back to the car. He quickly returns and together we walk up the gravel path at the front of St Stephen's. Stepping through the heavy oak door, inside the church is cool and the congregation quiet. Sunlight floods through the stained-glass window, illuminating a bright blue cross. We walk slowly down a side aisle before Sarah leads us into a pew in the middle of the nave. We shuffle across, Sam squeezing past Annabel to seat himself next to me. With his head twisting like a meerkat, he is never off duty.

'That's our MP,' he whispers in my ear as he briefly nods in the direction of a woman in a neighbouring pew. 'She should enjoy herself while she can because she'll be gone at the next election.'

'I'm not sure coming to a funeral is enjoying herself.'

'The wake's at Mailer's. She's the sort who'll be taking home a goody bag. And two rows in front of her, that's the council leader. She won't like sitting behind him.'

'She's lucky to get a seat at all,' I reply, turning around to see every pew now filled.

Sam elbows me in the ribs. 'Who've we got here?'

I turn back around. 'That's the new vicar. She replaced Adrian Withers,' I reply, as the Reverend Louise Eden stands beside the pulpit.

'Seems young?'

'Sam, everyone's young compared to you,' I reply. 'That's her husband, Harry, on the second row.'

'I hear on the grapevine he had a link to Aaron Welsby. Do you think he'll be called to give evidence at Taylor's trial?' he asks.

'Word is Taylor's pleading guilty, so probably not.'

Organ music fills the church and Reverend Eden invites us to stand. We turn and I bow my head as, in full dress uniform, Dani and PC Karen Cooke lead the pall-bearers carrying the coffin of Detective Sergeant Lesley Barnsdale.

CHAPTER 88

Detective Barnsdale's mother, Anne, walks directly behind the coffin. Dressed in a tailored black suit, a pillbox hat conceals her grey hair. A small veil partly covers her face, but her eyes remain fixed forward on her daughter's casket. Beside her is Phil Doorley, who I know has supported her enormously over the past three weeks. On the night of her daughter's murder, the security officer in the PDQ gatehouse called Phil to the site. From his upstairs office window, Phil saw Taylor sprint across the warehouse floor. His intervention, risking his own life, came with the intention of stopping Taylor taking further lives. Tragically, Lesley Barnsdale sacrificed her own life to save his. As they approach the front pew, Mrs Barnsdale takes hold of Phil's arm, and together they sit.

Following behind them is a procession of police hierarchy, led by Deputy Commissioner Dame Elizabeth Jones. Beside her is Chief Inspector Bridget Freeman, before Lesley Barnsdale's colleagues from the Haddley Police and representatives from stations across London. Dani and her fellow pall-bearers carefully rest the coffin in front of the altar, before respectfully stepping away. I chance a brief look in Dani's direction, and she raises her eyes to mine before taking her seat next to her husband. Today is a day for unity within the police force.

Reverend Eden leads us in prayers before we all join in the singing of 'Abide with Me'. When we sit, it is Haddley's senior officer who moves forward to the lectern to lead the tributes.

'We all knew Detective Sergeant Lesley Barnsdale as an officer of great professionalism, with an indisputable eye for detail, a sharp intelligence and a love of process.' Chief Inspector Freeman pauses as a gentle murmur passes among her colleagues. 'But she was also a hero of the most outstanding order.' Looking across the aisle I can see Dani touch away a tear as Freeman recounts events at the PDQ warehouse three weeks ago. On that night, unflinching in her duty, and perhaps with some devotion to Doorley, Barnsdale acted without a second thought. In the weeks following, her bravery has led many within the Haddley force, and some outside, myself among them, to reconsider their views of Detective Barnsdale.

'In giving her life in protection of the public,' continues CI Freeman, 'Lesley Barnsdale made the ultimate sacrifice. In serving with her, the honour was all mine.' She steps away from the lectern and standing in front of Barnsdale's coffin solemnly bows her head before returning to her pew. Dani moves into the aisle, and I watch Freeman slip her white-gloved hand into hers before retaking her seat. Bowing her head, Dani walks solemnly forward. Standing behind the lectern, the brave and beautiful woman who led the pallbearers into the church suddenly appears so fragile.

My stomach tightens. Every day for the past three weeks, I have thought of the shot that ricocheted off the warehouse conveyor before grazing Dani's arm. I wake in the night, paralysed with fear, convinced the final fatal shot hit Dani, not Barnsdale. When I sit up in bed and look at Dani sleeping beside me, I know how desperate I am to never let her go.

Dani turns towards Barnsdale's coffin, before moving back and facing the congregation. She lifts her hands to the lectern but still says nothing. Her words are prepared but I can see her still collecting her thoughts.

'DS Barnsdale acted as my supervising officer for the past three years.' There's a crack in Dani's voice and she stops. She closes her eyes. 'For three years,' she says, somehow summoning the strength to continue, 'she listened, she cared and was unflinching in her support.' Dani takes a deep breath. 'But she was also relentless in her desire to uncover the truth. Yes, she always followed process. No, she didn't go rogue.' Dani looks directly at me. 'She never flouted the rules but that made her no less determined to get results. And she was kind.' Dani stops and gently smiles at Anne Barnsdale. 'Following the knife attack on my husband and my extended period of leave, when I returned to work DS Barnsdale was the first to welcome me back, to take me back into the fold. Not with great banners and celebrations but by making me feel part of a team.' Dani looks directly at her husband. 'She made me feel like a police officer again, and not once,

404

never, did she question or doubt my abilities. I would not be standing here in front of you all today if it weren't for DS Lesley Barnsdale. Last year, she championed my move into CID, delighted at my success but always pushed me to achieve more.' Dani pauses, gathering her final thoughts. 'My one regret was not to know her more. We'd recently arranged, for the first time, to spend some time together, just two colleagues getting together after work. I know she was looking forward to it and so was I.' Dani takes a step towards Barnsdale's coffin and speaks directly to her. 'I saw you as someone I could trust, confide in. I will miss that, but I will always work in the honest manner you taught me. I'm sorry we never got to have our drink but today I will raise a glass to you. Goodbye, ma'am.'

CHAPTER 89

'Such a very special lady,' Łukasz Nowak tells me, as we stand on Mailer's riverside terrace. With the inside of the restaurant packed with members of the Metropolitan Police, I've made my way outside.

'You knew her well?' I ask.

'I was with her the very day she died,' he replies, reaching for a Thai shrimp. 'Her great skill,' he tells me, raising his finger, 'was she listened. She took what I told her and unravelled a complex crime.' He moves a step closer to me. Dropping his voice, he continues. 'It was me who led her to the school and all its horrors. But now, of course, I wish I hadn't.'

'You can't blame yourself, Mr Nowak,' I reply. 'Dominic Taylor was the criminal in this case. Everything happened because of him.' From the corner of my eye, I spot Madeline stepping out onto the terrace. 'You'll have to excuse me,' I say to Mr Nowak, 'my boss is after me.'

'I've escaped,' says Madeline, taking hold of my arm and leading me to a small table where the terrace narrows. 'Those two are driving me insane.'

'They mean well.'

'I'm sure they do,' she replies, removing her sunglasses for the first time. The deep purple bruise beneath her eye has faded, but the scars from where she required surgery on her nose remain raw. 'My mum spotted a property in Como so she's heading back tomorrow to sign the contract.'

'That'll be a relief to Sam.'

Madeline smiles. 'She runs him ragged, but he lets her. I've told him to stand up to her.'

'He prefers complaining behind her back.'

'That's his favourite sport.'

'But nice to have them talking?'

'Something good had to come out of this.' A waiter approaches our table and offers us a plate of oysters. Madeline splashes one with Tabasco sauce before swallowing it down. I politely decline, reaching instead for a prawn croquette.

'You don't know what you're missing,' she tells me, and I smile.

'East does put on a decent funeral lunch.'

'I hope the Met Police drink him dry and it burns a fucking hole in his pocket.'

'You two getting on fine now?'

She laughs. 'One day I might forgive him, but not until I've screwed a lifetime of free dinners out of him.'

'He should have told you Billy Monroe had been released.'

'Of course he fucking should but, hand on heart, can I say I would have behaved any differently? No. I know exactly what I'd have said to him – stop being such a worrier.'

'Why didn't he tell you?'

407

'On the night of Sam's birthday dinner he was about to, but then we got into a stupid argument about social media. Irony is he's getting more coverage now than he'd ever dreamed possible.'

'It'll pass. Him and Will not good?'

'They're done. East will keep the restaurant but they're selling the house. Don't you dare tell my mother, or she'll make them an offer.'

'It wouldn't be nice to have her nearby?'

'No,' replies Madeline, reaching for a glass of wine from a passing tray. 'And anyway, it's you she adores. She'd expect you to be popping over every other day.' She sips from her wine. 'I might not have said it, but thanks for all you did; both with them, but also in risking your own life.'

A hand rests on my shoulder. 'Ben always likes to jump in with both feet and put his life in danger.'

I stand to greet Dame Elizabeth Jones. 'I'm truly sorry about DS Barnsdale,' I say.

'Thank you,' she replies. 'You all did everything possible that night, but when you're dealing with a maniac . . . ' She turns to Madeline. 'I'm pleased to see you're recovering.'

I offer my seat to Dame Elizabeth and step away, leaving the two women finally to talk. Walking across the terrace, I see Dani speaking to Shannon Lancaster. I stand for a moment looking out on the river. When I feel a hand gently touch my back, I turn.

'Let's go home,' says Dani, quietly.

CHAPTER 90

Dani and I step down from Mailer's terrace and follow the river path up towards St Marnham Bridge.

'Taylor stumbled upon Shannon Lancaster's home after a conversation with her mother-in-law?' I ask.

Dani nods. 'Discovering she would be alone the following night, he planned to attack her.'

'After everything he'd done to her in the past.'

'He's a sick human being. He watched her sleeping, waiting for his moment. But, when she woke, she flew at him and pulled at his mask. He panicked and fled.'

'How's she coping?' I ask.

'It's tough for her. She feels guilty about not stopping Taylor sooner.'

'She was a fourteen-year-old girl, and he raped her.'

'I know,' replies Dani, 'but that doesn't stop her thinking she might have acted differently. After Aaron's murder she was paralysed with fear, but when Madeline told the world Billy Monroe had murdered Aaron, Shannon felt nothing but relief.'

We walk on up the path. 'You spoke wonderfully about Barnsdale,' I say.

'It's what she deserved. She was a good officer.'

'That night in the warehouse, nobody could have been braver.'

'I'd have liked more time with her.'

I take hold of Dani's hand. 'You planned to speak to her about Freeman?'

'How did you know?'

'Because I love you.'

Dani smiles. 'That's not an answer.'

'You trusted her, valued her opinion. That's why.' Dani nods. 'And now?' I ask.

'I've watched Freeman throughout this case. I cannot fault her in anything she does.'

'She could be a good officer and still in the pay of the Baxters.'

'And I could be completely wrong,' replies Dani. 'Right now, there's nothing more I can do.' She stops and let's go of my hand. 'And I need you to do the same. We have no evidence. All we can do is wait. You have to be comfortable with that.'

'I am,' I say. 'If it's what you want, I absolutely am.'

'Thank you,' she says, kissing me softly on the cheek.

We wait to let a cyclist pass before, in the warm sunshine, we follow the path up to the bridge. Beneath the Victorian structure, we stop again.

'These shoes are bloody killing me,' I say, rubbing my heel.

'You can change them when we get home.'

I look at Dani. 'That's twice you've said that.'

'Said what?'

'Home.'

'I guess it is home, if you'll have me?'

'You mean for ever? Not just the odd night.'

'Maybe we take it a day at a time, but, yes, kind of for ever. I spoke with Mat last night. He's started his new job, his life is back on track and, deep down, he knew when that happened, I wanted to go.' Dani kisses me. 'Despite all your crazy, impulsive, reckless madness, everything you did for Sam and Annabel was because you cared for them. And for Madeline. I wouldn't change you for the world, Ben Harper.'

We kiss again. 'I love you, Dani.'

'I love you too,' she replies, and I smile.

'One more thing,' she says, putting her mouth to my ear to whisper, 'I'm pregnant.'

THE REINVENTION OF
BILLY MONROE

by Madeline Wilson

Five months ago, a man named Billy Monroe kidnapped me. He held me hostage in abandoned farm buildings on the southern fringes of Nottingham. I escaped after seventy-two terrifying hours. For the following six days, I was placed under the excellent care of the doctors and nurses of the Queen's Medical Centre, as I underwent nasal reconstruction surgery, including septoplasty to reshape my crushed septum – crushed by the agonising force of Billy Monroe's fist.

On leaving hospital, so great was the interest in my story, I agreed to hold a brief press conference. In a packed meeting room at the nearby Orchard Hotel, one of the first questions asked of me was, *Did I now regret my pursuit of Billy Monroe, fourteen years earlier?*

My response? A categorical no. My only regret was my failure to ensure Monroe didn't receive an even longer sentence.

In the days that followed, newspaper columnists, along with social media opinion formers, dissected my response, critiquing my view of Monroe. Abuse of me on social media followed, depicting me as the offender and Monroe as the victim – my victim.

Their logic? Billy Monroe was a casualty of all of society's ills. Nobody ever gave him a chance.

Didn't I understand? As a child, Billy's father abandoned him before birth. He lost his mother, a drug-addicted prostitute, when he was only seven. Crippled by ill-health, his grandfather had no other option but to place Billy for adoption. Mistreated by his adoptive parents, he spent days on end, alone, in the attic room of their home. Rejected and returned to social services, Billy drifted into adulthood working as a builder's labourer, seeking shelter on whatever couch he could find. Issues with his mental health left him open to exploitation by others, most distressingly by the natural son of his adoptive parents. Manipulated into killing Aaron Welsby, Billy served an overly harsh sentence. Upon his release, crippled by paranoia, he entered into an ill-judged scheme that ended with his own brutal murder.

Fourteen years ago, the narrative around Monroe's conviction was why not longer? Today, the reborn narrative is why did he serve any time at all?

All Billy needed was for someone to care.

In the court of popular opinion and among keyboard warriors, I became culpable. Culpable because I campaigned for his original conviction after he savagely murdered an innocent man. According to them, I fought for his conviction when all Billy needed was help.

413

Still now, five months later, the question posed to me the most frequently is, *Have I reassessed my opinion of Billy Monroe?*

My answer remains no.

Why?

Billy Monroe ambushed me in my own car. He brutally assaulted me. Bound, gagged and, without sight, he terrorised me. Chained in a room, he humiliated me. Repeatedly, I feared he would rape me. Constantly, I believed he would kill me. I have no sympathy for Billy Monroe.

Every action he took was his own. He had a precise plan and the decision to execute the plan was his.

The only person responsible for Billy Monroe's actions against me was Billy Monroe.

Others may choose to reinterpret and forgive, but I never will.

I'm often told, *Billy Monroe's grandfather saved your life. How can you not feel sympathy for him? He was a good man. He sacrificed his own life for yours.*

To Tosh Monroe, am I eternally grateful?

Yes.

But he sacrificed his life to the actions of his grandson. And perhaps to his own actions, in raising, or not raising, his family.

I'm told of Tosh Monroe's exceptional bravery.

In my story, the exceptional bravery came from Detective Sergeant Lesley Barnsdale, killed during the apprehension of Dominic Taylor; of Detective Constable Dani Cash, of Ben Harper and of Phil Doorley.

And of my own parents, Sam Hardy and Annabel Wilson.

My parents led the pursuit of Monroe and Taylor, never faltering in their determination to rescue a daughter to whom they had already given so much of their lives. Both placed themselves in mortal danger without giving a thought to the possible consequences.

Throughout my life, both have taught me honesty, love, persistence, and a little bit of obstinance. Our family lived by those principles. They gave me the hope that ultimately saved my life.

A final question posed of me is, *Do I accept that Dominic Taylor is the real villain in my story?*

Dominic Taylor is a monster. Sentenced to a thirty-year term, I hope he rots in prison for the rest of his life. He planned to rape and kill me. He terrorised countless other women. And he murdered DS Lesley Barnsdale, as well as my friend and colleague, Dennis Thackeray.

Dominic Taylor twisted and abused his family. A sadist and a psychopath, driven by a desire for money, he controlled them. Police interviews reveal how Taylor manipulated Monroe's displeasure at failing to secure work as a labourer on the Haddley Grammar School sports pavilion construction project. Teaching him violent homophobic hate, Monroe became a deadly weapon. Needing to conceal his sexual abuse of two schoolgirls, Taylor launched his assault weapon directly at Aaron Welsby.

During Billy Monroe's years of incarceration, Taylor didn't rest. Through occasional prison visits, he drip-fed poison into Billy's mind, feeding an insatiable hatred of me.

Reloaded, Billy was ready to fire.

And Taylor fired him directly at me.

ACKNOWLEDGEMENTS

This is the third book I've been fortunate to publish with the team at Little, Brown. While it might seem a slightly strange thing to say, one of the biggest things I've learned during the writing and publishing of those three books is publishing a book truly is a team effort. And captain of my team is, without a doubt, my primary editor, Rosanna Forte. Rosanna has as much determination to create the best possible story as I do. After reading my manuscript she always arrives with great insight into each of the characters and understands every element of the twisty plot. She shares my commitment to publish a book that entertains readers until the very last page. Her work ethic is incredible and my enormous gratitude goes to her.

Big thanks must also go to the rest of the publishing team at Little, Brown including Charlie, Ed, Gemma, Laura, Niamh and Zoe. Thanks once again to Duncan for the brilliant cover design, and his unending patience; a wonderful trait present in so many great art directors. And huge thanks to Hannah and all of the LB sales team for being such amazing champions of my books.

In the small Robert Gold team, nothing would ever have been achieved without my wonderful agent, Juliet Mushens, and her own brilliant team at Mushens Entertainment. Thanks also to Lynsey for her patience with me in answering her questions.

For the character of Max I remain indebted to the real Max. His brilliant personality is the inspiration for so many of the lines spoken by the younger characters throughout my books. Thanks also go to my family for their never-ending support and understanding, especially as I constantly seem to be working on my next book. Special thanks and love, as always to O, H, and W for the loan of the name.

This book is dedicated in memory of my mum, Christine. Nobody could have been more excited and proud than she was when I published my first novel, *Twelve Secrets*. She was thrilled when it reached the *Sunday Times* top 10, a feat largely achieved by her hand-selling the book to everyone she ever met, while also moving copies to the front of display in every shop she visited. She was a fantastic supporter and offered nothing but great encouragement throughout my life. When I started this book she loved hearing my new plot ideas and how the story was coming together. Never did I imagine she wouldn't see the publication of *Ten Seconds*, but after a very short illness she passed away not long after I'd begun writing. Wherever she is, I know she will still be busy hand-selling copies now.

And, finally, my thanks go to you the reader. An enormous number of books are published each year and it still now blows my mind that you took the time to choose mine and invested your precious time in reading it. I hope the story kept you entertained throughout, with a few surprises coming right at the very end.

Thanks for reading.

Revisit the first Ben Harper mystery . . .

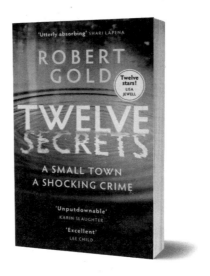

A SMALL TOWN. A SHOCKING CRIME.
YOU'LL SUSPECT EVERY CHARACTER.
BUT YOU'LL NEVER GUESS THE ENDING.

Ben Harper's life changed for ever the day his older brother
Nick was murdered by two classmates. It was a crime
that shocked the nation and catapulted Ben's family and
their idyllic hometown, Haddley, into the spotlight.

Twenty years on, Ben is one of the best investigative
journalists in the country and settled back in Haddley,
thanks to the support of its close-knit community. But
then a fresh murder case shines new light on his brother's
death and throws suspicion on those closest to him.

Ben is about to discover that in Haddley no one is
as they seem. Everyone has something to hide.

And *someone* will do anything to keep the truth buried . . .

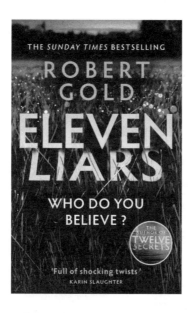

'Packed with explosive twists and impossible
to put down' *WOMAN & HOME*

Journalist Ben Harper is on his way home when he sees
the flames in the churchyard. The derelict community
centre is on fire. And somebody is trapped inside.

With Ben's help the person escapes, only to flee the scene
before they can be identified. Now the small town of Haddley
is abuzz with rumours. Was this an accident, or arson?

Then a skeleton is found in the burnt-out foundations.

And when the identity of the victim is revealed, Ben
is confronted with a crime that is terrifyingly close to
home. As he uncovers a web of deceit and destruction
that goes back decades, Ben quickly learns that in this
small town, everybody has something to hide.